For
Ca
Best
Dora Dicum

Radha

A novel inspired by true events

by
Dora Pushpa Dicum

Argentiere Publishing
London

Published in 2011 in Great Britain by Argentiere Publishing LLP,
31 Gwynne House
Lloyd Baker Street
London WC1X 9BG

ISBN 978-0-9567158-0-7

Printed in France by
DFS+
ZI Les Milles-Actimart
1140, Rue Ampère
3, Allée des Ingénieurs
13851 Aix-en-Provence Cedex 3

Argentiere Publishing LLP makes every effort to ensure its books are printed
on paper that is natural, renewable and recyclable. Also that the logging and
manufacturing processes conform to the environmental regulations of the
country of origin.

Be to her virtues very kind
Be to her faults a little blind

Acknowledgements

I am deeply grateful to my husband and my daughter, without whose generous help, interest and extraordinary patience this book would not have reached publication.

And a big thank you to all the remaining members of my family (with a special thanks to Virginie) for their continued support and enthusiasm.

I would also like to thank Argentiere Publishing for all their hours of dedicated work.

And I am greatly indebted to the following friends for their countless suggestions, all of which helped to bring this book to its present state – Carys Ampofo, Gillon Aitken, Margaret Amor, Olivier Azières, Michelle and Stephen Barker, Sandy Baer, Simon Cannon, Susannah Clapp, Peter and Brenda Coop, Ann Croft, Kim Cutler, Saskia Fitzwilliam-Lay, Paul Freeman, Angela and Rodney Heath, Cécile and Greg Henley-Price, Linda Lorentz, Lennox Money, John and Caroline Sullivan, Florence Swarzstein, Barry Winkleman and, last but by no means least, Diana and Michael Wood.

Forward

What follows is about my cousin Radha and her marriage to Doctor Mentem.

It should never have happened because Radha and I were in love with each other and had been from our earliest childhood. I am still haunted by the loss. At last I have decided to set it down on paper to see if it makes more sense.

When Radha was nine, her family moved to Saigon. I was fourteen. Despite my tender years, the separation was hard to bear, but not for a moment did I doubt she'd come back to me. And she did.

Radha was seventeen when they returned to Pondicherry. That first moment when I saw her again, I must have looked like a simpleton – I couldn't help staring at her. I had never imagined so much loveliness, such a bewitching balance of coquetry and sweet shyness. The certainty that my love was returned made me so light-headed I just kept grinning.

Even the memory of that moment mocks me now. But then, how could I have foreseen a stranger would suddenly appear to wreck my dreams of a lifetime.

I left for Kuala Lumpur to set up my law firm there, and, intentionally, missed her wedding which I heard was a very lavish affair.

Immediately after their marriage, the Doctor and his bride settled in Kuala Lumpur close to where I lived so that I found myself once more within the same orbit as Radha.

From then on, I kept her in my sights, learnt everything there was to know about her.

In writing this story, I have tried to be objective and, to that end, have used the third person in those passages where I appear. You will judge to what extent I have been successful. Above all I wanted to paint a true picture of my dearest cousin Radha.

Chapter 1

Malaya, 1929.

S ounds of insects in the air; the uneven grind of metal
wheels on tarmac – a cart trundling past. Tall canes of
bamboo bending and rustling in the breeze; screech of
kingfisher with flash of electric blue. Twilight over Kuala
Lumpur.

The Doctor sat on the veranda, hearing nothing, lost
in a distant future. When Radha handed him the lime juice,
he took it from her, tasted it – no sugar – and nodded
mechanically.

'How was the English lesson?' he asked.

She placed the other glass on the low table, a quick
glance to take in his mood, then, pulling her chair closer to
his, sat down.

'I put it off till tomorrow – don't look cross. Promise
I won't do it again. I finished my letter to my mother; told
her about our bungalow, especially this veranda, our two
new wicker chairs. Ah, what's that lovely smell? Jasmin! I
told her about the lantern, the potted plants; all my favourite
things.' She looked eagerly at him, but when he said nothing,
she resumed, 'I don't miss home, I mean, Pondicherry, and

I've found a girl to help round the house.' This time he smiled his approval, and she went on, 'you'll be pleased to hear I've put the last touches to the painting on the screen. A day of finishing things; a day of achievement.' Fingering the gold chain round her neck (her most treasured wedding gift), she asked, '*Atha*, why do I have to do English? My Tamil's top grade.'

'Forget your Tamil; it's not worth a fig. Nothing but a primitive language, fit for a backward race entrenched in its ignorance.'

Radha stared at him in disbelief. How should she handle this? She fleetingly toyed with the idea of sitting on his lap, running her finger along his chin to make him smile; it had worked the other day. But no – that was the other day. She went up to the railing, too upset to sit still. Leaning against it, she smiled at him. The scent of jasmin was stronger than ever. He never seemed to notice things like that, except that he didn't like her to wear it in her hair.

Silhouetted against the balustrade in the twilight, she looked like some rare bird of paradise, trapped against the metal bar, fragile, young. Her light cotton sari moulded her slender form; she was playing with the single plait which she'd pulled round over her shoulder. Her voice, teasing, cut into his thoughts with his own words.

'Primitive language? Backward race? *Atha*, you don't mean that.'

A vision of beauty. Must be on his guard. What use was beauty if it couldn't further his dreams?

'You don't have to be part of it,' he said and swatted a mosquito on his arm so suddenly, she flinched. He continued, 'by all means write to your mother in the language she admires. I'm aware your script is thought to be fine; but here, at home, as soon as you've made some progress, we'll use English. Only English. You should make more of an effort; the tutor tells me you have ability but aren't interested.'

'I prefer French. *Veux-tu danser avec moi, mon chéri?*' she asked coquettishly, the light pink folds of the fabric swaying this way and that as her hips moved gently to and fro.

How could he tap into this energy and make it work to further his plans?

'Your French will be of limited use to our children; English is the international language of the future, and this is an opportunity for you to stay one step ahead of them. If you persevere and become fluent, then, when they're born, it could be said to be their mother tongue, after a fashion.'

She smiled to show she understood his joke but went on swaying and humming softly. If only there wasn't such a gap between them, she thought. Ten years was too long. Here they were, a whole month together since their wedding and, if anything, he seemed more of a stranger than ever. Oh, their wedding! – that had been wonderful! Her sari, shimmering folds of gold; the very best from Kanchipuram. He in his new white suit, looking so tall, so lean and *so* handsome! All the women envying her; not daring to look at him; a bit stern, unsmiling. Like now. She'd change that. Just needed time.

'Their real mother tongue,' she said, her tone teasing, 'you haven't forgotten, have you? – I'm Tamil, and so are you for that matter. The only difference is I don't mind being Tamil; quite like it really.' Now, holding the *mundani*, the embroidered end of her sari, she was doing a sort of dance of the veils.

'Then there's no hope for you,' he concluded, leaning his head back, eyes closed in an attempt to shut out the enticing image.

'*Atha*, please don't say that!' She was stooping down towards him, tenderly.

'We might as well start straight away – these figures of speech are meaningless. Calling me *Atha* doesn't make me any more your husband than I already am. Nor does it tell me something I don't know. Besides, it proves your unwillingness to improve yourself, and that's not likely to endear you to me.'

'What can I call you then?'

'Why call me anything when it's clear you're addressing me?'

She didn't answer. Couldn't tell him that for her it had been a term of endearment. Turning away, her gaze pierced to the confines of the garden; the road just below that ran east-west made her think wistfully of another country where life had been so easy. So recently. Except in bed, communication with the Doctor, instead of becoming more fluent, was almost at a standstill. Would she end up envying his patients who told him their problems and he listened?

The next morning, as always, he got up before her to do his 'fitness exercises' in the next room – twenty minutes of lying on the ground, first on his stomach, bobbing up and down on his arms (it reminded her of the previous night's activity and she stifled her giggles under the sheet), then over onto his back, his dark curls flattened against the floorboards (they'd be smoothed down with water before he left for work), a pair of weights, one in each hand, lifting them off his chest till his arms were straight, then down, then up, then down. His lean frame had already developed bumps here and there. At this rate he was going to look like a coolie with bulging muscles. That made her smile knowing how much he despised physical labour.

She lay in bed, her eyes closed except for the odd peep through the open door, pretending to be unaware of all that energy being wasted so early in the morning there on the floor of the sitting room, which was still dusty from the day before. Would the servant girl turn up on time, she wondered.

When he stopped, she shot out of bed to bathe before him – another of his odd ideas – to wait after an exertion before washing off the sweat because, he said, it was better for the body to cool off first. Such strange ideas! The tub filled up quickly and she dipped the tin can into the water and poured it liberally over herself taking care to keep her head dry. One last canful over the floor to clean it, then she swept the water with her feet towards the hole in the corner. Quick look round to make sure the soap was in the saucer, the can next to it, his towel on the wooden hook, then, wrapping her towel round her, she slipped back into the bedroom.

As she got dressed behind the bamboo screen – he hadn't noticed her painting on it, or at any rate, there had been no comment – she hummed a tune to keep up her spirits while making the last folds of the sari.

'You should consider throwing out these yards of material you wind round yourself,' he said as though he could see her through the screen. 'Give them to the servant; she'll be happy to have them.'

'Yards of material?' Radha asked, poking her head round, '*Ath*' she coughed to cover her near blunder. Hiding behind the screen once more, she continued, 'You mean my saris? D'you want me to buy new ones?'

'Certainly not! Six or more yards to create the same outfit day after day! You can have three different dresses for that, each with its own style. You'd look good in a dress.'

'Dresses! But nobody wears dresses. And they all look the same to me, not nearly as different as one sari and another. Anyway, I'd feel silly showing my legs, it's immodest.'

'Merely a convention. Is it less immodest to wander about exhibiting a bare midriff? And when you say nobody wears a frock, you're speaking of Indians. Set your sights higher. Study the Europeans, their clothes, their ways. Now that you're in Malaya, there's no one here to disapprove of what you wear, and I, as I was saying, would be happy to see you in a European-style dress.'

She knew that the 'no one' referred to her mother. Radha said nothing, but the notion of changing into a dress as if she was playing a part in a play, seemed to her far from setting her sights higher. She quietly finished the folds and tucked them in at her waist knowing that this was one wish she would not fulfil.

Bad start to the day. This continual harping against all things Indian was getting through to her. Whenever they spoke, it seemed to turn into an argument which ended in silence.

There must be a way out of this. If there was, she'd find it, but it had better be soon.

Chapter 2

The Doctor left each morning and took a rickshaw to the top of the hill on the other side of town where Government Hospital stood. Sometimes, he had the use of the hospital car and he took Radha for a drive. She was aware how few wives enjoyed such a treat. Her husband, despite being the youngest surgeon at the hospital, was already valued far beyond his years.

One evening, on returning home, instead of asking her about her day as he usually did, he remained silent and absorbed, pacing the veranda with long impatient strides. She waited till he calmed down, then went up to him.

'A hard day?'

He gave a nod and stared into the black night, one hand gripping the rail of the balustrade. When he finally spoke, it was little more than to himself.

'How is it possible to believe in a benign God when there's such unspeakable suffering wreaked on innocent creatures?'

She kept quiet knowing this was not the moment to mention Faith. He turned and looked straight at her. By the light of the lantern, she saw perplexity in his eyes.

'Same age as you. A little while ago, she'd have been running round the playground with her classmates. Today, all I could offer her was six months. Six months of hell, ending in nothing.'

'Poor woman! Were you able to give her something to lessen her pain?'

Without turning, he put his arm round her shoulder and drew her to him.

'Yes, I was able to do that.' Then he repeated in a lighter tone, 'you're right – at least I was able to do that.' And a smile crossed his lips.

'You should take a holiday. No one else works without a break.'

'Holiday! If you knew the level of incompetence of some of my colleagues!'

'Your health ...'

'I'm all right. Perhaps one day I'll be able to hand out the palliative without seeing the patient. Come, let's have something to eat. It's well past supper time.'

The Doctor rarely brought home his troubles and Radha, sensing his need to leave them behind, rarely questioned him. She was happy making their home his haven. She had the help of a girl, a Tamil, to clean as well as to work in the kitchen though she did most of the cooking herself. It was what she enjoyed most although at first it was hard for her to accept spices shouldn't be used, at all. Not even pepper.

A gardener came each evening to tidy up and water the plants. Blue plumbago, purple bougainvillea and red hibiscus grew with abandon. So did the wild convolvulus with its large trumpet-flowers that she asked him to leave to clamber up the bamboo. Gardenias were given pride of place.

Sundays, after church which she attended on her own, her cousin, Pradeep, sometimes came to lunch. Later, when he married Vida, he brought his wife with him. Occasionally they went to Pradeep's, though it soon became apparent the Doctor preferred to eat at home which made it easier all round given how fastidious he was about his diet.

'I like your cousins,' he said finally, 'but Sunday is my only day off; I'd like to be on my own with you. If you want, you could see Vida during the week.'

Radha accepted joyfully. The atmosphere between them had improved and she felt they'd reached a new level of understanding.

*

Almost three years later (there'd been a miscarriage the previous year), Radha lay in bed propped up by pillows, the babe at her breast; she'd just given birth to Julius. Her husband stood next to her, stroking her long hair that was damp with the effort she'd been through.

She closed her eyes, drifted in and out of sleep; remembered, of a sudden, that Sunday nine months ago, the sun already high as they sat on the veranda over breakfast. Their first holiday, and this, the first day of the two weeks that lay before them.

'Pack some things together; we'll take a summer break of a few days.'

'Mmm, nice – don't think I've had a "summer break" before.'

'In that far-away place I've told you about, there are four seasons in the year: everything starts sprouting in spring, grows all through summer. In the autumn leaves on trees turn bright red or gold – imagine what a sight that must be! – then drop off, so that, in a cold year, ice can settle on bare branches without harming the trees.'

'Why do people stay in such a place? Sounds so cold!'

'During summer, they take a break, somewhere near water to dip in and cool off from the hot sun.'

'Aren't they afraid the water might be infected?'

'I'm talking about the sea. You're right about rivers; it's hard to understand the Indian fixation with foul water, forever dunking themselves and their clothes in murky pools. If you want, Anna could join us later; perhaps during the second week. Would you like that?'

'Oh, I would! She's the sister I never had. Are you sure her husband can spare her?'

That was their first visit to Port Dickson; no children nor dog as yet. The bay before them, still as a pond, the house, enormous for just the two of them with a wooden balcony that ran the length of the first floor. No other house in sight. Water lapping gently on the shore, whispering a thousand secrets into her enchanted ears.

He came out of the house and joined her on the shoreline, dressed in a curious striped garment, 'Come on, let's have a dip before the sun sets,' And he was already

*pulling her towards the sea, ignoring her mild protests.
'Don't be afraid; I won't let you go in too deep.' The sea
was warm and caressing and so gentle she wasn't afraid,
not with him holding her. When it was time to get out she
lingered, feeling self-conscious, the sari clinging to her
body. 'See,' he was looking at her appreciatively, 'that's
how you'd look in a dress. If only you'd listen to me!'*

*'How can you want everyone to see me like this? I feel
naked.'*

That, then, must have been when Julius was conceived,
she mused, during that summer break. Her husband's voice
broke into her thoughts, sounding different, warm and gentle.

'Radha, this is an historic moment – you've matched
your beauty with performance; in your arms you're holding
a future statesman of our country.'

She leant her head against him, too moved to speak.

'I too am happy it's a boy,' she said at last. 'Look,
funny little squiggle of a curl! So sweet. He'll be brilliant
like you, I know he will.'

'With my mind and your looks, he'll go far,' he
reflected dreamily.

'*Atha*, not so far I can't smother him with kisses,' she
sighed, pressing the baby's fingers to her lips. He smiled
and didn't scold her for reverting to old ways. In fact, he
hardly noticed it.

A little later, she listened with greater interest when
the subject of English came round with renewed force. No
doubt at all, they were communicating well. Yes, she was
an achiever – a boy for their first child, and she'd regained
her shape in no time at all.

'One day,' he confided, 'I shall send all our children to England to be educated; first to take their School Certificate at boarding school, then on to university, preferably Oxford. It's what the better class of British living here do.'

It was an astonishingly bold idea for a young doctor with limited means, nor was it at all usual even among rich Indians. But he'd read a lot, and his ambition knew no bounds. And in time, except for his daughter, Leela, who had a learning disability, this is what he'd do.

Radha nodded in agreement. She was aware she had no idea what he was going on about. All the children? He *can't* mean that, not girls, if they have any. How was she to prepare them to be good wives and mothers if they were somewhere miles away? Anyway, he'd never take little Julius from her to send to some nasty boarding school in another country, cold and far away. Nobody could take him from her. She wouldn't let them; that's all there was to it. With that she rolled over on the mat, laughing and hugging the baby to her.

'We must prepare him to assume the responsibilities he'll have one day. In the meantime, let him enjoy a carefree infancy. These photos I've taken of you playing with him will serve as a record of this period. See, I've put the date and place on each. An aid to memory.'

'No need, I'll never forget this moment,' Radha said, feeling the joy of motherhood.

About a year later, the Doctor who'd known for some time he had a goitre problem, felt it was time to have it operated upon. A good opportunity, he decided, to kill two birds with one stone. He would go to London for the operation, that would allow him to have first-hand knowledge of the country where his children would be educated one day.

It was long-drawn out; the crossing alone took a month each way, but the plan worked. The operation was a success, and, during that month in London, he familiarised himself with the major landmarks of the city.

On his return, he was pleased to see Radha had survived his absence without any difficulty. This augured well for the future. His wife needed to be an independent woman.

Chapter 3

Paula was born three years after Julius. The noticeable resemblance to her paternal grandmother made the Doctor laugh and Radha saw he was happy. Yes, a daughter for their second child was a good thing; especially as she reminded him of his mother.

'One of each,' he remarked, 'you've organized it well. Couldn't have hoped for more.'

'*Atha*, I did my best just for you.'

'We make a good team,' he whispered as he bent down to kiss her forehead. 'Sad my mother will never see these children!'

'Yes, sad,' Radha agreed. 'If she'd been alive, we could have taken them to Pondicherry to show her. I think that would have made her happy, don't you?'

The Doctor contented himself with a muffled, 'hmm.'

Paula was a handful from the start. A battle of wills in which Radha usually lost. But now, as well as the servant girl, there was an ayah, also Tamil, to help with the children.

There followed years of happiness when Radha's letters to her mother were full of their son, Julius, followed by accounts of the wilful antics of little Paula. Above all, her husband had softened, kept buying her jewels, and laughing because he found the children amusing. Years of joy that promised to stretch far into the unforeseeable future.

Roy was born the following year. If he hadn't reminded her so much of her brother Ravi, Radha might have found the pace of production too exacting. As it was, though she said nothing, knowing what the Doctor thought of her brother, when she was alone with the baby she cooed and petted him with sheer delight.

Leela came two years later; an unmistakable likeness to the Doctor though he seemed unaware of it. Finally, two years after that, Mena. Mena broke the boy/girl sequence. She should have been a boy, but Radha couldn't find it in her heart to hold it against her. She reminded her of someone – her mother? But she wasn't sure.

Each child, except for Julius who had the distinction of having two English names, had an English as well as an Indian name. In the earliest years, the Doctor indulged his young wife, but eventually the children were called only by their English name.

There were bunk beds for the boys in one room, two narrow beds for the girls in the other as well as a cot for the baby. The room occupied by the parents stood on the opposite side of the corridor.

It was in the sitting area between these rooms and the front of the house that Radha hung the two oval portraits, one of him, the other of her. Photos taken at the wedding, coloured in by hand afterwards. How young she looked! A flower still in bud. And he, a proud creature, caught and caged against his will. It made her smile. He looked different now.

The two servants slept in the shack behind. Finally, there was Ted, the large hairy dog, who spent most of his time on the veranda, lying flat out, panting in the shade. Ted, a family pet, as might be found in an English home; a dog that came indoors at night. Not a guard dog.

Full house.

The time was ready, the Doctor judged, to begin the next phase.

*

With five children to think about (Julius already eight and struggling with tutors), the Doctor dwelt frequently on the subject closest to his heart: their education. Radha was shaping up well in the areas that mattered. Pity their mother tongue continued to be Tamil, but generally speaking, she was proving to be more than pliant in carrying out his wishes. He put his arm round her waist and drew her to him.

'The tutor tells me you always have Julius ready and keen to start the class. He's lucky to have such a clear-sighted mother.' She lay her head against his chest, smiling with contentment. He continued, 'Leo has written to say he's got a teaching post at St John's Institute; Julius will be in his class. He'll no doubt be dropping in on us one of these days.'

'Good. I really like your brother; and Anna and I get on wonderfully well. They're my favourites of your family; we're lucky to have them here in Malaya.'

'Leo is certainly a great champion of yours.' The time had come for him to expand further about the children's education. 'When our children are at school in England, you could go over, stay a couple of months during the long summer holiday; that way we'll be able to keep in touch with them without having to bring them home every year as the cost of that would be inhibitive.'

'The family broken!' she cried in consternation. 'Are our children not to see their father from one year to the next, and their mother just two months of the summer break? Is that the right start to life?'

'Start to life?' he cried, 'Are you not aware how far advanced we are already? All I'm asking is for you to keep in touch with them.'

Though she said nothing, he saw the refusal in her eyes and turned away. Rebellion! He was the architect of the scheme he had in mind. No one but he could fulfil that role. But an architect needs a mason to lay the stones one by one while he himself remains at a distance to view the work from a perspective. She was his mason and she was refusing to cooperate.

From that instant the first seeds to exclude her from his dreams were sown.

Doctor Mentem confided his misgivings to the Chinese nurse who had recently been assigned to him. She stood at his elbow, ready to run whatever errand he may have. On this occasion, he needed to voice his doubts. Her reply in broken English showed understanding.

'Your wife, she too much Indian, maybe?' the nurse asked.

Why, of course! Radha was too Indian; he'd always known it. She was downright backward: hadn't made the slightest effort to learn English, wouldn't listen to him about saris, still called him husband. And now it was clear she'd put a spanner in the works by refusing to go to England. If only she had the insight of this young nurse! Instead, Radha was ineradicably stuck in the mediocrity of her background. All her deficiencies came to the fore.

There was her addiction to church and incense and Sunday Mass, priests mumbling Latin to an illiterate congregation. Babies, baptised within a month of their birth. Couldn't risk having them end up in Limbo. Limbo indeed! Where did the Church think up these quaint ideas, he wondered. And, even more remarkable, how did they manage to convince their aptly-named 'flock' to take them seriously?

And all this bounced on them just two generations earlier! Their grandfathers, practising Hindus, threatened with hell and damnation by those Catholic missionaries, had switched to Christianity. The Doctor wondered if the transaction had been done via an interpreter.

He himself had no time for the Church or the Bible (both of which meant so much to his wife though, he noted with a wry smile, she'd not completely abandoned Shiva and his gang). Radha's refusal to extend her horizons reminded him of the servant from the parable in the New Testament who buried his money to keep it safe instead of letting it multiply. No doubt, although the parable came from her favourite reading, she wasn't familiar with it.

Though uncommonly pretty and with an attractive veneer of social grace (yes, she was competent in French, but then, what use was that beyond these little songs she sang to the children? and yes, she had a good voice for what that was worth), she didn't let him forget she was Indian. A beauty queen who couldn't share his vision, he told himself, was like the proverbial 'swarm in July'.

The fact that she became animated and was perceptive about subjects that touched on Indian culture merely irritated him (except perhaps where he owed something to the Karma Sutra for, in that one area, she satisfied him). He'd told her Indian culture was unworthy of her attention. Her persistence suggested a perverse wilfulness, a mind that was closed to new ideas. He must find ways of minimising any ill effects she might have on their children. The essential thing was to keep her out of their lives.

Radha noticed he suddenly became aloof, his work all-absorbing, his nights restless. Words, thrown out from the depth of sleep. Names. A foreign name. She told no one. The years of happiness, so recent. Will-o'-the-wisp glowing in the past. A past that daily grew more nourishing as the present became arid and the future uncertain.

There was now the *ayah* who helped with the children; all the same, Radha was busy from morning till night. So busy and absorbed at being the perfect wife and mother, there was little time left to fret about anything.

But there were things to fret about and she knew it. Her husband's sleep – she told him it was restless; told him he was talking in his sleep. She didn't mention he'd changed; that he'd stopped talking about the children's schooling. It made her uneasy; even more than his plans to send them abroad. English had crept in insidiously by way of tutors for Julius. Would Tamil be marginalised completely, used only for practical instructions and to servants?

As the Doctor's fame increased, the gulf between him and Radha widened accordingly. He knew it was time to move to a bigger house, but he delayed, sensing that changes beyond his control were on the way; changes that would sweep away the existing order.

Radha too knew this and dreaded it; there'd already been too much change in her life; each time it took away what was familiar and dear to her and replaced it with something different, not better. Change did not usually work in Radha's favour.

Chapter 4

For months there had been talk of war. Japan was on the move. Rumours hardened into blatant manoeuvres to the north. Fear wormed its way through her and paralysed her will. She prayed to the Virgin Mary, made promises to the Goddess Lakshmi, lighted candles, sweet-scented joss sticks. Promises and prayers. And tears. Rivers of tears before the sacred images to carry her desperate pleas. But all in vain.

The day came when the Doctor and Radha stood facing each other on that same veranda where twelve years earlier, he'd first talked about her English, or the lack of it, and she had teased him playfully. And now, must she really leave this home and this man who meant more to her than life itself? Did he know how much he meant to her? She doubted it. And yet, she still felt loved. Was it merely a yearning that nourished itself, ignoring harsh reality? No! There had to be a deep current of love between them. A two-way course that fed him as much as her. Why else had he spent so much time making plans for their future?

So argued Radha and found comfort in this reasoning. She waited, knowing there was nothing she could do to stop what he was about to say.

'Now, you must realize war is a certainty. The French have caved in; given the Japanese their military base in Indo-China. It's a matter of weeks if not days before they overrun the whole peninsula. I've delayed your departure too long, far too long.' He stopped, not expecting an answer. She'd already been astonishingly persistent.

She had to try one last time, the very last. Nothing emotional. She would appeal to his commonsense.

'The Japanese,' she began, tears threatening to spoil her argument, 'if they invade Malaya, they'll have to face the British. They won't want that; you said so yourself.'

His voice barely held in check as if dealing with a recalcitrant child, he corrected her.

'That was before. Now the British have their hands full in Europe. You know that. And you know why the Japanese will come – there's the rubber. And tin. Most important of all – the strategic port of Singapore. Men have killed and plundered for less. Does any of that sound familiar to you?'

She ignored the sarcasm and repeated what would certainly sound familiar to him.

'Your position as doctor will keep us safe because they'll need you. A doctor is even more useful in war than in peace – we agreed on that. No harm will come to us if we stick together.' He said nothing but she understood his silence meant dissent.

'It's the last thing I want,' he murmured finally, 'a disruption of this sort in the children's education.'

The children's education! Was that all? She was astounded. What about the disruption in *their* lives, his and hers? To be separated from her – did it mean nothing to him? Nothing at all?

'There's nothing I can do about it. Hopefully it won't last long and their studies won't suffer unduly.' He paused before adding, 'I've managed to secure a passage on the *Rajula* for you to leave on September the first. I'll accompany you by train as far as Port Swetenham; the crossing will take five days, your brother will meet you at Madras and take you to your mother.'

In years to come Radha would trace all her troubles back to this moment when there was nothing left for her to say. God knew she'd tried; used every trick in the book: begged, pleaded, reasoned; gone far beyond the point a wife should try her husband. Wept, though he hated tears. Refused to admit defeat when all was lost. Now, the last lingering sparks of hope were spent. Standing before him, alone and helpless, she knew nothing would be the same ever again.

She lowered her eyes afraid he might see the panic in them, but he wasn't looking at her. She understood what he was saying – at a time like this, five children, the eldest no more than nine, were too many possible hostages to fortune. And yet every particle of her cried out that to be separated from him would injure them in untold ways far more damaging than anything the Japanese might inflict. She'd told him so. But there were as many arguments and more, not to mention cold facts, to negate the warnings of the heart. Now, only the fear in her eyes might have communicated these unspoken words, and he was deaf to that language.

'The drive from Madras to Pondicherry will take the best part of a day. I've forwarded enough money for your brother to hire a car for the journey; it'll save you being bumped along in a bullock cart for days on end. Make sure the children are properly fed; no rubbishy snacks from the roadside. These Indian stalls – filthy – no idea of hygiene. While you're with your mother, give them plenty of fresh fruit and vegetables; you should be able to get hold of that. Remember what I've told you about proper diet. Not enough attention is paid to it even here; you no doubt remember what it was like in India.'

She remembered, and knew her memories and his had nothing in common.

'I've made arrangements with Barclays Bank for payments to be made into an account in your name; your mother's present means will be significantly improved by my contributions. The arrival of five members of my family will be to her advantage. That is how I wish it to be.'

There! He'd said it all; or almost all. He sank into the wicker chair that creaked with age, and was glad of the dark night.

The light from the lantern was so feeble she could hardly make out his face. Her heart pounding, she gripped the metal bar of the railing for support as she corrected him, knowing he would not have made a mistake.

'There'll be six of us, not five.'

'Julius is nine; he'll remain here with me so that I can supervise his studies. You ...'

'Leave Julius behind, alone?!'

'Not alone. I said he'll be with me; and someone has offered to help out if necessary.'

'Someone?' Her voice was shrill.

'You needn't worry about him.'

'I am worried, worried sick!' she cried, almost hysterical at the thought of leaving Julius.

'Rest assured; someone, as I said, has offered to help if need be; Julius will be well looked after.' He continued as though he hadn't heard her sharp intake of breath, 'You'll have plenty to do with the four younger ones to look after. Paula and Roy should have private tuition as the standard of education out there will be abysmal. I'm arranging for Roy to go to All Saints in a year's time; that is, if you're still in India.'

'Still in India in a year's time!' Radha's head was spinning and she couldn't trust herself to move. Everything had been decided. Nothing remained to discuss between them. No Julius! A stranger (that Chinese nurse?) to steal her son from her. Only her son? O, help me, God! Roy in All Saints in a year's time. In a year's time, still in India!

The heavy scent of jasmin reached her, bringing back a blinding image of another time – was that really the two of them, her and him, on this same veranda with purple velvet stretched across the evening sky? Twelve whole years ago. Oh, how different the world was then! The future so full of promise, and love a near certainty .

She shut off the tantalising image. The tenuous thread that still connected Julius with her wouldn't stand the strain of separation; she tried not to think of a proxy mother in his life, especially not that woman. If Radha accepted what her husband meted out, it was because she hoped that in due course their life would return to what it had been before.

The decision to send the children away with his wife, far from his supervision, weighed heavily on the Doctor, but there was no alternative. He had seen to all the details for their departure: tickets, her Indian passport now included the children, cash for the journey, even new shoes for the children. She merely had to get her own things together and this she had still not done. Instead she was wandering around trimming the potted plants on the veranda as though she had nothing better to do.

It was true. Radha moved as in a daze. She knew better than to show the depth of her misery; he would never accept that this distance that now lay between them was sapping her life-force. He avoided her probing questions, but her intuition warned her and filled her ignorance more completely with dreadful intimations than if he'd taken her into his confidence. And now, he left her with nothing to take with her into the lonely future. Therefore, she went about her daily routine, making the imminent separation seem less real.

Finally the day arrived and a taxi took the family to the magnificent, domed railway station in the centre of Kuala Lumpur. Paula and Roy looked in awe at what might have been a palace in red and white. The place was seething; Radha felt numb: they would be together for just a few more hours. How strange that although every thought was centred on him she felt so empty. The unaccustomed noise and bustle barely registered on her consciousness.

In the carriage, they said little, sitting cramped, children on their knees, people jostling against them. She was aware her husband resented the heat, the smell of bodies and the jolts that threw them all together. Two whole hours to Port Swetenham and barely a word uttered between them. Where do you start when there are so many months of silence to be squeezed into these desperate few minutes before the ship's horn blasts you apart?

On arriving at the port, the confusion was so great there was no time to think of anything but hold on to the children. She wished she had more hands. A hellish commotion, seemingly directionless, ants whose nest is under siege. And the noise – officials blowing whistles, vendors yelling their wares, children shrieking, bicycle bells, and dogs barking and scratching and getting in the way. Bedlam. And there were soldiers everywhere.

Amidst all this, the Doctor remained stern and silent. Most of the crowd set off for the steamer, heavily encumbered with their luggage, but he was among the first to hire two porters to carry their bags onto the boat. He accompanied his family aboard, checked their cabin and settled them in as far as possible.

When the moment came for Radha to part from her husband, she clung to Mena, her twenty-month-old child, in a vain attempt not to cry. She knew her tears would displease him, not only because he would interpret them as a sign of immaturity, but for the effect on the children. The tears came anyway. Mercifully the children were too absorbed in their unusual surroundings to notice her sobs. She thought, if only he'd take me in his arms, hold me while I drown in my sorrow, I'd have a memory to comfort me in the months to come. *Atha*, please, hold me, and tell me you'll miss me; *please*, just this once. But it would have taken more than her prayers to reach him as he stood there, reserved and distant.

He embraced them stiffly, each one in turn, she was one among the rest. Later she tried to recall if she'd been first or last or somewhere in the middle. No parting words of tenderness unless his assurance he'd write counted as one.

He disembarked taking Julius with him, leaving her standing there, alone and rent in the throng on the deck, the toddler in her arms, the three older children grouped about her. As the steamer slowly pulled out of the harbour, she kept her eyes fixed on his tall figure till she could make him out no more. Still her eyes lingered on the watery blank as she wondered how such emptiness could be so unbearably painful.

Chapter 5

The five-day crossing, though uncomfortable, was without a mishap. Radha had little time to dwell on the unhappy separation. She fell into her bunk each night so tired sleep rescued her from all but a fleeting moment of anxiety. The cramped space brought her comfort; this, for the moment, was her universe; here, at least, she was in command.

Mornings saw the five of them taking the air round the upper deck. Radha taught the two older children to play with cowry shells. They were happy to play on their own, scooping the shells with their tiny hands, while she attended to a few chores such as washing their clothes. And if Paula, her eldest daughter, looked challengingly at her, she did nevertheless what she was told: brushed her teeth, combed her hair, placed her shoes by her bunk each night, the clean socks neatly folded inside each shoe. It could have been worse. Paula, who was six and a half, took charge of Roy who was five, so that Radha's main task was to look after Leela and Mena. It was manageable.

The image of her husband was before long accompanied by that of her mother on whom she'd relied unquestioningly until her marriage. The thought of seeing her again partly made up for the loss of him. These two people whom she loved hadn't taken to each other. She remembered that look of listlessness on her mother's face immediately after their meeting with the Doctor; she'd remained unusually silent, looking at her daughter every now and then, a frown on her face.

She knew so little about the man she'd chosen for her son-in-law. Her husband's work had kept them in French Indo-china too long. The Doctor too had been living abroad, in Malaya, where his father had worked till his retirement. Both families, typical of so many Indians who had left home in search of work. Her probing enquiries brought little light. In the end, she knew, everything was in the hands of the Gods.

Radha's husband had made it clear from the beginning what he thought of her mother; 'domineering and backward', he'd called her. This had pained Radha but before long he ceased to mention her; she was far away in South India and had become an irrelevance in their lives.

The most wearisome part of the five-day crossing was having to mingle with the other passengers on deck or in the dining hall; to sit with strangers and smile and talk to them. All of them fleeing from the horror of war, their lives torn apart. 'Everyone in the same boat!' they shouted gleefully a thousand times over. It seemed to bring them comfort. In what way was misery lessened simply because there was so much more of it all round?

The ship called at Penang to pick up more passengers. It was already crammed to bursting. Radha was not used to crowds and was glad when, at last, they docked at Madras though the bustle here was worse even than the crush in Port Swetenham. The noise was deafening, coolies running in every direction, some so encumbered with luggage they were a moving jumble of cases, bags and boxes. Except for a few Europeans showing their ankles, all the women wore saris. Not a single Chinese anywhere in sight. So different from Malaya. It was good to be back.

Her brother Ravi was there to meet her as planned. He'd become a good looking, suave young man. Surely her husband would think better of him now? Almost the same height and broad like him too. But in other respects so different with that mischievous smile. Ravi, her little brother, always getting up to tricks!

'Surprised, huh?' he exclaimed, aware of her appreciative gaze. 'Twelve years is a long time. Hey, imagine that – I was exactly twelve when you left. I'm taller than father used to be.' He would have added, and more handsome, but remembering how his sister used to dote on their father, thought better of it. Instead, he smiled winningly across at her and said, 'you, on the other hand, don't look a day older; husband must be treating you well.'

'I ...' Radha began, but her brother had moved on to the children.

'These kiddies – what, not feeling shy, are you? It's your uncle Ravi, come to take you in a motor car.' He playfully cuffed his nephew's ear, then, noticing Paula, teased, 'Hey Radha, no kidding, you have a rival in the making! Come on everyone, car's over there; you can't see it with those urchins crowding round it.'

So saying, Ravi, the proud owner (at least, for one day) of a motor, pushed his way through, holding a child's hand in each of his. He tilted his seat forward and ushered the three children into the back while Radha settled in front with Mena. Boys clambered onto the mudguard of the little Morris and all but onto the roof.

'Here,' Ravi shouted, throwing the end of the rope to one of the two coolies, 'You, take the other end and fix it over there. Pull hard, harder; I don't want it coming loose as we're speeding along, I'll hold you responsible if it does.'

They were laughing and tugging as they fixed the rope and Radha watched in wonder thinking how subdued this same scene would be if her husband were conducting the operation. Undoubtedly, it would be done in half the time and the knots probably secured more tightly, only, nobody would have enjoyed the task. Perhaps his training as a surgeon had made him meticulous and serious – having a life at your finger-tips was no laughing matter. And yet, there had been lighter moments. A long time ago.

When everything was in place Ravi started up the engine with the handle, then took his seat and put his foot down. There was an almighty roar but the car refused to budge. In the back, Roy, who'd been barely able to contain his excitement, was suddenly deflated.

'Car's not going,' he said in a small voice, 'Breakdown!'

'Ah,' Ravi rejoined, 'Quite right; brake down! I should have thought of that; there, off we go.' And with that he let down the brake and the car leapt forward and stalled.

'Breakdown, breakdown!' Roy chanted, bolder now and more excited than ever.

'Hand brake's down, so it can't be that. Think I overdid the foot brake. So many different brakes – *I* need a break!' Ravi got out and tinkered first with one end of the Morris - where he clearly didn't find what he was looking for, then the other. Meanwhile there was no shortage of advice from the crowd that had suddenly re-grouped from nowhere.

Radha watched her brother and smiled; she couldn't help noting that the few times her husband had used a car, they hadn't had these problems. But it was nice to see how good-humouredly everyone set to.

Eventually they edged forward till he was clear of the jostling crowd. Getting onto the road seemed to take forever as the little car jerked forward and almost stalled countless times. Finally they made it and were bumping along on the way to Pondicherry.

'I never dreamt I'd be here like this,' Radha said, the wind snatching her words through the open window of the little car.

'What was that? Weren't you going to see us again?!' The car veered wildly as he turned to look at his sister, 'Hey, *Aka*, my little big sister, weren't you ever going to come and see us then? Not even when I get married? – which I shall one day.'

'Might have been difficult. My husband – but it's amazing to see you like this, driving a car, knowing your way about; a comfort to *Umma*, I'm sure.'

'Hmm, she doesn't always share my sense of fun, but I try. So, Manicasami's –'

'Oh, you mustn't call him that! He's known as the Doctor. Everyone calls him the Doctor, and so must you.'

'*The* Doctor? We got word he was the best surgeon in Kuala Lumpur, but is he really the *only* one there? What's the matter with Manicasami, perfectly good name, I'd have thought. What's he like *The Doctor*? Going to the top, from what we can make out.'

All those feelings Radha had kept stored up in the last two years, could she, she wondered, tell her brother about them now? Open the sluice gates at long last? Tell him how much she missed home, what had been her home here in Pondicherry. Missed her mother and him, Ravi. Longed to be with them, to feel once more cosseted, a life shared with others.

'Yes, well, he commands respect wherever he goes, but I'm not sure he shares my sense of fun either; so, there we are.' Radha laughed and turned away to look out once more, but she wished she could think of something else to say, something warm and inspiring.

'Serious business, being a surgeon,' Ravi observed. 'I kept well clear of that.'

Through the window a reddish slurry of fields, women bent from their waist, their cotton saris tucked in, ankle-deep in water. They were planting rice. Open country. So different from over there where he was: miles of dense plantations; tall, dark rubber trees; secret forests, their canopies warding off the rays of the sun. Jungle. Lonely tappers gathering the viscous fluid in the uncanny silence of rows and rows of shadowless trunks. The air suffocating, saturated, still. She should be over there with him; who knows what might happen to a man on his own in such a place.

Chapter 6

Lusty singing from Ravi brought her back to her surroundings. Everything was different here, even the air – drier; people darker and wiry; open faces, ready to break into a smile. Radha smiled back at the women who had stopped to stare at the passing car.

Except for jeeps with French soldiers, there was little motorized traffic on the narrow road which had been damaged by the recent torrential rainfall. The odd army truck, not much bigger than their car, rattled along though, more often, it was at a standstill, having a tyre changed or cooling off with bonnet raised, cloaked in mystery within clouds of smoke. Each time they approached a vehicle, horns blaring, Ravi as much as the other driver gesticulated wildly and seemed set on collision course with neither of them willing to give way, both uncertain which side they should pass the other. It was not much better when it was a buffalo cart.

Radha sat with the imperturbability of one who knew nothing about driving. But the last near-encounter was a little too close and Ravi leant out of the window, shaking his fist at the disappearing truck as he hurled insults into the vacant air and almost landed in the ditch.

'Should be locked up; scoundrel!' Then with the contempt of a seasoned driver for a mere learner, he spat out, 'Thinks he can drive! I tell you, Roy, here, could do better.'

'Ooh, uncle Ravi, can I try now? Please, you said I could,' and the child began to clamber over to the front.

'Shush, Roy, don't distract your uncle,' Radha said, turning round. 'Sit down quietly; you'll get your chance all in good time.'

'You still haven't told me what he's really like,' Ravi pursued, 'I want to hear all about him. Think I'll be rich and famous like him one day? He is famous, isn't he, *Aka*?'

'Oh, yes, he has quite a reputation though he's only just forty.'

'And he must be rich to have told me to get hold of a car. It was the easiest thing on earth renting it – actually, belongs to a friend of a friend; he was happy to have the extra cash. We have Manicasa – the Doctor to thank for this bit of luxury.'

'When it comes to money, he's generous ... Ravi, you really are clever to have learnt to drive like this!' she remarked, changing the subject adroitly.

'There's nothing to it; I could probably do it with my eyes closed and no hands – see!'

'No, Ravi! Think of the children! Whoa! What happened there?'

'Relax! We're back on course. It's easy, actually, if you've got a knack for it.' At this point, Ravi leant right over to help the car turn the corner.

They stopped three times to re-fill from the cans he'd put in the boot as they covered the hundred-and-fifty kilometres between Madras and Pondicherry in Southern India. In places the road was little more than a mud track.

Coconut palms threw sharp silhouettes against a flat white sky; mongrels scratched their emaciated bodies, turned dry incurious eyes on them and returned to their scratching. She'd forgotten how many cows there were, wandering lazily, their long tongues curling round torn-off bits of banana leaves. Or they just lay in the middle of the road, resting. Radha's heart was still with her husband, but this was home.

Every strip of water seemed to have washing of some sort or other, brown bodies that dipped and glistened in the sun, clothes beaten against boulders; sights her husband would have found distasteful. She remembered his words, 'Indian fixation with dunking themselves in filthy water', and yet, they looked so happy, she thought.

At last, with darkness falling round them, Ravi brought the car to a dramatic stop outside the old house. Radha put down the toddler and reached out to enfold her mother in her arms.

'It's been a long time,' the grandmother said. 'God be praised! I thought this day would never come.' As though a dam had burst, Radha hugged her mother to her and sobbed her heart out. 'Ah, problems? I guessed as much, though you said little in your letters. My poor child, a woman must endure. We'll talk later.' Noticing the children, she exclaimed, 'Look at these little things, they must be exhausted. Come, a cold drink – lime – I made it myself; nice and sweet; and some rice and tomatoes; then to bed.'

'No,' said a voice.

Turning round, the grandmother saw one of the children, must be Paula, she thought, tall for a six-year-old. Her eldest grand-daughter, pretty, in a short dress which was just about understandable given her age, but there was something else oddly European about her – might have been the short hair or the socks. Perhaps the unfriendly air. Her sisters too all had short hair, no doubt a whim of her son-in-law.

'What d'you mean 'no'?' she asked, looking at the child sternly.

'Oh, that's just Paula,' Radha explained, 'Always says no, but she'll have some anyway.

Taking her brother's hand, Paula went inside to explore. Leela, in the meantime, clung to her mother's sari, hiding her face within its folds the moment anyone looked at her; Mena held onto her mother's hand and seemed to be singing or talking to herself.

Inside, the two older children perked up and began to look around. Everything was so different from what they were used to. A long staircase going straight up from the middle of the house! In their home there'd only been a few steps from the garden onto the veranda. No garden here with grass where they could run around and play with Ted, the dog. Ted was old now; very old. No dog here. Just a courtyard. Where were they going to play?

They climbed up the stone steps to the upper floor: their bedroom with two single beds, one for Paula, the other for Leela; a cot in one corner. Where would Roy be sleeping? There were other doors further along; probably in one of those rooms, Paula thought.

The door to the terrace was locked. Standing on tiptoe they looked through the upper glass section; the stone terrace that overlooked the street had a parapet all round. The window in the bedroom was too high for the children to reach. It let in warm evening air with sounds of voices and bicycle bells. Crows cawed raucously and somewhere nearby a dog barked setting off a noisy chorus of mongrels.

Ravi attended to the luggage with the help of the two young servant girls.

'I've lost him,' Radha whispered to her mother, tears springing to her eyes.

'Oh, my poor child! What a time to be away from him.'

'Oh, I tried to resist, didn't want to leave; but in the end ...' the words died away.

'We'll speak tomorrow,' the grandmother said, 'You too need a rest now.'

They gave the children their supper and put them to bed. Radha retired to her old room, to memories of days filled with laughter, to a time when the quiet innocence of her heart was untroubled by thoughts of love. Or the fear of losing it. At last, she fell into a deep sleep.

Chapter 7

The next morning, with the children in the care of the ayah who was little more than a child herself, the two women sat in the intimate darkness of the bedroom where the blinds were kept half closed to keep out the heat.

'I've no proof to back up my feelings,' Radha confided. 'Nothing at all unless you accept what he mumbles in his sleep. The first time it happened, I asked him what Luk was.'

'Luk?'

'It's a name; it means six in Chinese – they call their children by the number in order of birth. They probably do the same for their wives or concubines.'

'Tch! What a notion!'

'I think this woman may be his –'

'A *Chinese* woman! Radha, it won't be anything serious. He can't forget his caste.'

'Listen, *Umma*, when I asked him, he stared at me for what seemed ages; the silence was awful; wished I hadn't asked. At last he said it was one of the nurses who work at the hospital. I knew it would be.' She waited for her mother's reaction, but there was none.

'All he said was "She works hard and is efficient", but something in his voice scared me. It was as though he found me wanting by comparison.'

'A man in his position can't have his wife working as if he couldn't afford servants.'

Position? Caste? How could she explain to her mother her husband had no regard for either? Indeed, that he despised them. That he thought married women should go out to work; that there was nothing wrong if an Indian married a European. Or, presumably, a Chinese. Her mother would never be able to understand these ideas. She wasn't picking up her train of thought at all, but she persevered.

'I told him again he'd uttered that – word – in his sleep but he said nothing more. Can you imagine, *Umma*, what it sounds like in the stillness of the night?'

Her mother didn't answer. Radha thought the situation must be too unfamiliar to her. Either that or she hoped to keep it at bay by not confronting it. Could one do that? Yes, she herself had managed up to a point. But it was a relief at last to bring it into the open.

'He doesn't let me call him *Atha*,' she said, knowing this might hit home.

'Ayoyo! How can you talk to him if you can't call him husband?'

'That's the problem – we don't. At first, I tried to stop, but *Atha* kept slipping in; he didn't seem to mind, by then; we were getting on well. You see, in the early days, he was trying to make me less Indian; then he stopped worrying about things like that.'

'I should think so! What else would you be if not Indian?'

'Now things have changed for the worse. I feel if I call him *Atha* now, he doesn't want to be reminded he *is* my husband.'

'Tch! He was lucky to get you, that's for sure.' Those ghastly rumours she'd heard at the time of the marriage about her son-in-law's father were more rife than ever. His poor wife had endured in silence, but since her death, things had gone from bad to worse. 'Tell me, Radha, how did he take the death of his mother? I remember he was attached to her.'

'Just mentioned it, that's all; I think he knew, with her heart, she wasn't going to reach old age, poor *Mamy*! It was your letters that told me all about it; her death, and the funeral.'

'Your father-in-law...' her mother began, then changed direction, 'I'll tell you one thing, your father was a saint, but on the whole, men aren't to be trusted. This separation ...'

'I know. I didn't want to leave him, I told you.'

'He must have been pleased when Mena was born,' she remarked patting the toddler who was busy pulling at her sandal.

'Not sure; think he'd have preferred a boy. Future plans were ready long before she was born; I think he was expecting a boy.' Radha hesitated a moment, '*Umma*, that doll I used to have when I was little, remember? it was on the shelf in my bedroom. You remember it, don't you, with a little pink sarong and almond eyes? I used to find myself looking at it a lot when I was pregnant. Mena looks just like it, don't you think? That too was a girl.'

'Mmm, there is a resemblance though I think little Mena looks just like you.'

'Really?' After a moment's silence, though there was no one about, Radha dropped her voice to a whisper, 'Recently, his touch has changed. I know I'm not imagining it.'

'It's better not to say these things,' her mother said decisively, cutting off any further discussion on the subject.

So that was it. Somehow, if it wasn't said, it didn't exist. Or, if it existed, as long as it wasn't mentioned, it wouldn't acquire the substance of something real. Radha needed to talk, to break out of the loneliness that married life had become. It was obvious her mother's experiences were too different from her own to be of any help.

She turned her thoughts to the next day when her in-laws would be here to see her. With a few exceptions, her husband had nothing good to say about his family whereas she loved hers deeply. Well, she'd get to know his, at last. Could be interesting, different; hers so small, his large enough to be a clan. She was eager to make a good impression on them.

Her mother watched, happy to see her daughter perk up suddenly as she went to the kitchen to sort out various ingredients – an almond and cardomom mixture, of all things! The servant had left the table clean but Radha wiped it vigorously before beginning.

'This has to be Manicasami's influence,' her mother said smiling.

'I've got used to it now, don't even notice it.' Radha looked up suddenly. 'Feels just like that other time when I did the sweetmeats for his very first visit!'

'Goodness!' her mother exclaimed, jolted by the memory.

'Do hope they like my almond cake; makes a change from the usual treats we make here. Nine adults coming, is that right?'

'Eight, I think. The eldest son won't be here; just his wife.' It was a wonder, the mother mused, she dared show her face in public when everyone knew the shameful truth.

'I met them all, of course, during those few days before we left for Kuala Lumpur, but there was so much happening, it was hard to take in everything; so many of them – mother, sister, nine brothers! Father, of course. Really sad *Mamy* is dead. She was nice.'

'Yes, I think she was.' After a pause, her mother murmured, 'She's better off where she is, poor woman.'

'Why?'

'Oh, just problems she could do nothing about,' her mother said vaguely.

The day after that visit which had held such promise, Radha lay awake at the hour of the siesta going over it step by step. It had not gone brilliantly.

Her father-in-law had been the first to come in and Radha greeted the head of the family with due deference, though she couldn't help noticing he was slurring his words badly. No doubt this was where her husband's aversion to drink had started.

'I know he'd have wanted to be here with you all,' she murmured, a white lie, dictated by etiquette, 'He often talks of India, of you – we were very sad about *Mamy*.'

His answer was both inappropriate and lacking in respect for the dead. Radha moved away slightly so as not to be overpowered by the smell of alcohol.

The three sons who'd followed soon after, gave her a perfunctory greeting then carried on their discussion about the rising cost of rice. No doubt they were in touch with Anna and Leo, even so, their lack of interest in her husband and son, there in a country where war was imminent, was dismaying.

Radha turned her attention to the children, plying them with cake and Indian biscuits, telling the girls how lovely they looked in their colourful *pavade suttae* with the long skirt.

'Paula's old enough to be in a proper skirt,' one of the mothers pointed out.

'I don't like them; they look funny,' was Paula's verdict.

'Funny! you're the one who looks funny in a little child's dress at your age,' came the sharp reply.

Radha was shocked by the attack on her daughter but before she could go to her rescue, other questions came thick and fast from various sisters-in-law: size of their bungalow; cost of servants; the Doctor's standing at the hospital. Then suddenly:

'Why didn't your husband come over with his family?' Something about the tone was full of menace even if the question was simply thoughtless. Radha registered they were waiting for an answer.

'With such a large family,' she began, 'it would be risky to start from scratch over here; it's taken him ages to get where he is.' There were no nods, no soothing murmurs of agreement. She knew better than to mention her husband's views on hygiene in Indian hospitals. 'Pay would be a lot lower here. Besides, the war won't last, if it comes at all. But while we're here, I hope we'll be able to meet often. Perhaps the children can –'

If Radha had been hoping for soft words to boost her morale, they didn't come. And the return invitation was unenthusiastic and deferred to a later date. It was discouraging; this was her husband's family. *Her* family. However was she going to strike a warm relationship with any of them?

As they left it became patently clear they would keep her at arm's length. Why were they forcing her to be an outsider? She had smiled throughout, but it had been an ordeal. If only Anna or brother Leo were here, she thought. Anna was stuck in Penang. Perhaps Leo managed to see her husband and Julius? Cousin Pradeep and Vida were still in KL; possibly, they too went over to see him from time to time. Dear God, let them all be safe, she prayed.

Radha had not taken in how far her husband had alienated his family. He had rejected them. His name was no longer theirs. Even if she didn't voice his views, they were well known, and in their eyes, she would always remain an appendage of the Doctor, her husband.

Chapter 8

Shrieks from her children put an end to all thoughts of in-laws and Radha ran out of her room to check. Seeing the creature twirl angrily was far from reassuring.

'Roy, don't touch it! she cried, 'It'll sting you! Don't!'

'He's all right. Don't worry, go back and finish your siesta,' her mother called. 'Lakshmi, you useless girl, get rid of it, at once. If you did your work properly, there wouldn't be scorpions lurking in the corners under the furniture.'

Radha went back to her room. Other snippets came through the closed door, "Paula, I do not want to hear you say no ever again. And don't just stand around."

Paula, the apple of her father's eye. But it was already clear *Ummuma* and her eldest granddaughter were not hitting it off. After the tussles Radha herself had had, this didn't come as a surprise. If Paula developed into a difficult young woman, it could present problems. It would reduce her chances of finding a suitable husband for her.

Radha shook herself free of these thoughts. She had to get on with her life here. How often had she dreamt of returning to this place! Now that she was here, she must somehow make a go of it, stop fretting about Paula, about her husband and Julius (poor Julius!). And about her in-laws.

She became aware how quiet the house was suddenly; her mother must have taken the children upstairs. Radha threw open the shutters only to close them again immediately – she was not in her bungalow with the grassy expanse bordered by trees and flowering shrubs. This was town, people passing to and fro, bicycles tinkling and the incessant rasping caw of crows. Leaving the shade of her room she walked into the open-plan reception area.

On the wall opposite, hung the two wedding photos, hers and her parents. A formal occasion; perhaps that was why he looked so stern. On another wall, a large framed picture of the Sacred Heart with a palm leaf tortured into a cross tucked behind it. She touched the cross with the tips of her fingers, then kissed them. Next to it, a plain clock ticked noisily, telling her time was passing even as she stood there separated from him by the deep waters of the Indian Ocean. Nothing she could do about it; she moved on.

Ah, the picture of the goddess Sarasvathi seated on a grassy mound, one leg gracefully resting on the other to balance the sitar. Radha's hand came to rest over her heart as she remembered that afternoon – it was before she met her husband. The beads on the goddess's sari glistened bright gold. Radha remembered the monsoon rain as it crashed noisily outside, and the calm inside this room as she sat fixing the beads along the sari's edge, cousin

Pradeep watching her, humming a tune, an accompaniment to the goddess. Happiness.

She sighed at the memory and looked down where her hands were resting – a vase of tall flowers on an occasional table. The perfume, heavens, nothing had changed in all that time! Not this, at least. The air was drenched with the scent of Madonna lilies, exactly as on that day, twelve years ago when Manicasami Nanamentem, accompanied by his parents, had come to ask for her hand in marriage. It had all been arranged beforehand between their parents so that this was merely a formality for the young people to meet each other.

The previous day, preparations had been frantic.

'*Umma*, hadn't I better make the sweetmeats straightaway or they won't be ready in time? No bait, no man!' Radha's hand flew to her mouth to hide her smile; she'd been too bold, lacking in modesty, could have been scolded. But her mother was preoccupied and appeared not to have heard.

'He will like them, won't he?' she asked, her self confidence suddenly gone. 'What if –'

'Of course he'll like them! Whoever heard of a man not liking sweetmeats! But make sure you do it yourself and don't let the servant interfere or you won't be able to say they're yours. When they arrive, you can be in the dining room.' She paused, working out the moves for maximum effect. 'Wait till I call you, then bring in your cakes and pass them round. A nice informal touch. Run along now and make them.'

Radha ran towards the kitchen then stopped suddenly and retraced her steps, hesitant.

'*Umma*, why do I have to get married? Can't I stay here with you?'

'Radha, we've been through all this: you were eighteen last week, a good age to marry.'

'Then, why not Pradeep?'

'Stop going on about Pradeep.'

'But, why not? He likes me, I know he does.'

'I'll tell you why, I thought of him before anyone else; but it's out of the question – your birth signs are not compatible.'

'There must be a mistake; we get on really well.'

'No mistake; I made the *sastrakar* re-check his calculations. He told me he'd compared your birth charts with the greatest care imaginable. It would be very irresponsible of me to ignore these warnings. Manicasami Nanamentem is the right man for you.'

'How do I know I'll like him?'

'What a way to talk! Marriage is a lifelong commitment; knowing that will help you to grow fond of him in a very short time. Have you forgotten how you used to get round *Uppa*? Well, it won't be different with your husband. Being some ten years older, he'll teach you all you need to know. One thing is certain, I can't keep you here forever.'

Her mother sighed as she thought of the difficulties of bringing up two children on her own. Of course, it would have been harder still if she hadn't had that miscarriage between Radha and Ravi. She was quite well off as far as money was concerned; her husband had worked for the French government so that she received a decent pension.

There was also the rent from the big house which would go to Ravi one day. The thing was, Radha was the right age. The match she'd made, though it wasn't ideal in one detail, in all others, it was highly satisfactory. Surgeons were in short supply and a *brilliant* surgeon a once-in-a-lifetime find.

'Look on the bright side,' she said encouragingly, 'Not only are the signs right but he's the right caste and your dowry has secured a worthy husband.'

'Pradeep's the right caste.'

'Radha, that is enough! The matter is settled; I want to hear no more on the subject.'

Her mother mused, this attachment to her cousin was nothing serious; they'd always been like brother and sister since they were tiny. In any case, it was out of the question. As for the Mentems, there were certain aspects of her future in-laws that were deeply disturbing: the father, she'd heard, was an alcoholic. There were still worse rumours about him: something to do with being too intimate with his eldest son's wife, God forbid!

What a burden this was! No husband to advise her, no friend to consult after so long an absence from Pondicherry. At least she'd been able to check on their birth signs. The Doctor was said to be exceptional, but did that mean he'd be a good husband? What if she were mistaken? A marriage is forever. Well, at least she could count on Radha. If disaster struck, she could be relied on to be steady.

'Your fiancé is said to be a serious man; perhaps a little stern, but in time that will be corrected by love. They say he's on the way to becoming a brilliant doctor. I have it on reliable authority, he's what they call an outstanding diagnostician.'

'An outstanding diagnostician! Heavens!' Turning suddenly, Radha asked, '*Umma*, what's a diagnostician?'

'Tch!' her mother replied impatiently, 'isn't it enough to know he's a diagnostician without wanting to know everything about him? Run along now and make those cakes.' Yes, she thought, all things considered, an outstanding diagnos - whatever he is, would make a suitable son-in-law.

Then the day had come.

Chapter 9

Radha now looked round the room, each piece of furniture a powerful reminder of the moment she'd first met her husband. Could the reality have been as piercing as these memories, she wondered.

He'd sat in the carved upright chair to the right; his parents in the sofa opposite the dining room, so that when she made her entrance, she fixed her most winsome smile on her future mother-in-law who let out an involuntary, 'Aah'.

What a find, the woman mused, gazing at Radha. She was very lovely in that shade of blue. And the gold necklaces looked wonderful against her clear complexion; fine gold bangles on slim wrists, but not too many; and something sparkled on her ears as she came forward, smiling. Beautiful! An abundance of smooth hair gathered behind, interlaced with silk thread that held a single, small gardenia – white on jet-black. A tiny curl had strayed onto her neck showing the smooth pallor of her skin. Her movements were so graceful she could have been Ganga herself wooing Shiva with every step; sandals glistened gold on slender feet.

In later years when his parents were dead, indeed, when there was no one left to contradict him, the man would claim, 'They sent me a photo beforehand, and I agreed to the match; told my mother she'd made a good choice. But that photo – it was a cheat; it had nothing to do with the person I finally saw and married. I would never have married her but for that picture.' So the man would argue and thus salve his conscience.

But on that day, though it was true he'd sworn to himself he wouldn't marry an Indian, never one from the South, he looked at her beauty and forgot his resolution. And although the day would come when his memory became selective, or downright inventive, there were many moments in their early years when Radha drew him into her world of the here and now, and they were happy together, a bright future ahead of them.

The day of the betrothal, her mother had placed herself as agreed in the armchair to the left so that Radha would be able to take the smaller upright chair to the extreme right, opposite the man. This arrangement would give her and her future husband a feeling of intimacy. Nothing but a vase of Madonna lilies on the inlaid table between them on this their first and last encounter before the wedding.

Radha offered her platter of sweetmeats which were readily accepted by his parents. And now another 'Ah' of wonder escaped from his mother on hearing Radha had made them herself. What a sweet, cultured voice the girl had! 'Talent to match her beauty,' the older woman murmured, unable to take her eyes off her future daughter-in-law.

A smile darted from the girl to her mother; it was true, she had made them herself without the help of the servant.

Radha continued her attentions to the older lady, but out of the corner of her eye, she could see her son: clean shaven in a white European-style suit and, goodness! was that a tie hanging round his neck? It had diagonal stripes. She should have guessed he'd be dressed something like this but she hadn't, and it caught her by surprise. His knees stuck out way past the edge of the chair. She tried to gauge his height: tall, very tall. More like a European. Standing next to him she'd not even come to his shoulders.

Now she moved towards him, was almost in front of him. White socks, black leather lace–ups that shone so bright she could see her silver salver mirrored in them; there were tiny holes making a pattern on the toe cap. Was all this to impress her? Or, suddenly she felt a flutter of panic, to intimidate her, to show he was different from all that was familiar to her?

She slowly raised her eyes, armed with her studiedly quiet smile, and offered him the bait. The look of anger on his face made her falter. What had she done? Had a fly somehow embedded itself among her cakes? She looked down in alarm. But no, there they were, as perfect and appetising as ever. She asked in amazement, 'Don't you want one? I made them myself.' She was about to move away when there was a sound from behind – his mother. His hand came forward and reluctantly took a *pal cova*. So much for her irresistible bait.

Her heart pounding, she put down the platter on the low table which had been placed conveniently near his parents and took her seat. The scent of the lilies was overpowering. Though she didn't raise her eyes from her hands that were tightly clasped in her lap, she was acutely aware he was looking straight ahead and not at her. It was as though, in this particular game, all the rules had been reversed: the Ace, usually the winner, turned out to be the lowest card.

For a second she entertained a wild hope – there would be no betrothal. This wasn't, never would be, the man for her. She'd seen in that fleeting glance he was good looking. But not in the way she knew. Her father's looks had been gentle in spite of a manly moustache, and his gaze had had a sweetness that had invited her to reach out to him. This man was different: wild, untamed. His deep voice cut into her thoughts.

'Did you mind living abroad?'

'I liked it. I was nine when we left Pondy; the whole family. Yes, I liked it.'

'Convent education, I suppose?'

'Yes.' He's waiting for more, to hear of my achievements. 'In my last term, I sang solo before the whole school. It was in French; everything was. But I kept up my Tamil.'

'Hmm, what about English?'

'English! No. In Saigon as in Pondicherry, French is the language in use.'

Silence fell between them. She sensed his disapproval. Had he guessed English had never featured in her priorities, and still didn't?

'What d'you want to know about me?' he asked.

'About you?' A glance of amazement as much as excitement, then she quickly looked down. Why did he look so angry? – could she ask him? 'Why do ... I don't know.' Help! 'I suppose I'll find out soon enough.' A smile to conceal her nervousness.

There was a deep rumble. Anger? Perhaps a laugh.
'Good answer.'

A laugh then. She sighed with relief. Now leave well alone, she told herself.

He too must have decided he'd found out all he needed to know. There were no further questions.

Now, so many years later, Radha looked at the chair where her husband had sat and felt a terrible longing for his nearness, to touch him, to feel his body hard against hers, to lay her head against him while he stroked her long, black hair. She'd known such moments of tenderness.

That afternoon, twelve years ago, when he and his parents had left, she'd been dismayed to find he hadn't touched the *pal cova*. It lay on the plate mocking her earlier confidence. She'd stood staring at it when suddenly, as if the god himself were sending her a message, she recalled the misunderstanding between Shiva and Parvati with its seemingly fearful consequences, Shiva's fury at finding the boy barring the door to his wife; how in his anger he had, there and then, severed his head. Parvati's distress. And then, the happy outcome with the god repenting his rashness which had led to the creation of Ganesh, the darling boy.

Perhaps Manicasami too would repent and this unhappy moment would be nothing more than a temporary misunderstanding. One day they'd laugh about it. She smiled to think she'd called him by his name even if it was only to herself. Then she said aloud, 'Manicasami Nanamentem'. There was no doubt the name had a heroic resonance, and her smile lingered as she felt the first intimations of love.

Chapter 10

The house in Pondicherry was exactly as it had been twelve years before.

'No point in making changes just for the sake of change,' her mother explained. 'I still get the outside painted every other year, but with just Ravi and me at home, there's been no wear and tear.'

'It's lovely. I wasn't here long before I had to leave, and yet this house is home for me.'

'Well, you know I'm leaving it to you, don't you, as well as your grandfather's mango plantation. Ravi will have the big house with the garden. Uppa and I felt that was fair.'

'Very fair. It's so peaceful here! Our bungalow over there is nice and quiet, a lovely garden, quite far from town. But it's not peaceful. Used to be. Now it's like waiting for something to happen.' She changed the subject, 'Are the mangoes from the back yard ripe? Oh, that reminds me – fruit – we must get some for the children. Those mangoes were the best I've ever tasted; such a gnarled old tree to produce such sweet fruit!' She smiled, remembering, then said, 'Just before I left KL, he mentioned the latrines; he knew they'd still be here.'

'They function perfectly well; why install a hole for everyone to share?' Her mother clucked her tongue to show what she thought of these new fangled, so-called improvements.

'The new sort isn't ideal, but I think there's room for improvement here,' Radha suggested. She remembered her husband's words, "Serious health hazard," he'd explained when installing a different system in the grounds behind their bungalow; then he'd added, "Jonah's antiques are best relegated to history."

The latrines in *Ummuma*'s house were of the most primitive imaginable: a square room with concrete floor, open to the sky; concrete foot blocks graded in size jutting from the wall on three of the four sides. Early in the morning, a coolie cleared the waste after which the servant girl cleaned the floor by sloshing water which ran out along the gulley on the fourth side and out into the open drain of the street behind the house.

In the old days, it had not seemed unhygienic to Radha. She realized how much she'd changed! Living with the Doctor had taught her all sorts of things, starting with a new language; not the English he used to go on about, but *his* language. He often talked in riddles; she'd meant to find out who Jonah was.

In spite of what her mother had said about him teaching her, she'd had to work things out for herself. It was what he expected of her, and she'd done it. Better than that; she'd learnt to extract words of approval, and finally, of love. Gradually, even his touch had become warm and tender.

Soon after they were married, the two of them were in the bedroom one day, she at the dressing table, he pacing up and down behind her somewhere. Suddenly he stopped.

'The first time we met ...'

'At my house, you mean?'

'Hm, not a good start. And then the church and wedding ceremony – worse still.'

'I can understand the church and celebrations wouldn't have suited you, but that first time we met, what went wrong then?'

'Heinous for a civilised man to have to accept the custom of arranged marriages, and then, for a doctor to be expected to celebrate with sugar-drenched sweetmeats – the cause of serious diabetes throughout India – frankly, it was anathema.'

Anathema – that didn't sound good at all but she had to know.

'Why then did you do it? I mean nobody made you. You must have accepted the idea of the arranged marriage and, to some extent, even the *pal cova*.'

'I was bewitched,' he rejoined, with what sounded surprisingly like a laugh.

'Oh heavens, bewitched!' she exclaimed with alarm, not yet familiar with his sense of humour.

'No, don't take fright – you looked – good. And there was my mother; she was pleased with the match she'd made.' He remembered her words, "Such beauty, and an ample dowry. Very fair-skinned; Mani, you're a lucky man; French education too". That had given her an edge over her peers. Above all, Radha was of the right caste, his mother's primary concern. How could she perceive the needs of her ambitious, curiously-westernized son when blinded by such an avalanche of blessings?

It was hard to say exactly when he'd turned so completely against all things Indian. The first stirrings of revolt had been against his father's philandering. Somewhere in the novels of Dickens, he'd read how dignified the English were in their dealings with each other. It was damnably unfair to have been born an Indian. There was no easy way round that.

It would have been impossible for him to acquire a European wife of the breeding and education he had in mind. If, by some miracle, he'd managed, his mother wouldn't have accepted her. She'd have been thoroughly ashamed of him for marrying out of caste. Strangely, for a man who felt so little regard for just about anyone, he wanted to please her in this area that meant so much to her.

That first sighting of Radha had, in any case, weakened his resolution. To his surprise, in a short time, he was actually happy with his lot. He even felt what might be called love.

'There was one great advantage in our getting married,' he'd continued, 'it meant I could leave India in a way that was conventionally acceptable. I shan't set foot there again.'

'What about our families, they're over there!' Radha cried in consternation, swivelling round on her stool to face him.

'A pack of wolves, waiting to pull you down into the slime, or pick your bones.'

'That's not how I see my family. My brother will get married one day, and we –'

'Your brother's a wastrel.'

'Despite the age gap, we're very close; like Anna and you. If you're not going to say something nice about him, I'd rather you said nothing.' He started for the veranda and she called after him, 'What about your mother, isn't she to see her grandchildren one day?'

'I repeat, I shall never set foot there again.'

Radha bit her lip and got on with painting the *puttu* on her forehead. In his answers (would that she'd never asked!), only his regard for his mother struck an accord. As she checked her make–up in the mirror, she saw her eyes glistened unusually.

Standing alone on the balcony, Doctor Mentem recalled his wedding ceremony. First the Nuptial Mass in *Notre Dame des Anges*: there was certainly nothing angelic about the singing. His new suit felt tight; the fellow had got the measurements wrong, trousers too short. They looked like borrowed garments. He should not have agreed to be the central figure in someone else's choreography. Standing there, gleaming white, bulls-eye for the congregation's curiosity. His bride in gold, so weighted down with heavy silk and jewels it was a wonder she could stand at all. The Mass dragged on, the priest uttering worn out platitudes. All the while his bride standing there, the *mundani* covering her head, cut off from her surroundings. Especially from him. Unreachable.

But however hard he tried to cut himself off from her, his mind dragged him into areas never before explored. She'd clearly never touched a man discounting her father; not even a handshake let alone other parts of the body. How well would he acquit himself? As long as there was no tittle-tattle about what happened between them. A quick glance at her profile that was just discernible amid the glittering fabric. Yes, all hell might break loose, but no one would be any the wiser. Good.

The reception in the ludicrously grand rented hall that followed the Mass was so typically Indian, it riled him to think he'd sat through that show. Two hundred guests in all! A hundred from his side, a hundred from hers. Unjustifiable extravagance since both families had lived abroad for years; they couldn't possibly have kept in touch with so many friends and relatives.

Given the atypical austerity of his in-laws house, the reception had been unspeakably showy with gold braid draped from pillar to post. Thousands of garishly coloured paper flowers formed garlands swathed from the entrance up to the absurd dais erected for him and his bride so that the two-hundred guests could gawk at them as at animals in a zoo. And there'd been that wretched photographer, refusing to buzz off however hard he scowled.

As for the musicians, thumping away on their drums till all hours of the night to the hideous accompaniment of a whining *nadesaram* fit to wake the dead. That was a trumpet that would never find its way into any civilized orchestra. Finally, a mountain of biriani and enough sweetmeats to kill off all those present. The whole show was meretricious beyond belief. A total waste of money, to boot, and to what end?

His father – "drunk as a lord" – the English say with that incomprehensible indulgence towards the aristocracy. Oh, the shame of it! Not that he gave a fig, or so he told himself, as to what the rest of them thought, but his mother, having to watch as her drunken husband lurched towards their eldest son's wife. And his brand-new, oh-so-superior mother-in-law watching, weighing him up, *him*, her son-in-law, through his father's shortcomings, and finding him wanting! Rage stirred within him.

Now fury mingled with pity as his eyes took in his sister Anna standing in the knot of women, tallest and youngest. A girl to end the long line of boys. A pearl. Fourteen and already wed. Married off before the groping attentions of her father shackled her forever to the family home, thereby adding to an overflowing cup of shame and disgrace. Revulsion choked him and he turned away only to meet the gaze of his bride's pert little brother, Ravi.

'I'm here to wish you luck, dear bro-in-law. Look after my sister, won't you? – she's the only one I have. You're a lucky man.'

Twelve-years old and talking like a boring old man! He made to move away but Ravi wasn't to be so easily shaken off.

'I can give you a tip – a sure way to get round her is to ply her regularly with *gulab jamun*, in fact, any sweetmeat will do. I've tried it, and it works.'

'That would hardly be the way to look after her,' the Doctor growled. Such an extraordinary mixture of ignorance and confidence was beyond comprehension.

To hell with the lot of them. He'll leave these people and start his married life in Malaya, another British colony, one he was already familiar with. His family had lived in Penang for years before returning to India; some of his ancestors had strayed over there as early as the previous century. He himself had done his medical training in

Singapore (where else could he have found a standard equal to his ability?). He'd then secured a post on the mainland as surgeon at Government Hospital in Kuala Lumpur. An upmarket bungalow went with the appointment; it stood a little out of town and had a plot of land round it with mature trees and shrubs. From the start his family would be cut off from the riffraff. And, when the first child was born, he'd get a pet dog.

He would change his cumbersome names, keeping just the part of Nanamentem that had a pleasing Latin sound. Appropriate too! And it had a ring of authority when coupled with the title: Doctor. Doctor Mentem – a name to describe the profession and the man.

When he announced to his bride, on their first morning as man and wife, they'd be leaving for Kuala Lumpur at the end of the week, she at first imagined he was talking of an extravagant western-style honeymoon. As the truth dawned on her, she showed neither curiosity nor annoyance but an acceptance which he interpreted as a sort of fatalism.

In fact, Radha was not sorry to hear of a complete change. Sensing she'd be making many mistakes before learning to please this difficult man, she preferred to set out on her new life unobserved.

Chapter 11

Twelve years since that wedding. A sense of hopelessness. How was she to retrieve all those hopes and dreams that had been lost along the way?

Her mother came in with the toddler and sat down next to her, sighing with contentment.

'Sweet little Mena!' Then a different sort of sigh, 'Ravi's such a worry to me! He's so wild.'

'Boys are always wild.'

'That's the point – he's no longer a boy. He's twenty-four!' She changed the subject, 'Tell me about my eldest grandson. Poor Julius, left over there without his mother!'

In fact, every time Radha thought about her son, Julius, the "someone" who was looking after him usurped his place and Radha found herself concentrating on her rather than Julius. It was also true that for the last three years her contact with Julius had changed subtly. But at the beginning, ah, how different that had been! How proud she'd been of him! Her first born and a boy! She thanked Heaven from the bottom of her heart for so great a blessing.

'Can't help thinking I should have breast-fed him longer,' she said, more to herself than to her mother. Her husband's words came back to her, "One month only; the baby will get all the necessary nutrients and you will keep your shape." Her thoughts were still far away when she added, 'A lovely baby ... now it's as though he's been weaned off me in more ways than one. Tutors come to instruct him in subjects I studied in my last years at school.'

'Tch! Far too young!' Her mother shook her head with disapproval.

'He was six when it started.'

'Six!'

'In the evenings, on returning from the Dispensary, his father conducts an informal question-and-answer session which, like the day-time tutorials, is in English.'

'What does he want all this English for?'

'He has his reasons,' Radha shrugged to show she didn't share them. 'At first Julius entered into the game excitedly, showing off while I sat nearby, embroidering, encouraging him with a smile or even clapping. It was touching to see the two of them – his father was so engrossed in him! Before long, it became less fun. You see, *Umma*, Julius couldn't stop when he felt like it: it was like a proper lesson. But, in another sense, it was still a game – bit like a cat and mouse. I came to dread it.'

'Poor child!'

'Yes, poor Julius. Awful, watching the change in him; he used to laugh a lot. We had such fun together! Now, he's like a frightened little boy. That's what he's become, a frightened little boy; sort of dithers before saying the simplest phrase. He has a stutter.'

'Of course, you couldn't say anything.'

'I did.' She half expected her mother to scold her for daring to question her husband. 'I couldn't just watch and do nothing. By then, we no longer agreed about anything. He reacted heatedly; told me to stick to what I knew. What I knew! Actually, in a way, seeing the change in Julius, I understood what was happening better than he did; but however hard I tried, I couldn't get that across to him, not even through tears.' She fell silent. Then, wanting to change the subject, she asked, '*Umma*, doesn't Roy remind you of Ravi? He makes me laugh with his funny antics.'

'Yes, he is like Ravi. You're quite right to be proud of him. But keep an eye on him; make sure he doesn't get up to too much mischief. A timely beating never did anyone any ...'

'Beating! Oh, he's never that naughty! Besides, my husband wouldn't have that and for once we're in complete agreement.'

'Hmm, you're making a mistake. Watch what he gets up to, – at least Julius has a younger brother to keep him company.'

'Too far apart,' Radha said with a shake of her head. 'In any case, Julius is expected to study most of the time. Listen to this, *Umma*, these are the plans: one day, Julius will go to England, just like Gandhichi and Nehru. He's to become a leading statesman or it may be a lawyer; he'll be studying law anyway. Roy is to be a surgeon; some sort of diplomatic thing for Paula; and medicine for Mena – imagine that! As yet, no plans for Leela; she's going to be a problem for him.'

'Strange, isn't it – she looks just like any other child, but there is something not quite right.' She was lost in thought for a moment. 'You know Radha,' she said at last, 'I hoped being with you would make Manicasami less headstrong; generally change him. But it hasn't happened. These poor children! Poor little Mena, a medic! I ask you, is that the proper preparation for a wife and mother of a family?' She shook her head in answer to herself, 'And Julius, why fill his head with such wild and empty dreams? Why take him away from his family to send him to a foreign country?'

Her mother had merely re-phrased Radha's own misgivings and yet, of a sudden, she found herself defending her husband as though only she had the right to criticize him.

'There's nothing wrong in making plans for one's children. Or to start teaching them at a young age, to set them on the right course. You yourself always said *Uppa* wasn't strict enough with Ravi.'

Talking about her husband had already become an obsession with Radha; but the combination of husband and children, especially Julius, was too painful. She started moving listlessly round the room.

'I need to get one or two things, maybe a sari and the odd blouse; some things for the children too. I brought only the essentials, what with so much to carry. The trunk he sent on ahead – I'm wondering if it's got lost.'

'Oh, you won't believe the changes in Bina Bazaar! Can't understand why your husband wants to chase after Europe when we've got the finest things right here. We'll go there before anywhere else; I know you'll like it.'

The outing was a success in that Radha managed to buy what she was looking for, but she was deeply disturbed by the gulf between her life and that of her husband. Hers, seemingly carefree as she wandered round shops buying pretty things; she might have been on holiday, bringing her children to meet their grandmother. His – in mortal danger, day and night, caring for Julius, caring for all of them; the burden of providing; that need to survive for the sake of others.

'Radha,' her mother suddenly called, 'I know what you're thinking. There's nothing you can do about what's happening over there; but you can make the best of your life here. Don't forget the children rely on you for their well-being.'

Radha nodded her head to show agreement. But she felt making the best of her life here, at this moment, was going to be extremely challenging.

Chapter 12

It hadn't been easy to get Paula into the convent where the standard of education was higher than the junior school, but Radha had done it with promises of embroidered altar cloths and donations plus a refusal to accept defeat. Ravi, who had watched her efforts with interest was full of admiration.

'The same old Radha who always gets her way!' he said as they were walking home after leaving Paula at the convent on her first day. Ravi did seem to take time off work all too easily, his sister thought, but said nothing. He continued, 'I was told women change when they get married, that they become submissive and undemanding. But there was no budging you till Paula was accepted. I pity the Doctor.'

'Don't. It doesn't work with him.'

'I'm sure you found a way.'

'I tried, and it did seem to work for a while. Then things changed and, in the end, I ran out of ideas. My last attempt, and failure, was turning myself into a slave, but perhaps, by then ...'

'What a monster!'

'Oh no! If you knew him as I do, you wouldn't say that. I've seen him racked through the suffering of his patients. In fact, he never thinks of himself. In all our years together, he's only taken a handful of holidays because he's so conscientious. And when it comes to our children, we don't agree about the way they should be brought up, but I can see he lives for them. You must agree, that isn't the image of a monster. He's just different. Perhaps that's why, despite everything, here I am wishing I was with him, wondering why I haven't heard for so long.'

They'd reached the house and on going in, Ravi was the first to see the blue envelope on the inlaid table.

'Look Radha – a letter!' he said, handing it to her with a flourish.

She snatched it from him and, running to her room, shut the door for complete privacy.

Feb. 15th
'42

Dear Radha,

An opportunity has presented itself so that I am able to send this via a trusted friend; it should therefore reach you safely. I may have to be circumspect in future correspondence; reprisals for any perceived infraction are pitiless.

There's chaos here, though I shall set your mind at rest straightaway: the occupation of KL was surprisingly smooth. An exemplary case of military planning. Their post conquest administration is quite the reverse: no postal service, schools shut down, the Hospital ... but I'll come to that later.

First, the occupation: they stationed themselves on the other side of the river on Christmas Eve. Our brave soldiers (mainly Australians), were busy preparing themselves for the festivities. The actual occupation took place on Christmas Day and Boxing Day during which time the afore-mentioned soldiers were either taken up celebrating or found themselves in no fit state to face the enemy. The evils of alcohol, yet again. The outcome was felicitous in that there was little of the anticipated carnage. In spite of that I have been kept very busy.

I evacuated Julius to Kachou with the matron from H. (You may remember the village; we drove through it when I had to see a patient in Serambam, a rich Chinese fellow who was in tin.) It looks as though it was an unnecessary precaution but I didn't want to take any risks. In any case, Victoria Institute has been taken over for housing aircraft personnel, so there are no classes for him to miss. I'll shift him to St John's when he gets back (probably next month), though the Brothers at St J's, being Catholic, are under house arrest; they are not allowed to teach. Food is in short supply. Rumour has it the

Brothers are having to trap monkeys.

Julius has made very little progress in the six months since your departure.

The problem re the Hospital is grave. They've taken it over, but we (surgeons, doctors and nurses) have not been paid since the end of November. The arrangements I've made for you are secure, but I am concerned. This is not a situation that can continue indefinitely and yet it looks set to do so. There are already serious food shortages everywhere.

I have therefore decided to take drastic action. I plan to quit Gov H next month and set up in private practice. The only good thing about the rotten admin is that they don't seem to be aware the bungalow is part of a surgeon's perks so that I shall probably be able to hang on to it when I leave.

I am also fortunate in that my ex-patient, the wealthy Chinese property developer (remember him?), has agreed to back me. I intend to open the Paula Surgery towards the end of April. It's right in the centre, somewhat cramped, but it has an area where I shall be able to perform minor surgery (nothing serious as I shall only have minimum equipment to work with); my main occupation will be as GP. Needs must. In the front of the premises, there's an area for a dispensary so that patients can buy the medication on the spot. I shall be wholly independent. As a GP I shall get paid on the

spot (though that may be in the form of a
chicken or six eggs. I shall count myself lucky in
either case).

I have already had to operate on high-
ranking Japanese officers; inside, their bodies
look much like anyone else's but their mentality
is very different.

I hope you've managed to do something
about Paula's schooling. Might be a good idea
to drop in on the Brothers though Roy will not
be there till the end of the year.

Are the children getting enough to eat?

Radha was touched by the shared memories. She looked at the pages and smiled – his Tamil was, of course, correct, but the writing – so cramped and angular! She pressed the letter to her lips, feeling a surge of overwhelming love and started reading it again.

This second reading, however, brought less joy. There was something that wasn't right. What was it? She read it a third time, attentively.

Julius, thank God, was all right; she knew the matron and was confident no harm would come to him though it was a pity he wasn't with his father. Change of work; what a leap in the dark! If only she was there by his side! Lucky indeed they still had their bungalow. He was having to depend on too many Chinese: the matron from the hospital, the wealthy property man... what about the dispensary? Who would be serving there to take the money and deal out the medicine? A vital person in his new life. No mention of any such person.

That was it! No doubt, no doubt at all – it would be the Chinese nurse called Luk.

She tried to imagine him returning to their home in the evening, alone, to be attended by the cook, no Julius there, and failed. O, God! just three sets of letters exchanged between them and she was already supplanted by another. Or had that happened long before?

The letter slipped from her hand, the flimsy sheets scattering on the floor. She didn't pick them up. From nowhere, a fearful headache plunged her into a dark cocoon. She lay back on the bed and shut her eyes tight, wondering what fatal sickness had struck so suddenly. After what seemed hours, the nausea receded.

This was Radha's first experience of the migraines she'd have, on and off, for the rest of her stay in Pondicherry.

Chapter 13

The weeks turned into months and still there was no end in sight of this war that was tearing lives apart. Could he have known it was going to be like this? He *must* have known, he knew so much! – Oh, no! Julius – on his own! *Of course* this woman wasn't ever going to look after him! That had *never* been on offer whatever she may have said. All she wanted from the beginning was the Doctor!

And Radha thought with anguish how she was stuck here, no way of returning to him, of throwing out the foul vampire that was sucking her family's life force. Could he not feel what was happening?

Sunday mornings took her to *Notre Dame des Anges*, the girls ranged on either side of her, her mother at the end, Ravi and Roy on the other side of the aisle with the men. A familiar space this, but the comfort she needed was no longer to be found here. She'd made her first Holy Communion here; had come here as a child to Sunday Mass, cousin Pradeep on the other side of the aisle where Roy was now standing. Nothing had changed during the years they'd been away in Saigon. She'd returned here to Sunday Mass and

Holy days of obligation, culminating in the most solemn ceremony of the nuptial Mass.

Radha knelt and prayed, head bowed low, eyes shut to the world. She prayed with all her might for her family, for Julius, but most of all for her husband, to give him strength to resist the evil round him. Then, back to the house to write him a letter that might or might not find its way to him, let alone to his heart. Not a word of what she most feared.

The house stood in a pretty street with all the buildings painted a startling white so that the district was known as *le quartier blanc*. The walls had bougainvilleas and jasmin trained up the façade, cassias had been planted along the pavement, casting light shade here and there. It was conveniently near the promenade along the seafront where a barrier of huge boulders had been erected against the encroaching sea.

The obligatory walk along the wide, raised promenade that rich and poor Indians indulged in brought Radha there on Sunday evenings to stand before the unlimited expanse of the Indian Ocean, her longing and pain and frustration masked from passers-by.

This was a weekly treat for the children, these early evening walks out in the open, the waves crashing against the black rocks, sending the spray high into the air. There were vendors with coloured balloons, others with trays hung round their necks selling spicy savouries the children were never allowed. So much colour and movement, once a week.

When it was time for Paula's first Holy Communion, Radha took on the task of instructing her daughter as well as making her outfit. Afterwards, at the celebration at home, there was no escaping the in-laws plus their children. They were back, as nosy, insinuating, wheedling and obnoxious as ever, but Radha felt immense satisfaction presenting a calm countenance to her husband's family. The party went well.

During the church service, as Paula turned from the altar steps to regain her seat, seeing her in the white dress with the short veil, a smile on her lips, Radha felt a moment of elation. One day, she thought, what a glorious bride Paula was going to be, swathed in glittering gold!

Gradually, the running of the house as well as bringing up the children fell to the care of the grandmother. For Radha, that will to make something of her stay in Pondicherry had dwindled as the letters from Malaya became less personal, the gaps longer. So little mention of their home or what he was doing! It was certainly not for want of asking.

Radha was plunged in these thoughts when the letter from her cousin Pradeep arrived:

My dearest cousin

I am deeply saddened to tell you my dear wife died last week on the 9th. She bore her suffering with great courage. The Doctor held out no hope so that after the initial shock, I knew what to expect. Even so, the end seems sudden and I'm having difficulty coming to terms with this great loss. Vida and I had been talking about you, Radha, so recently!- wondering how you were; thinking it was fortunate you were all in India.

This morning's news – rumours of the
Japanese advance in Burma – is most disturbing.
Thank heaven the monsoons will stop all action
for the next several months. The presence of the
French army in Pondicherry is also reassuring.

Here in Malaya, the war shows no sign of
abating. Poor Vida, her last days were hard.
Supplies are miserably low. Work is at an all
time low. Nobody has the inclination to take on a
lawsuit at a time like this. We're seriously
considering opening a branch in Madras; the
majority of our customers are Tamil and still
have interests in India.

I pray the situation will improve.

'Poor Vida! And poor Pradeep! it must be so sad for him.' There were tears in Radha's eyes. 'To make matters worse, he's clearly having problems getting work.'

'He's a good boy,' the grandmother rejoined. 'Sad losing his wife so young, and no children, poor things! though, in view of what's happened, it's probably just as well.' They remained silent for a while, then her mother asked, 'Don't you think it's strange they seem to know what's happening here better than we do?'

'Nothing ever happens here; bands of soldiers walking along the streets – French of course; and some African, looking very tall and black next to the French. Noisy. But nothing happens. Perhaps it sounds worse when you're not here to see this nothing. God, how I wish I was over there with him!'

'Radha, how could you with all these children? It sounds really terrible over there.'

Yes, thought Radha, terrible over there; but worse here to be losing the battle without a fight.

As is the way with children, Radha's were unaware of their mother's trial; they found ingenious ways of amusing themselves. Paula and Mena played hopscotch for hours on end while Leela, who couldn't balance on one leg, sat among the potted cannas and miniature gardenias, giving a running commentary on the game without having the faintest idea of the rules.

Hair-washing, followed by the torture of combing out tangles was so unpopular Radha decided to have their hair cut short as it had been on their arrival. Her mother was against it, but Radha pointed out it would have to be done anyway when it was time to return to KL.

Friction between Paula and her grandmother increased. Radha did not intercede on behalf of her young daughter, thinking instead that correction from a new source would, in the end, be to everyone's advantage. Thus Paula's trust in her was further eroded.

In the morning, the two older children left for school accompanied by uncle Ravi who then cycled on to his office. The ayah fetched them home at one. Lunch was followed by a siesta, then there was homework to be done. This routine still left plenty of time for Paula's inventiveness to find ways of filling in the hours enjoyably for herself and the other children.

One weekend, she had the bright idea of playing 'hospitals'. A rare memory of seeing her father at the hospital came to her aid and she improvised their costumes. As Sister of the ward, her blue cotton blouse with the sari under-skirt from her mother's wardrobe, a white handkerchief folded diagonally and tied round her head to form a natty little cap. An old discarded white shirt of Uncle Ravi's made an excellent overall for Doctor R; a plain dress fashioned out of a tablecloth for assistant nurse, Leela, and for Mena, the patient, clearly nothing but her bare skin.

'No, not bare skin,' the patient complained.

'All right, keep your pants on,' Sister Paula agreed, 'but stop shouting. And stop saying 'no' all the time. The patient just has to lie there – pretend you're dead.'

'Dead,' Doctor R repeated nervously, 'Not sure how good I am at resuscitation. Now, let me see, this is a case of appendicitis.'

'Doctor, are you sure her appendix is up there!' Sister Paula exclaimed in fits of giggles.

'Maybe not. Let's see, down here, d'you think? Hey, Patient, keep your eyes shut. Remember you've had – Sister, what's she had?'

'Anaesthetic, Doctor.'

'That's it, and that means you can't see or hear anything; so keep quiet.'

The doctor probed further and the patient started to screech,

'You're tickling me-ee.'

Sister Paula was now in stitches. Looking up, she caught sight of nurse Leela who was transfixed, mouth wide-open, staring at the door. Their grandmother had come in.

'That is enough,' the old lady thundered. 'Enough of this filthy game. Child, get dressed; you'll catch pneumonia in that state. Paula and Roy, follow me.'

They went downstairs, knowing what was to come. The grandmother, cane in hand, called the other two children to come down.

Leela and Mena cowered behind a pillar, sure their turn would come, but it didn't. Such preferential treatment didn't endear them to the two culprits who'd been punished. Rather, it engendered a deep-seated grudge that endured years after the memory of the beating faded.

Chapter 14

When Roy started as weekly boarder at All Saints School for Boys, Paula found herself more isolated than ever. Friends from school had been discouraged on the grounds they were not quite of her social standing, while relatives kept their distance in silent protest at Radha's asceticism. Paula's age didn't allow her to join the adult world but, except for the odd game of hopscotch which had also somehow lost its appeal, she didn't belong in the nursery games of her younger sisters either.

Radha hadn't confided her fears to her mother knowing they wouldn't be understood. The letters from her husband in war-torn Malaya had become infrequent. They no longer spoke of shared experiences. Mention of Julius was never good:

> *You didn't mention if you'd found a tutor for*
> *Paula. I'm particularly anxious about her standard*
> *of English. Hopefully the Brothers will attend to*
> *Roy but you will have to move heaven and earth to*
> *find someone of a reasonable standard for Paula.*

Don't allow the children to run around outside. They must be accompanied by an adult (someone responsible) if they wish to step out of the house.

Also, make sure the children get fresh vegetables and fruit. At least there should be no shortage of milk and eggs.

It isn't easy here but we're surviving. Julius is persevering as best he can. I started him on the violin last month but fear it's not his instrument. We'll no doubt find something else.

My regards to your mother and your brother,

M.

PS Your cousin, Pradeep, came round and spent some time talking to Julius. He's very alone since the death of his wife, but doesn't seem to want company. It appears he might be transferred to Madras, to set up a branch there; he may get in touch with you.

This particular letter with news of her cousin was more personal than most. Each time she saw his writing on the envelope, she hoped, still hoped, for something different. Then, after reading the thin insubstantial pages, there was an awful sense of anticlimax.

Radha thought of Pradeep, still grieving for his wife. Vida and she had been good friends yet Radha had never confided in her. Was it pride that had held her back, or the way she'd been brought up? Now she thought perhaps there'd been altogether something else. Reluctantly, Radha asked herself if she'd envied her friend her life with Pradeep; so much easier than her own. Less complicated and more loving. Had she been jealous of her?

That night, not for the first time, Radha lay in bed and wept. She longed for her husband. To feel his hand along her body, his touch tender ...

She shook herself awake. She'd been dreaming. Her heart was racing. The image of him lingered in her mind's eye. He'd looked strangely different: slightly shorter and smiling, wonderfully relaxed, for a change. And loving. Radha smiled and fell into a quiet sleep.

The next morning, she went through his letter again, then put it aside. No mention of love, not one word to say he missed her, or wanted to see her. Just a list of instructions for her to carry out. The dream had made up for all that was missing in the letter.

Well, she didn't carry out his instructions. Paula was making perfectly satisfactory progress at the convent; a tutor would only take her beyond the rest of the class, leaving her bored. But she saw that Paula was gifted in those womanly attributes that would secure her a good husband in spite of being headstrong. Like herself, Paula had a talent for needlework and embroidery; the only point they had in common. Under her mother's guidance Paula began to produce beautiful, decorative needlework. The embroidery, alas, highlighted the neglect in intellectual development which was the only area that interested her husband.

Mena was five now and attended the junior school, as did Leela. Time was marching on while they sat in a haze of ignorance in the noisy, disorderly classroom.

Radha saw all her children would be tall like their father. Hopefully they'd inherited a bit of her love of India. She was pleased Paula and Mena were light coloured like herself. One day, she'd have no difficulty finding them prosperous husbands. Leela, with her disability, was a different matter; who knew what life held in store for her? As long as she herself was there, Leela would be safe.

Thus Radha kept the future of her daughters in the forefront of her mind.

The war that was raging round her husband and eldest son was less real for Radha than his possible betrayal of her love. There were no images on screens nor even in newspapers at that time to bring home to her the horror of the Japanese occupation. The Doctor's letters contained few references to it. Somehow he saw to it the payments arrived regularly into her account. As long as there was no telegram, all was as well as could be.

The grandmother, sensing Radha had lost heart of late, thought up ways of cheering her up. There was shopping, the market, dress making, hair-cutting. Even cooking on certain occasions. Sometime in the fourth year there was an unusual outing: a day-excursion to their mango grove. Until then the grandmother had made the yearly visit on her own, but this time, she decided they would all go. A rare midweek adventure during the children's holidays.

The excitement ever since it was announced at breakfast was intense. Not only an outing in a bus, their first ever, but there'd also be a picnic; food to be eaten in the open air on shiny banana leaves instead of plates and, naturally, fingers so as not to puncture the leaves. Even Paula was anxious not to annoy the old lady. At the bus stop, they joined the group of people who were already there, chatting and laughing excitedly as though they too were on a special excursion.

The *char à banc* arrived; this primitive bus, was little more than a motorized cart with an awning to fend off the worst of the noonday sun. It was full to bursting but they climbed in anyway by way of the metal step. Room was made for the two women on one of the benches that ran the length on either side of the cart; the children squeezed themselves near them or onto their knees.

The little motor laboured with its load even though the ground was level. Half an hour later, they were out of the town and the grandmother made a sign to the conductor. He tapped the driver's shoulder to stop and they climbed down onto the dusty road. The bus then continued on its way towards the neighbouring village.

A narrow path invaded by thorny undergrowth led to the plantation. The children walked along, concentrating, holding their arms tightly across their chest so as not to get scratched in the enclosing tunnel of vegetation. They arrived suddenly in a wide open space and stood still, awed by the immensity of their world.

Tall trees cast pools of deep shade, the sun reverberating on the gloss of their leathery leaves. A bird was singing somewhere close by. Otherwise, all was stillness and silence. The grandmother too stood for a moment and looked about her without saying a word; then, she took Radha's arm.

'This plantation, see how beautifully it's kept; I'm lucky to have a trustworthy man. The boundaries trim, never a complaint from neighbouring owners, and saplings over here.'

Radha was about to point out the plentiful yield that year but her mother was in a reminiscent mood.

'This was your grandfather's treasured spot; he used to bring me here. In his father's time, it was a plantation of coconut trees. Then, one morning, he asked me to choose between mangoes and coconuts. I must have been same age as this child. He said, "I'll make sure you never go short of mangoes; nor will your children's children ..."' She paused, those words still fresh in her memory. Finally, with a slight pressure on her daughter's arm, she said, 'I told you Ravi will inherit the big house with the garden, but this plantation will be yours, as will the house we live in. You've always loved both these; I want you to have them. And after you, your children will inherit this land.'

A smile came to Radha's lips. She was touched to think of a time when her children, returning home after their exile in Malaya, would once more tread this plot on Indian soil that had been in their family for generations.

An unusual sense of peace touched her as she laid out the picnic in the grove, her mother's voice a soothing note in the background, Leela standing close by her side, Mena not far off, the two older children running in and out among the ancestral trees.

Neither of the two women foresaw the day when Ravi, beloved son and brother, in an act of sheer opportunism, would appropriate house and land, thereby robbing Radha's children of their inheritance.

Chapter 15

One torrid afternoon, there was a sudden commotion. The servant girl ran to the grandmother, blubbering hysterically that there was a robber in the house. It was the hour of the *siesta*, Ravi hadn't come home for lunch that day as happened sometimes. The hullabaloo woke everyone.

A houseful of women with the grandmother, the mother and her three daughters. And now, this desperate looking robber in their midst. Radha ran across to shield her children who had come running down. If only they'd stayed upstairs!

The ruffian's beard was tangled, his eyes so bruised they were terrible to look at, a sack covered his matted hair as he stood in front of them, brandishing a gun. He was concentrating on the grandmother.

'Rupees, *Ummaaa*!' he whined, waving a dirty cloth bag at the old lady.

'What?' the grandmother asked, her voice tremulous as she stood by her bedroom door. 'My son will be here in a moment. He'll ...'

This prevarication made the robber mad.

'*Oodanay*! *Oodanay*!' he shouted wildly and there was a distinct click from the gun.

'No, don't!' Radha cried. 'Give him what he wants, *Umma*!'

Her mother immediately parted with the bundle of notes in her handbag. The robber left as suddenly as he'd appeared but the two women were so shaken, all they could do was shut themselves in and wait for Ravi to come home.

That evening when her son returned from work, the old lady recounted the full story.

'What could we have done if he'd grabbed one of the children?' she ended, 'As it was, I had no choice but to hand over all the money in my purse. Thank goodness I'd put half in my armoire drawer when I got home from the bank this morning. I don't know what this world is coming to, really I don't.'

'These are bad times,' Ravi agreed, 'but there is a solution. What we need is a chain with a padlock. I know someone who'll do it; I'll make sure it's done tomorrow.'

His mother praised Heaven he was there to protect them and Ravi proved to be as good as his word. His mother gave him the money and the work was done the very next day.

*

A few days later, the women had got over the worst of the fright from the robber, when the grandmother remembered she had to sew on a loose button on one of Ravi's shirts; she therefore went to get it from his wardrobe. There she found the full paraphernalia used by the 'robber' together with Roy's toy gun which had so scared them. There lay also most of the money she'd handed over, though not quite all.

She immediately sent the cook and the girl home, telling them to return early the next morning. She made sure the children were in bed by the time her son returned.

That evening when Ravi came home from work he knocked. Since the incident of the 'robber', the chain was always in use and had to be removed before the door could be opened.

'Radha, how come the chain wasn't on? It should be permanently slotted,' he said as he stepped in.

His sister's eyes were fixed on him but she said nothing. Then he saw his mother; she was standing by the low table which looked unusually cluttered. Without taking her eyes off him, she pointed to the heap of things piled on it. His disguise. Ravi swallowed hard. This was going to be tricky.

'Yours?' his mother asked.

He nodded knowing more was expected from him.

'Yes,' he said at last. 'It was – it was a bet.' It sounded horribly hollow even to him.

'A bet?' she repeated with a slight inflection. 'Who with?'

'With, with one of my friends – Doraj actually.'

'Ravi' his mother pursued, 'how old are you?'

'Why, *Umma*, I was twenty-six last birthday.' A tentative smile. This felt like less dangerous ground. 'You very kindly gave me this magnificent watch.' A flourish of his wrist to show off the gleaming gift.

'But this,' and his mother indicated the bundle on the table, 'This is the work of a ten year old; an irresponsible, dangerous prank.' She paused. 'If a man of twenty-six behaves like a ten year old, it's only right he should be punished like a boy of ten.' As she went to the corner where the cane was kept, she said in a flat, resigned voice, 'Take off your shirt.'

Ravi removed his shirt without a word. He glanced at his watch and after a slight hesitation, undid the clasp and laid it by his shirt. He then knelt down. But for the watch, his movements looked well rehearsed.

Radha watched the scene in horror. There were so many conflicting emotions warring for precedence she had to steady herself against the chair. When Ravi admitted to the hoax, there'd been a moment of wonder: it had been well-timed – nobody about at that hour – and well-executed. They'd been completely taken in.

If, at the end of that moment of silence, their mother had dismissed it with a laugh, would Radha have felt, to use her husband's vocabulary, that it had been strategically planned and brilliantly executed? Maybe. But the emperor's thumb had gone down and Ravi had had to suffer the consequences.

He got up, keeping his eyes averted, and escaped to his room, knowing with something like relief, there'd be no supper for him that night.

'This is what happens when there isn't a man about the house,' the old lady sighed, then continued, 'Your father was too indulgent towards him. This is the result. How am I to find him a suitable wife if this sort of behaviour gets out? Do you honestly think a man of his age should waste his time playing such pranks?'

Radha conceded it had been irresponsible and thoughtless. She could never imagine her husband ever resorting to anything like this. As for anyone daring to whip him in such a humiliating way, it was unthinkable. She realized how much her views had changed over the years. Surely, in the old days, she'd have thought it normal for *Ummuma,* in the absence of *Uppa,* to punish Ravi like this? Now she found the scene uncomfortable and distressing.

Radha thought, living there while their mother ran the house, Ravi, and she too, perhaps, may have abandoned their sense of responsibility, and reverted to their childhood. And yet, she knew this anxiety that tormented her days and robbed her nights of sleep only had lodging in the adult world of betrayal and broken vows.

*

The subdued gloom which had been with them deepened as a result of this mischief. However, the story of the robber did not leak to the outside world. Some months later, Ravi's mother found a young woman who, although she would not have been her first choice, being dark–skinned and her education rudimentary, was from the right caste and background, Franco–Indian. They became betrothed and within a year Ravi and his bride, like Radha, were married in the French Church.

Ravi now moved into the big house with his bride; just two streets away, to the house that *Ummuma* made over to him.

Radha was profoundly happy for her brother. Her lethargy gave way to a wave of creativity. She made the children's outfits and prepared the house to receive guests for celebrations, although the main feasting was to be organized by the bride's family.

On the appointed day, she found herself in church, not far from where she'd stood sixteen years earlier on the day of her own wedding. How different she'd imagined her life would be! The enormous vault of *Notre Dame des Anges* suddenly felt sucked of all air and Radha might have fallen if she'd not reached towards Leela who was standing next to her and clutched her small hand in hers. She knelt down and prayed her brother's life would be blessed with happiness.

The group photo was taken with the bride to Ravi's right, beyond her were several in-laws clustered in a smiling mass, the richly–clad figure of his mother stood on his left, followed by Radha who looked remarkably young for her thirty–four years. Next came her three children: Paula, serious and composed; Roy, the image of his uncle; Leela, grinning into the camera. Various other relatives from the bride's side dotted further back. Mena, who was one of four bridesmaids, was in front of the groom, her grandmother's proprietary hand on her shoulder. She looked sweet in her *pavade sutte*, the long Indian skirt. The sash and satin pumps added a Western touch, a fine coronet of pale silk flowers encircled her black hair.

Chapter 16

With Ravi safely married, conversation between the two women now touched more often on outside events. The Japanese had, that very month, been defeated in their attempt to invade India. Surely this at last heralded their imminent collapse in Malaya? Radha waited from one day to the next to receive details of her return. But the letter did not come.

Often in the evening, once the children were in bed, *Ummuma* reminisced about a distant past in Saigon, when the father of the family had been there and their life had been joyful; or even before that, here in Pondicherry itself when Radha was a little girl and her cousin Pradeep had lived round the corner. Hardly a day had gone by without him coming round to be with her. Radha detected a note of regret in her mother's voice but knew better than to question her or, still more dangerous, dwell on it in her thoughts.

Within the uncertainty of this present, there was one assured comfort to be found for both women – their country, beloved India, was in the safe hands of the Mahatma; a light that slowly but surely would lead them to the desired goal of Independence. Here was a true Indian, and proud of his origin. If only other men followed his example ...

And that brought them to the Doctor. From time to time, Radha expressed the hope the long separation might tip the scales in her favour. They say "absence makes the heart grow fonder," don't they? And she looked away wistfully, the familiarity of the words shielding her from the pain as well as from the emptiness of the promise in the proverb.

*

Almost a year later, the long-awaited letter arrived telling Radha to prepare for their homeward journey at the end of August. At last Julius was back living with his father, thank heaven! The war had been over since the end of '45 and, yes, she understood, it was still dangerous though peace had been declared. Knew too there was a lot her husband had to do to ensure the safety and comfort of the family before they returned. Yes, she understood all that, and yet, heavens, how hard it was to wait.

Her migraine dissipated from one day to the next and she was charged with frantic energy. In two months she tried to do what should have been gradually evolving over the last two years or more. He would see immediately how little had been achieved. God! If only she'd managed to keep going!

Their first year in Pondicherry – she remembered how she'd confronted the Mother Superior, managed to get Paula in a whole year early; visited the Brothers at Roy's school, won them over with her smiles to accept him at seven.

Embroidered table cloths and napkins to give to the Sisters of The Assumption. There hadn't been enough hours in the day to do all the things she had to do. And all the while written long letters to let him know she was with him, never hinting how tortured she was by her doubts.

All that had been at the beginning. Then had followed the years in Limbo, and she'd lost heart.

It was not only Radha who now woke as from a deep sleep. Paula sensed a sudden elation; Roy something of a misgiving that energized him and put him on his guard; Leela and Mena, an uncontrollable excitement which was not related to anything in particular.

A tutor was found who, since the holidays had begun, came every morning except Sundays, to teach English, mathematics and geography. He concentrated his efforts on the two older children who responded well to his attentions. He then set them work while he tried to see what could be achieved with the two younger ones who appeared to be totally unschooled – not much was the answer, but he did his best.

In the afternoon, a young woman came twice a week, to teach Paula and Mena classical Indian dance. Radha watched with heartache, wishing she'd not waited so long to set these classes in motion.

Every spare moment was spent on embroidery and Paula could boast three separate pairs of pillow cases, each with rich, silk motifs, two squares for occasional tables and a set of napkins. The motifs were, at times, bizarre, and on one occasion, she actually objected.

'Cockerels! But this will take ages, and anyway, funny to have them on pillow cases.'

'Look how well it'll show off your work!' Radha argued. 'And such beautiful colours; there's no other pattern with colours like these.'

Paula did as she was told and got on with it.

Radha undertook the task of teaching Leela and Mena the alphabet. It was obvious the teacher hadn't got very far. She saw at once that Leela, while being wildly enthusiastic, would always be illiterate, but she made headway with Mena. Again she wished she'd started earlier. Just one year earlier and she'd have had something to show her husband.

Radha would have liked to parade the children in front of his astonished eyes and accept his applause, her heart bursting with pride. That would not happen for she hadn't followed the postal instructions with which he'd bombarded her. All her energy had been sapped, fretting about what he was up to. She'd set out with good intentions; but the migraine, the doubt ... she had become a sleepwalker.

Now, at this eleventh hour, she too needed sprucing up. No more of those sweetmeats she'd taken up in his absence. How was she ever going to lose enough weight in so short a time? Would he understand – pining for him she'd needed some consolation?

They were going to meet again after five long years apart. Sight of her must bring back for him the fondest memories of their past. Her sari – a soft colour, perhaps even cream; he always preferred light shades. And it would be silk, with a quiet sheen.

At last the day came for their departure. She checked her passport and the tickets a thousand times. Everything was in order; the children were ready and Ravi had come over and was even now fixing the luggage onto the roof rack.

She smiled lovingly as she saw him handle the heavy cases as if they were weightless; his wife had given birth to their first child the previous month – a boy. They'd called him Julius after her son. Poor Julius! Fourteen now. Would she recognize him? Would he remember her?

She moved listlessly from room to room realising with a pang she'd been sort of happy here over the last five years. She'd managed to keep her fears at bay.

Whatever awaited her suddenly loomed menacingly – what if he no longer wanted her by his side? She winced involuntarily, then pulled herself together; she was letting her imagination run wild. Where was her faith in God's goodness now, she chided herself.

And the trial hadn't even begun.

But she did love this house, this room with the staircase that led to the floor above and the terrace, the photos that were dotted about. A new one of Ravi and his bride had joined the other two wedding photos.

And suddenly she was standing by the little inlaid table and she closed her eyes as memory blurred her vision. It was here, in this chair that he'd sat and she'd seen him for the first time. God, how handsome he'd looked, so tall, with that piercing gaze … the cakes … it had been a warning but it was already too late. So many hopes and dreams had invaded her poor heart and it was he, Manicasami Nanamentem, who had opened the door to them all.

With him she'd left her home that first time, to begin a new life as his wife and to bear his children. And now, to join him once more, she was about to leave this home for the second time. No, not the second. The last. And this time, her heart was full of doubt and foreboding.

She'd learnt a lot since that first departure, from her own experience of life with him. Learnt that however much she loved him and yearned for his love, only he could give her that love. Soon, her children would talk in a foreign language; there would be no Kuttekali dancing however gifted the child might be; no Indian outfits; her mother's name would never be mentioned and Pondicherry would be a part of all that should be forgotten. Radha knew with desperate sadness, she would never return to this house again, nor to this country – India, her home, the only place on earth where she belonged.

Someone touched her gently. Turning, Radha saw her mother standing next to her.

'It's time.' They held each other and wept silently. At last her mother said, 'What a comfort you've been to me! Pray God you'll find the happiness you deserve.'

'We've been a comfort to each other,' Radha's voice was a whisper, 'If only I could take you with me. Perhaps one day …' but she stopped.

They both knew the moment of separation had at last come. Turning wordlessly away, the grandmother caught sight of Mena, her youngest granddaughter, and she felt a great love.

'My, don't you look pretty in that little cotton frock! *Yenne cunne*! Come here and give your old *Ummuma* a kiss.'

But the child was too busy twirling round and round, chanting:

'I'm off to see my daddy!' She didn't register the look of pain in her grandmother's eyes.

Chapter 17

As on the outward journey, the boat made various landings: from Madras, it carried them to Penang, then went on down to Port Swetenham where they disembarked before it continued to Singapore. Radha had forgotten this cloying humidity that made her blouse stick to her body. She couldn't breathe. Her hands, the right one holding Leela, the left, Mena, felt sticky. Telling Paula to hold onto Mena, she dried them with her handkerchief, then took out the fan from her bag to cool her face. A different crowd from the ones in India; many foreigners here, Malays, Chinese, Europeans, some Indians. She'd forgotten.

They boarded the train for the two hour journey back to Kuala Lumpur. Unlike the outward trip, he hadn't come to the port, saying the line of patients spilled into the street and past the next building; but he'd meet them at the station in KL. The children were so much older now, Radha had no difficulty managing them, but, however true his excuse might have been, that stab of foreboding was reinforced and she drew a deep breath to quell the unease. Once again she pulled out her fan, then put it away; it was useless. She hadn't foreseen this build up of tension as each station brought back vivid memories of that other journey five years before.

The country outside the window looked unfamiliar, too lush, threatening. What deadly creatures lurked in those impenetrable branches dripping with poisonous, sticky fluids? Had she felt this when they'd first landed here? – she, the bride, with her so very English Indian husband? She couldn't remember. Perhaps she'd trusted him to protect her from harm. Then. And now?

She automatically began fanning herself in the airless carriage and prayed more fervently than she'd done in a long time. St Jude, patron saint of lost causes, headed the litany, followed closely by St Joseph, finder of lost objects, though it wasn't certain as yet exactly what had been lost. The Virgin Mary served as the chorus to link the various saints.

The children were, on the whole, subdued after the long boat trip. Perhaps they were apprehensive at the thought of meeting their father at long last. Paula alone looked forward with confidence; his image was clear in her mind.

As for Roy, he hoped in the bustle of the various encounters to pass unnoticed. He suspected with more than a slight dread that in spite of the efforts of the Brothers, his academic level would fall short of expectations. He must not attract attention, that's all there was to it. He practised the name 'Julius' though he had no recollection of his brother. There was a photo that now lay in their grandmother's album to tell him what he looked like, that is, if he hadn't changed.

At last the train edged its way into the palatial station at Kuala Lumpur. The moment they alighted from the train, she saw him – he stood out head and shoulders above the seething crowd, the white cotton suit making him look startlingly European. He'd always dressed like that but somehow she'd forgotten how white the cloth looked. However hard you try to cling on to things, they slip through your fingers in a gap of five years.

He looked foreign. But now she saw he hadn't changed: the same domed forehead, lofty gaze, forbidding and distant; did she really expect him to have changed? Holding Leela and Mena by their hands, she ushered the other two towards him. Saints in Heaven, she thought, how cold he seems! I shall never reach his heart. Holy Mary, come to my aid!

'Well, well,' he said, 'So, you've got here in one piece. Yes, this is your brother, Julius, lurking behind me somewhere; yes, changed beyond recognition though whether it's for the ... Oh, I think he's trying to shake hands with you although the way he's going about it, it's not too clear; a case of the blind leading the blind.' Then, putting his arm round Paula's shoulder, he looked at her and nodded with approval, 'Good. Looking well, hm?'

'Happy to see you,' Paula said in English, the words sounding almost familiar to her after all the practice.

'Good, good,' he responded with a smile, and Paula recognized the man and the image she carried were the same. He then glossed over the rest of his family and stopped when his gaze landed on his wife.

'No shortage of sweetmeats, I see, in spite of war time restrictions.'

Had he always sounded so much like a foreigner when he spoke Tamil – halting, searching for the right word, his pronunciation all askew? Or was this something new, five years of being separated from her? Radha smiled at him, in the hope it would take the sting out of his words. He almost responded.

'So, this is little Mena,' he said picking up his youngest child and holding her in the crook of his left arm. As they started walking through the crowd which parted before him, he held his handkerchief to her nose and said, 'Blow, and again. Leela, put your hand in front of your mouth when you cough; I'm sure you don't want to share your germs with this rabble.'

Radha realized with a pang her son, Julius, hadn't understood a word of what she'd said. He no longer spoke Tamil. He was darker than she remembered, gangly and awkward and refusing to look at any of them. She felt miserable as she tried smiling at him while he averted his head at an imperious angle away from her; away from them all. There was something the matter with the way his eyes shifted uneasily. Had his voice broken? It sounded odd, halfway between a whisper and a rasp; and the words he uttered were, of course, foreign. Julius, her first-born!

They piled into the tiny, black Morris Minor, the four older children in the back and Mena in front on Radha's knees.

'Nice to have a car!' Radha exclaimed to fill in the silence.

'I bought it a few months ago. Things are going cheap if you have the money to buy, but there's little choice.' He was having considerable difficulty finding the right word.

'The new house, not that it's newly built, is further from the centre; some sort of transport was necessary. For the time being, this car was the best I could find.'

The luggage had been stacked on the roof rack and secured with stout straps. Her husband looked too big to fit in the driver's seat. His frame was more powerful than she remembered, no longer skinny and long, probably a thing of age, helped, perhaps, by those exercises he used to do. Did he still do them? Yes, he looked fit. And unsmiling.

Here we go, thought Radha, with another prayer on her lips.

Chapter 18

It was suffocatingly hot in spite of the windows being open. The air was much more humid and cloying than in Pondicherry. Through the small window of the car, the streets looked so orderly, Radha stared in wonder. Everything moved up one side and down the other, no one suddenly darted out to overtake at a mad pace. Had it always been like this?

'The house is quiet and large,' he said, 'there won't be any problem of space.'

Space, why, of course, after all this time with just Julius and him living together, now, having the whole family back could have created a problem of space. But as always, he'd seen to it and there'd be no problem; not of space. He continued in a low voice which was just audible to her, 'You may remember the nurse, Luk, she's been living with me and will continue to do so ...'

'No!' Radha screamed, 'No! You should have told me! I wouldn't have come!'

A sudden roar from the engine almost drowned her anguished cry. Had he really said there'd be no problem of space? There would never be space enough in this world for someone else to share her husband with her! Space! Why, let him give her a palace, let him heap palaces one on top of another, not all the palaces in the world could be space enough for her to live with this other woman. No consolation, none whatsoever to have been right, to have sensed the evil, pined for him through long, dark years, knowing and yet not knowing until this cursed moment, this now when she at last knew the truth which had all the while been vitiating her life-blood, her heart, this man, her heart. God in heaven, what had she done to deserve this?

'She's eager to meet you, to get on with you,' he went on in a low voice as though she hadn't cried out, 'I hope you'll make an effort to do the same with her. Of course she doesn't speak Tamil and I see you've not followed my instructions regarding English. You may remember, life here revolves in three major languages. Tamil isn't one of them. You'll no doubt muddle along as best you can.'

No, of course he hadn't told her before, *knowing* she wouldn't come if he did. He'd used her to bring the children back. They were the one ingredient that had always been essential to make his dreams come true. She'd never been part of that dream. Not then; certainly not now.

The car turned into the wide unmade road which led to the house. Jalan Inai. Radha saw it in lurid patches of shapes and colours: a deep ditch; the gate, approached over a flat access; the land opposite – a plantation of coconut trees reaching high into the sky, creating a jumbled, mysterious chequerboard of trunks below. A right turn over the flat bridge brought them to the drive which swept round gently till it reached the colonial-style porch.

The house loomed large. The land round it would have to be cleared to make a garden. Gecko on the branch of a tree, staring with an unblinking eye. A warning, she thought, but too late. A huge tree – what was it? A rumbutan; she'd forgotten. Five years is a long time; long enough to forget trees; even those you count among your favourites. Long enough to lose all that is dearest to you.

Heavens, how different this homecoming might have been! She forced herself not to think. Just keep looking at what stands there in front.

The wings on either side of the house were recessed so that the centre jutted out from under the gable, tall and imposing. Windows ran the whole length of the upper storey. There'd be plenty of light throughout. The servants' quarters were presumably at the back as there was no sign of any other building in sight. Yes, it was big, and her heart contracted painfully.

What a contrast to the bungalow she'd lived in with her husband and children when she was last here! House with a veranda, scent of jasmin, the evening air filled with birdsong. It seemed to her they'd been happy there. No venomous snake had lurked in its interior. Five years ago. What aeons separated this searing now from then! Five years of yearning for him. Five years that finally led to this harsh, bitter reality.

How old was *she*? If it was more children he wanted, she was back to bear him as many as he chose to have.

Thirty–four wasn't too old. She hadn't wanted to leave in the first place. He surely remembered that? She'd do anything he wanted but not, *please,* not this.

The car came to a standstill. Out. Now. Take hold of that child's hand; it will bring some comfort. And – no tears.

Radha stumbled out and, taking one of her younger children's hands, walked round the front of the car towards the two shallow steps of the porch. Beyond, she could see the living area. The broad, wooden staircase cut off the view of the dining room. A lizard suddenly darted into view, clicking as it looked down. If that too was a warning, Radha told herself, it was all far too late. The open–plan made it airy and peaceful. But the walls were bare, too bare. Where were the two portraits of herself and her husband that should have been hanging there? Where were they?

She saw the wooden rail of the stairs lead the eye up and then curve back towards the front of the house. On the upper floor, the bannister formed three sides of a rectangle. Julius was watching from above. He was crouched down almost to floor level. She hadn't seen him run upstairs but now she tried to smile at him. He appeared not to see her. No, he no longer knew her for his mother. And now she knew why. He'd been too young when she'd left. No, when she'd *had* to leave. A child needs a mother at such terrifying moments as war. Finding himself alone, he turns to the nearest substitute.

It wasn't only her husband that *she* had stolen from her.

Turning she saw where her rival stood with outstretched hand. The mistress of her husband and her house was greeting her with a smile. It was the smile of a hypocrite. She saw through it at once; did it really fool him? God! What did he see in her? Such an ugly, flat face! No, she, Radha, would not touch this shameful woman.

Out of the corner of her eye she could make out the grim smile on her husband's face, but it made no difference, she would not touch her. What on earth did he see in her? A little younger than herself, maybe, but not much. Of course she was fair-skinned, being Chinese. Why did he have to choose a Chinese of all things? Didn't he know they weren't to be trusted?

Radha's hands came together in a formal greeting as she backed away to stand with her children.

Chapter 19

Julius surveyed the new arrivals from the safety of the railing round the upstairs landing. His lips turned down in an expressive sneer belying his fourteen years. A bunch of Indians, that's what they were. And not a word of English between them! They'd almost crowded him out in the back of the car. Fortunately he'd hung back 'politely' and got the window seat so that he could look out the whole time and ignore them completely.

He'd become used to life as an only child with his irascible father and Aunty. Aunty, who wasn't his aunt at all but someone who'd moved in when his mother moved out. That day he'd felt odd from the moment he'd woken up, but especially as he saw the boat move slowly out of the harbour. His mother's blue sari blurred with the sea and the sky. A sort of hiccup came from nowhere and he was pleased his father didn't hear it in the tremendous noise of the port.

By the time they got back home it was pitch black but the lights were on in the house and there was a Chinese woman waiting for them inside. His father said, 'This is

Aunty. She's come to look after you. She'll be staying here with us. Now, have some supper and get off to bed. Tomorrow we'll be back to normal.' Julius had sat in front of the plate with bits of food on it but found that the tube in his throat where the food usually went down was shut off and water kept coming to his eyes.

The next day dawned and Aunty was standing next to him when that hiccup came back. Huge, salty drops of water spilled out of his eyes and trickled down into his mouth. He tried to blink them away because they made Aunty look like a hazy wicked dwarf. She smothered his face against her but the smell wasn't like his mother; nor could she speak Tamil, so that the hiccups came faster and faster till he thought he was going to choke. A small, reedy squeak made itself heard. It sounded like *'umma'* till it was muffled against the hard little buttons that went across Aunty's top.

Julius missed his mother. Missed his little brother, Roy. Even the others, a bit. Aunty kept saying she wouldn't tell father, and she didn't. Aunty understood what was good for her.

Far from everything being back to normal, everything changed. There were no more curries for a start, not even mild ones. And with the curries went the cook as well as the Indian servant to be replaced by Chinese ones. The old gardener still came for a while and Julius trailed after him as he watered the plants in the evening.

There were noodles and sticky balls of rice with very little taste. Sounds too changed: when his father was home, they spoke English which Aunty had great difficulty mastering. Otherwise, it was Cantonese with the servants and whenever Aunty spoke she sounded as though she was starting a fight. By now people no longer thought of gardens and flowers and one day the gardener didn't come back.

Over the years, Julius stopped missing his mother and the others. He liked Matron who looked after him for a while, then he returned to their home and Aunty was still there, smiling and joking and sometimes sticking up for him when his father was being difficult. And now his real mother was a stranger to him as were his siblings, whereas Aunty was – well, Aunty.

He wished the rest of them hadn't come back, bringing these uncomfortable memories. What was worse, Aunty hadn't been nice to him in the last few days; he couldn't be certain she'd go back to liking him if they stuck around. To think he'd missed them once and wished they hadn't left him behind! They looked so foreign! – like a family of refugees, though he realised refugees aren't usually dressed in silks, and that, if he wasn't mistaken, was a whole lot of silk draped round his mother.

Aunty and the three Chinese servants all wore trousers and tops or, when Aunty was dressed up for a special occasion, a *cheong sam*. His mother's sari was a foreign garment like the yards of garish cotton worn by the driver's dark–skinned wife. And like the driver's wife, she had a bun at the nape of her neck and a white flower stuck in it, though this looked like a gardenia, not a string of jasmin.

Nor had it helped when, at the railway station, he'd held out his hand to shake hers and she'd almost burst into tears as though she'd never shaken hands with anyone before. Totally uneducated, that's what it meant. No wonder his father was so scornful of all Indians, though, of course, he was one himself. For the time being, Julius decided not to ponder over that mystery.

At the station, his father had picked up his youngest sister, Mena, a skinny little thing, and walked to the car still holding her. She'd looked mighty smug at the distinction conferred on her, looking down on everyone from her lofty position. If she but knew! Julius had smiled to himself with the secret knowledge it was far safer to put some distance, in fact as much as possible, between himself and his father. It was hard for him to think of him as 'their' father as well, after having had him to himself for so long.

And now he could see as he peered through the banisters that his mother, that is, his biological one, was on the verge of tears yet again, just because father was introducing Aunty to her. (What had his father meant, 'the blind leading the blind?) Anyway, he felt like prompting her now, 'Come on, just shake hands politely. It isn't that difficult! You can do it if you try.' But no, she was doing a strange sort of Indian greeting and going backwards. The peculiar thing was, Aunty went on smiling. It was a hopeless situation.

Not that it had been a perfect life before. If he were to be honest, he'd always been more scared of his father than of the whole Jap army put together. Although he, Julius, spoke English well (that could not be said of Aunty even after five whole years), and like his father had become less and less familiar with Tamil, and could strum passably on the banjo, he soon understood from that downward turn of his father's lips he was a failure. He'd practised that sneer in the mirror and now imitated it almost to perfection. It had been gratifying to have been able to use it so fittingly on these uneducated immigrants.

That the instrument his father had finally chosen as suitable for him was the banjo and not the violin, was a denigration of his musical ability. It hadn't been at all clear to Julius why such a choice had been made – as far as he knew, there was no known 'Concerto for Banjo and Orchestra' that he'd be able to perform one day before an audience of thousands. Julius had been rather pleased with the noises that had emanated from the violin whenever he'd practised, and the smile on his father's lips seemed to confirm his talent.

He soon realized a smile didn't always indicate appreciation of excellence. And so, one day, he found himself wielding a banjo instead. He could now strum away though the better he got the more monotonous it sounded. Couldn't be helped. In any case, here he was, so clearly superior to this riffraff that had landed in their midst, unable to speak English or play an instrument of any sort. He'd stay aloof. That was the thing to do. He had nothing in common with them except the accident of birth.

Chapter 20

That first evening, the Doctor led Radha into the spacious bedroom downstairs. From the outside, it would have been to the left of the entrance, balancing the sitting area which was to the right. Here, the shutters were kept closed for further privacy. It was sparsely furnished: a bookcase against the wall as you went in with immensely heavy tomes, mostly medical treatises – they looked familiar. The walls were bare; no portraits, nothing.

'The arrangement is discreet,' he indicated, 'the children's rooms are upstairs.'

There was a large double bed on the right. She stood, numb, bewildered, uncomprehending.

'Since this is our first night together after a separation of five years,' he explained, 'Luk will occupy the single bed over there.' His face was a mask. A blank.

Had she heard right? She looked across at the single bed against the wall. It was there all right, one end by the door to the bathroom, the other next to another door which was bolted; it supposedly led to the dining area. *She* would be sleeping in that single bed tonight while they ... every part of Radha tingled with revulsion.

'I can't believe it! Five whole years, not a day without thinking of you, fretting for you, longing to be with you, I come back, bringing the children to you, and *this* is how you treat me? Do you honestly expect me to accept this shameful arrangement?' Turning round on him, she suddenly caught sight of Luk who had crept in and was watching the scene with interest.

'Out!' cried Radha, not caring whether Luk understood Tamil or not. 'Get out of here at once! And may the Gods bring down on your thrice cursed head all the misery and anguish tormenting me at this moment!'

'Luk,' the Doctor said in English, 'I have not finished. Will you ...' His eyes shot angry rays. She was out of the door before he'd finished.

This wasn't good. Why wasn't he defending her from that hell-cat, wife number one? Five years of planning; were they to be dashed so suddenly?

Turning to Radha, he reverted to Tamil, his voice fiercely kept in check.

'I don't think you've understood the situation. I'm not interested in your opinion. This is the arrangement. If you don't like it, you may leave.'

'I shall! Immediately! You won't see us ever again.' With that, she tried to push past him, but he towered over her, barring her way.

'I said *you* may leave. Forget the 'us'. The children are staying here. And if you're thinking of any heroics, I should remind you you're not an independent woman.'

'I'll find the means. I will not leave the children to be infected in this brothel you've set up in my absence.'

'Enough! Don't you dare speak to me like that! Now, listen carefully; this is the choice you have: you may remain here as my wife, but on condition you accept Luk amicably in our household. Alternatively, you may leave, on your own.'

Horror of horrors! The idea of staying was so repellent to her she shook with impotent rage. He was right – she had no means. God only knew what had become of her dowry. If only she could turn her back on this man and his filthy set-up. But how could she leave the children? Or him? There were ties she could never break.

'I will not share this room with that woman. There are plenty of rooms upstairs; the girls can all share one room; it's what they're used to anyway. And if you wish to be with me, you'll have to come upstairs.' She went quickly past him and made straight for the servants' quarters at the back.

Mainly by signs she told the servants to move the single bed upstairs to the second room where the girls were and her luggage into the first bedroom. How fortunate that the children were not yet in bed; she'd give them a moment to settle before going in to say goodnight. No bedtime songs tonight. Perhaps never again.

And what about the fourth bedroom, the one opposite hers? She looked across and saw the door was closed, a slit of light below – Julius poring over some book, constraint turning the pages unenthusiastically. Or was he listening to the uproar she'd created? Could she go in to say goodnight? She must. Had to start straightaway on this first night; just a light tap, then a quick 'goodnight' before closing the door once more without expecting or waiting for an answer. Julius, her first-born.

The two sets of rooms on either side were well thought out, spacious and independent with a separate door into the bathrooms that stood at the angle between them.

The servants went about their work efficiently and quietly, clearly aware of the delicate situation. The third bed in the girls' room was almost assembled and Radha's luggage was already in the main room.

Holding back her sobs, Radha opened her suitcase and drew out the four silver boxes in the shape of brooding birds that contained her make-up. She placed them carefully on the central panel of the dressing table. She laid the silver backed comb and matching hand-mirror alongside. The exercise calmed her. Sitting down on the stool, she removed the gardenia and the three long hairpins that held the plaited bun. She pulled the plait round and shook out the thick tresses to comb her hair smooth. How long, she wondered, before the first grey streaks through the curtain of black.

A glint from the bevelled edge of the mirror caught her attention – the dressing table – polished rosewood. Lacework under the glass that covered the panels on either side. The stool she was sitting on – also rosewood, the top upholstered in deep red velvet. She went over to the bed. Sweeping the mosquito net to one side, she ran her finger along the smooth polished wood of the footboard that curved back elegantly towards her – rosewood. A matching set.

A double bed for Paula, when the other children each had iron bedsteads like the single bed that had been downstairs? Why, this room was never meant for anyone other than her. That charade downstairs was to make it look as though it was her own choice that had brought her up here! Was the man really as devilishly calculating or was she getting carried away through her unhappy imagination?

And yet, when had she ever been more than a pawn in any of his moves? From that first moment when he'd placed the gold chain round her neck which had 'allowed him to leave India in a suitably conventional way that wouldn't upset his mother' – were those not his very words? – she'd been used by him. Used to bear and rear his children. Used to carry them to the safety of India away from the horrors of war. Used to return them safely to him at the end of the five years. And now that she'd delivered them into his keeping, her term of usefulness was at an end; there was 'someone else who would look after them' now.

Ideally, she should return quietly, without making a fuss, back to where she'd come from. Neither pester him nor, indeed, come in contact with the children ever again. He would reward her services by opening an account in Pondicherry in her name, and the payments would inflate her mother's income considerably. That is how he'd wish it to be.

But that was not how it was going to be. Radha would never abandon her children. Nor would she leave this space that housed them. Nor, indeed, leave him. Her husband's arrangement, so repellent to her, had one saving grace – this was the way, the *only* way left to win him back. Love would triumph over evil.

That night, the act she'd thought of a thousand times during the long five years was performed. But oh, how different from what she'd imagined! It was as if she weren't there at all – as if all that was vital in her, her feelings, her emotions, had all been removed, leaving this slab of flesh for the man to use. She felt nothing. In that void, Radha sensed her doom.

Afterwards, she became aware of a suffocating silence. Not a sound in the house; the man lying next to her, presumably asleep.

Tears trickled, slow and inexhaustible, out of the corners of her eyes. This was desolation. Gradually she felt her heart thud in her breast and she began to pray, 'O God, before whom I was married to this man, You see where I lie, dishonoured and brought low; in Your mercy, let this not last forever.'

But on this night, the usual solace she found in prayer was denied her.

Chapter 21

What soon became clear was that the arrangement suited no one. Luk's smile disappeared in a remarkably short time as she made out 'Wife number one' was calling her a whore and other equally unflattering names. For Radha the situation was downright nightmarish. The Doctor's dreams of an amicable settlement were soon dashed.

He found solace in work where he could immerse himself in the luxury of the sick. His Tamil had so deteriorated through lack of use he now had an interpreter as the majority of his patients were either Chinese or Indian. Luk helped out with the former. Despite this limitation, patients flooded in from distant places because of his reputation for being the best.

Doctor Mentem was way ahead of his time not only in understanding the importance of hygiene but in detecting the connection between health and diet. But where he excelled most was in his gift of diagnosis: at a glance, he sensed what was wrong with his patient. The rumours Radha's mother had heard all those years ago of his being an 'outstanding diagnostician' proved to be accurate.

The mastery he displayed in the dispensary was lamentably lacking in his home. The day started well enough with exercises followed by shower and shave. The Doctor always dressed in white: shirt, suit, socks, handkerchief His ties varied their stripes and his shoes of gleaming leather were sometimes brown, sometimes black. Seven-thirty, he turned on the radio in the sitting room pacing up and down, listening to the BBC World Service, of particular interest at the moment: *Negotiations for Indian Independence.* All very well, he mused, Gandhi's Passive Resistance which appeared to confuse and confound the Brits; it would surely be ineffective in the chaos that was bound to follow.

Breakfast at eight with everyone present so that he could keep an eye on their table manners and direct the conversation. Then he and Luk left for the Dispensary. Heavy silence in the car, but so what? When term began, the ferrying of children to school would complicate this departure but for the time being, the exit was smooth.

The problem began when he returned home. To be wedged between a distraught wife and a mistress defending her territory with tooth and nail was no place to be.

He'd read texts on various Chinese emperors whose dynasties belonged to the fairly recent past, who had had a bus-load of concubines without any problem. Luk herself had assured him it was still the practice for a man to have several wives. She'd also said the women all lived together as one, happy family, adding she'd be more than willing to cooperate. What, he wondered, had gone wrong? For all her brave words, she was no more cooperative than Radha. Perhaps two women were more of a problem than a bus-load?

His original plan, based on a familiar British pattern, would have been to house Luk at a convenient distance where he'd be able to visit her whenever the spirit moved. This idea had not gone down well: Luk saw herself gradually marginalised with the Doctor enfolded within the heart of his family. In fact, she'd have none of it.

So, the Doctor had come up with the idea of the *ménage à trois*. Within the Muslim context of Malaya, this arrangement could merge seamlessly. Radha's church-going with the children might provoke a few raised eyebrows, but that was her problem. Luk, sensibly, had no interest in any spiritual pursuit. He'd be waited upon by two women, both competing for his love. The situation had its appeal; it could even catch on. He was to be envied, possibly, having the means and the charisma to enjoy two women within his household.

The Doctor was indulging in an uncharacteristically fanciful scenario. Given the two women in question, the chances of his plan succeeding were nil.

There was one detail he'd overlooked – his role was horribly demanding and, frankly, beyond him. That Radha had accepted him that first night had felt like a triumph and he thought he'd acquitted himself reasonably well. Since then, things had taken a downturn. The siesta downstairs the next afternoon had been challenging: just when he needed sleep badly, Luk had made impossible demands. That evening, anxious to establish some sort of routine, he'd presented himself upstairs once more only to be met with stiff resistance.

He realised Radha had only accepted him the first night because she hadn't understood the new arrangement.

They were a long way from a peaceful settlement. The children barely made a sound as they waited for the next explosion from their father. During the day, they hung around the garden, just outside the window, drawn against their will by the sounds of fury and distress. The sounds at night were mysterious and undecipherable.

*

The years of separation inevitably worked against Radha; she was the intruder in an established relationship between the Doctor and the other woman. Each day saw her, his lawful wife, left behind at home to direct the servants in the morning (a task she was ill equipped to perform as her grasp of Chinese was, as yet, minimal), and in the afternoon to supervise the children's homework. There too, if they needed help, which they often did, it wasn't easy for her since everything was in English.

In the morning and again in the afternoon, she watched with a heavy heart each time her husband climbed into the car and the driver held the door open for the Chinese woman to get in. That was her husband the woman was leaving with. Radha watched her rival in disbelief: the slits of her *cheong sam* revealed too much – stocky legs, fat knees and thick thighs. Her face was broad and flat, and permanently set in a scowl. Pigface! That's what she'd call her! – Radha felt a moment of jubilation.

How wrong her mother had been! Having no caste made not the slightest difference to her husband. She'd known it wouldn't but where was the joy in having been right?

Could he really have forgotten his children's welfare to be behaving like this? He was breaking up the family and she saw no way of stopping him.

Now as she turned round, Ayu was standing by her, arms held out in a gesture of an offering – the sari, blouse and the underskirt she'd worn the day before, carefully ironed and folded. This preferential treatment was bound to get her into trouble.

The day before, Luk had laid into the servant for not having her *cheong sam* ready. It was still rolled up tight under a pile of other clothes waiting to be ironed. Radha had come in to see what the hullabaloo was about, whereupon, gesticulating wildly, Luk abandoned her Cantonese and launched into English.

'You no light asking servant iyon sarli. I, working girl; you stay home. You not working.'

Radha responded with great reserve in French.

'*Vous criez comme une poissonnière, ce qui ne m'étonne pas d'ailleurs; mais essayez au moins de respecter les convenances. Si mon mari vous entend, il ...*'

'English speaking. Doctor say no Tamil.'

Hearing the word 'doctor' Radha erupted,

'*Cela suffit. Tu oses me parler de mon mari!*'

At this point Luk became more excited than ever,

'Tamil no good language. Why you speak Tamil?'

'That's not Tamil; it's French,' Paula corrected, coming in on this bizarre scene.

Luk stared at the child then at Radha, wondering if she was being tricked by a conspiracy between mother and daughter. Radha saw the red lip stick smeared across thick lips and, once again, wondered that her husband allowed himself to be seen in public with a woman who painted herself to look like a prostitute. In the sudden silence in the room, Luk stomped out, muttering, 'I, working girl, you no one.'

In spite of that scene, here was Ayu, the very next day, ignoring Luk's outburst. Radha murmured, '*Dor je,*' thanking her in Cantonese, whereupon Ayu clapped and poured out a stream of words meant to encourage Radha to become fluent in her language.

Radha now clung closer to her children; not Julius for he was too far out of reach. Her heart ached on seeing he didn't want to know her. She tried to protect her other children, but hardly knew how to go about it. Mena, for one, was becoming withdrawn; how could it be otherwise? They were banished upstairs as the rows raged. Radha could see their legs through the railings of the landing: they saw and heard everything. These would be their childhood memories for the rest of their lives.

She shut her eyes tight to keep back the hot tears of pity. At least Roy and Paula seemed to be weathering the storm; they were a comfort to her. They kept their distance from Luk, she could see that. Whatever came from that woman would be tainted with the misery she wreaked on this family.

But the strain of the Doctor's ménage was too great. The solution he'd been trying to find was now provided by Radha herself who wittingly or otherwise, came to his rescue by forcing the issue.

Chapter 22

It was first of April and the *ménage à trois* had already lasted a little over half a year. The children were on school holiday but breakfast was at seven-thirty as usual. Despite the subdued silence which was customary, as the Doctor looked round the table, he thought he discerned a new alertness in the young faces round him. Yes, one day, he'd make something of them. They would rise far above the average. If the war hadn't intervened, by now they'd be far more – no, no good speculating what might have been; the important thing was – it was not too late.

In a playful tone (though it was still too challenging, but there was nothing he could do about that), he began.

'Who can tell me what the date is?' Something easy to start with to give them confidence.

'April the first, Father,' came from at least two voices.

'Well, well,' an approving glance that was only just less menacing than his usual look. 'I see you're wide-awake this morning. Good. April the first, as I'm sure you all know, is April fool's day.' Anxious peeps to left and right plus furtive nods. 'But, does anyone know where the tradition of April fool comes from?'

Total silence while more nervous glances flitted around. No one looked in his direction. Well, he'd not expected an answer; he'd inform them.

'There are several possible origins, but the one I favour dates back to the Romans: when Proserpine was gathering spring flowers in a meadow at the beginning of April, she was carried off by Pluto to the Underworld. Her mother, Ceres, hearing her daughter's cries for help, ran after the echo of her voice in an attempt to find her.' The Doctor raised the pitch of his voice to imitate Proserpine's cries, '"Help! Help!" resounded from every side. Needless to say, trying to locate Proserpine from the sound of her voice which came from every direction, was a fool's errand.' He paused, then shot out, 'Why?'

One or two of them jumped at the suddenness of the question, then quickly ducked their heads. No one dared answer, possibly because they hadn't understood a word of what he'd said.

Into the sudden silence Leela joyfully repeated, 'Help! Help!' trying as far as possible to mimic her father. Radha, who was sitting next to her, put out a hand to hush her, but it released the tension and there was an uncontrolled burst of laughter from everyone.

'Yes, Leela is proving the point,' the Doctor replied, without looking at her. 'You see, an echo is merely a reflection of the sound-waves as they hit upon a surface wherever it happens to be. The original sound might be a long way away and from a completely different direction.' He stopped and no one said anything. Then realizing the explanation was over, several heads nodded in eager agreement and there might even have been the odd 'yes'.

As he left for work, the Doctor felt in a good mood. He advised his children to pay attention when the tutor arrived or else they'd end up fools and it wouldn't be limited to the first of April. A sudden bit of giggling – good – it meant they'd understood his joke.

Luk had just entered the dispensary and the Doctor was about to follow when the driver ran after him shouting, 'Master, please.' This was a most unusual interruption. 'Sorry master, writing on back. Sorry.' He still didn't understand what the man was going on about. Finally, the driver, hardly daring to touch him, peeled off his back, a square piece of cloth, the size of a man's handkerchief. Scrawled in large letters in navy ink were the words:

APRIL

FOOL

*

That day, on returning home, the Doctor went in the main entrance as usual and the driver took the car to the back so that Luk could use the side door. The scene that was to follow was strictly between the man and his wife.

Radha stood, diagonally across from him, facing him, a carving of Resignation. No sign of the children – she'd have told them to stay out of sight. He felt an immense weariness and for a moment wished he could stop time. If only he could go back. Go back? No, there was only one way open to him, and that was forward. His gaze never left hers as he took a few steps in. She looked so small, so alone.

An importunate memory came to taunt him: rays of the setting sun, the sea warm, glinting purple and turquoise, laughter as she clung to him, arms round his neck:

"We'll come here every year. Would you like that, Radha?

"Our summer break at Port Dickson! Will you always hold me, not let me drown?

"Always, ... *later, we'll come with the children.*

"And later still, when our children have children?

"Then it will be just the two of us again ...

"You can put me down now, it's not so deep here.

"Next year, you'll be in a bathing costume; not these yards of dripping cloth."

He looked at her at the other end of the chasm that now separated them. Two statues sculpted of breathless stillness. How had they ended up here on this desert waste?

Of a sudden it seemed to him it was she who had stopped dead the wheel of fortune. She had refused to shake off the disadvantages of birth, refused to catch up with the twentieth century. She had wilfully and single handedly destroyed all the chances that had been there.

When he finally spoke, his voice was surprisingly under control.

'Did you?'

She gave an almost imperceptible nod, eyes on him.

He imagined her taking the cloth from one of the children (Paula? No, more likely, Roy); there would have been gum pasted on the corners; her hands would have reached for it and she'd have smoothed it on his back as she kissed him good bye. He'd been too distracted to feel any change in her touch as her fingers flattened it against his jacket; perhaps the children were creating a diversion. Yes, there'd been that moment, and this – play-acting – explained their excited state at breakfast. It had been planned beforehand.

Black fury flared up so suddenly and violently he didn't immediately trust himself to speak. Eventually a sound, barely more than a rasping breath, forced its way out.

'My patients – how would it have looked if they'd seen?' Her face was expressionless. 'D'you know who pointed it out to me?– the driver!' he spat out the words.

He didn't hit her for he knew a civilised man does not hit his wife. And he was past scolding. He made up his mind there and then to leave her. Which is what he did, without any ceremony or delay for, after that experience, time was of the essence.

Surely he'd known it would end like this? He'd not wanted her to return to Malaya. That part of his life was over; the war had put the final seal. But there'd been no choice – the children. Once she was here, he still hoped she might go back to her mother, but she'd refused. And so he'd set in motion the alternative plan. The *ménage à trois*. There was a slim chance it might work. It *should* have worked. Wasn't it reasonable to expect his wife to run the house and Luk to work outside it? He'd tried to please both women, tried with a grim determination to make the unconventional arrangement work. But he'd known for some time it was hopeless, and, accordingly, had made contingent plans.

Chapter 23

His departure was so sudden Radha was left in a state of shock. And although in the true sense she'd lost Julius many years earlier, that too came home to her in the days that followed. Julius, with no mother, no brother, no sisters! The double loss of husband and son was so devastating she was unable to savour the absence of the Chinese woman.

He would surely come back? Just him and Julius. She would never return to the loathsome arrangement of sharing him with that woman. Never that! This ending seemed so brutal and final. As the end of relationships between men and women had to be.

No, this was not the end. She'd learnt from her mother marriages are forever. There could be no going back on vows. No change of heart.

But he was so different!

Even so, he had to come back, not only because she was his lawful wife joined to him in Holy Matrimony, but because there'd been all those years of planning for their family, their children. Four of them were still with her. She still held four aces. He'd come back.

It had been Roy's idea and she'd seen the poetic justice of the prank. The piercing pain of all that she'd lost cried out for recognition even more than vengeance.

And there was one other element that urged her towards this ruinous act – her situation was so intolerable she had to end it, irrespective of the consequences.

She wrote to her mother, knowing how much it would grieve her. Not only had her daughter been abandoned, but it was for a Chinese woman. Someone outside the caste system, and therefore, beneath consideration. The old lady had thought he'd never stoop to such ignominy. Did such words have any meaning for him?

Radha's thoughts ground painfully in an ever descending spiral. How was she to get him back to his home and his children if he'd not let her see him? She couldn't go round to the Dispensary, screaming like a fishwife; not there where *she* presided, a death-dealing tarantula at the centre of her evil web.

Her husband told her she wasn't to get in touch with him. He'd arrange for monthly payments into a bank account in her name. It was already done.

That the allowance was generous was of no interest to Radha. She bitterly resented having to make the withdrawals and felt humiliated by the transaction which was made necessary by his absence.

The children tiptoed round the house, holding their breath for the next debacle. But nothing followed. All the sound and the fury was spent. But the silence was full of menace. From Radha they soon picked up that a separation of this sort in a respectable family was exceedingly out of the ordinary and shameful in the extreme.

Paula ruefully envisaged her life shut in within the limits of Radha's vision. But the thought of moving into the same space as Luk was worse. For the rest of the children, as the days went by, there was no denying the daily routine was more relaxed and there was an unspoken sense of relief. The thunderous explosions had come to an end. Gradually they stopped speaking in whispers.

However, the stigma was there. Not one of them mentioned to their classmates, not even to their best friends, that their parents were separated. That was too shameful a secret to share with anyone but each other. And, on the whole, best kept to oneself.

*

Despite the fearful emotional upheaval, life had to go on. The Chinese servants who had followed their mistress, had to be replaced with trustworthy Indian ones. Radha knew no one. But a few enquiries at church brought her a good cook, and through her, Radha found a reliable servant girl to clean the house. The girl lived in while the cook arrived each morning and left after the evening meal. She still had the gardener who came daily for a couple of hours of watering the plants, weeding and keeping the grass within bounds. It was a modest set-up but it would suffice. Radha didn't foresee entertaining in the near future.

The days already held enough of a routine within them to establish a fragile normality. In essence the Doctor's timetable remained established. Radha even managed to get the BBC World Service. The radio with its walnut casing, assumed a special significance since her husband's departure; it was almost as if it was he who turned it on each time. Mealtimes were fixed with military precision as were the children's bedtimes. Within this framework, Radha moved with increasing flexibility.

Sometime in mid August the long-awaited news of her country's Independence reached her. Her heart filled with joy and pride and she thought of her mother with whom she might have shared this moment. Had her husband been with her, she was certain he wouldn't have felt her elation. The children understood nothing, but they enjoyed the array of sweetmeats she'd made to celebrate the event.

Then she heard of the massacres even before she'd finished her letter to *Ummachi*. The Doctor had been right, after all. The horror, for the most part, was contained in the North and Radha prayed that the Mahatma would bring peace before it spread to other parts. Alas! he was so alone. His close friend Nehru, was being hailed as a great politician. But in Radha's eyes he was seriously flawed – too many European ways to be a true Indian.

Then, a few months later, the horror of Gandhi's murder, and by one of his own! To meet such a violent end for preaching peace made no sense at all. Radha wept, wishing she could share her grief with her mother.

She was at this unhappy period when, one Sunday, just as she was ushering the children out at the end of Mass, Radha caught sight of the woman who was to become her close friend, indeed, her only true friend.

Agnes was about the same age as Radha, and the same build, and on that particular Sunday, even their taste in saris was similar: organdy with small pale flowers dotted here and there, embroidery along the border and the edge of the *mundani*. With the years, Radha's beauty had softened, become more gentle and now matched Agnes's so closely they might have been sisters, their smooth hair twisted into a bun at the nape of the neck. Radha saw Agnes was not wearing a ring.

On other Sundays, she'd noticed her leaving by the side entrance at the end of Mass though. She always seemed to be on her own. They'd smiled at each other, sometimes given a shy nod. Agnes now introduced herself.

'I was wondering if you and the children would like to have some light refreshments with me?'

'Thank you; the problem is, the car.' and Radha felt the blood rush to her face at having to explain she had limited use of the car.

'I understand,' Agnes came quickly to her rescue. 'Besides, Sunday morning is not the most convenient time. But if you find yourself free at some other time –'

'Would it be possible for you to come and see me during the week?' Radha asked. 'You see, the children are at school; if you came mid-morning ...'

So it was that the very next Tuesday, Agnes took a rickshaw to Jalan Inai, got off just outside the gate of no 10, and, since it was her first visit, she told the man to wait, unsure how long she'd be. She was standing at the gate, wondering how best to attract the servant without shouting, when the girl came running to open it. Agnes walked down the curve of the drive and was met by Radha who'd been trimming the plumbago on the parapet of the porch.

'How pretty your flowers look.' she remarked, 'These are my favourite; we have that in common.'

'Yes, a lovely blue, but I hope, for your sake, there aren't too many things we have in common, that is ...' Radha gave a slight cough to hide her confusion; she'd not meant to plunge her new friend so suddenly into her emotional state. 'Come in; I ...'

They sat downstairs beneath the overhead fan and the servant brought two glasses, a jug with lemon drink, ice cubes bobbing on top, and a plate of small Indian cakes.

'I haven't been back long,' Radha began, 'These are such terrible times. India. My husband and eldest son were here on their own, I ...' She stopped, realizing this was grossly inaccurate; 'on their own' didn't simply mean 'without me and our four other children'. She started again, unsure of the best way to re-phrase what she wanted to say. 'What I mean is ...'

'I know,' Agnes interrupted. 'The Doctor's so well known, he can do nothing without everyone knowing all about it. You have my sympathy; may God bring him back soon.'

'I too am convinced it will be soon,' Radha said, interpreting Agnes's wish as an opinion. A lizard clicked and Radha made a gesture to mean it was in agreement. 'How else should it be?' she continued, 'In the end, he won't be able to do without his family. I've even started teaching myself English; to surprise him. He always wanted me to learn. It's coming along quite well; a little late but better that than never.' Radha smiled, optimism lighting up her eyes. She hadn't talked as much with anyone for weeks, perhaps months. Nor indeed so openly, ever. It was a great relief.

Agnes thought the Doctor had managed well enough without his family during the five years they'd been away, but she said nothing. Why snuff out that little spark? Besides, she was impressed by Radha's unshakeable faith, and recognized how similar her own upbringing had been. She enthusiastically seconded Radha's plans and launched into broken English.

'Friend, this is your instructor, standing in front of your two eyes. That's as sure as eggs are eggs. I'm diplomed in English and on this day pledge myself to instruct you to the end of my ability and best of my life.'

'That is wonderful,' Radha replied in Tamil, somewhat taken aback. 'I understand what you say for the most part; the Doctor has always had reservations about too many eggs. Unfortunately, it won't work; I'm not yet up to that standard.'

'I'm seeing no problem. Here I am speaking English to your ears, and there you are speaking Tamil to me, and we're understanding one hundred percent minus one percent for eggs. Net result: your husband will be overwhelming at your outlandish knowledge. That I am guaranteeing to you.'

The arrangement was sealed, and the two friends parted agreeing to deepen their friendship as well as to repeat the English lesson the following Tuesday. A lizard clicked again and Radha confirmed to her new friend that Providence was clearly on their side.

Chapter 24

R adha racked her brains as to how she might open the
line of communication with her husband. Both her
letters had met with stony silence. If the servant girl hadn't
delivered them by hand, she might have blamed the post.

Then, quite unexpectedly, a solution presented itself:
Mena suddenly developed such a high temperature, there
was genuine cause for alarm.

'What am I to do?' Radha rung her hands in
consternation.

'You could try phoning him; that's what this
contraption is for,' Paula suggested.

Radha looked at the phone as though noticing it for
the first time. It had been installed quite recently but it might
have been an ornament for all the use it was put to.

'He'll think it's a trick!' she murmured. Then she had
a bright idea, 'Paula, you ring. He's more likely to listen if
it's you.'

'No problem.' Paula meant it. It was the beginning of
her role as go-between.

The response was immediate. Never has a doctor said
less while attending to a patient. He saw, however, that the

call was justified. His face, an angry mask, he spat out in Tamil the instructions for the medicine, then left, promising to return the next evening.

Mena recovered quickly but Radha never found out what had been the matter with her. She saw these visits didn't herald his return. She had to create a life round the children. First, however, she'd re-arrange things to her liking.

The garden – it would take years for it to reach the maturity of the old bungalow which was why she had to start immediately. She bought three gardenia bushes to be planted along the drive. She'd given up wearing flowers in her hair but they'd provide the occasional bloom to put in a vase. The area of lawn shone bright green with the flat blades of grass gleaming in the brilliant sun. Everything had been cut back and trimmed when they'd arrived to make it safe for the children to play without fear of snakes. Thick bamboo hedges enclosed the perimeter with red hibiscus that had sprouted at random. On the left, just inside the gate, stood the rumbutan tree where she'd first seen the gecko which appeared from time to time, as it darted from one branch to another. Beyond that the tall coconut palms waved into the sky. She planted the new low-growing variety in between.

It was a peaceful spot where she liked to wander in the late afternoon in that brief moment when the heat of the day was over but the sun hadn't yet set, nor the mosquitoes come out in force.

Inside the house, she started with the main wall downstairs. Above the radio set, she hung the two oval portraits of herself and her husband which she found in the storage room. The three porcelain vases, a tall Chiang Chi and a pair of lustreware, early presents from grateful patients, were placed on the dining room sideboard.

The room downstairs which had served as the master bedroom was purified and converted into a prayer room. A statue of the Virgin Mary as she appeared at Lourdes stood on a tall table. On either side, candles were lit for evening prayers and in the tiny vase in front, a single gardenia sent out an elusive perfume.

On the upper floor the Goddess Lakshmi ruled supreme, conferring wealth and prosperity upon the household from the large reproduction that hung on the north wall. The polished wooden planks of the floor were left bare. On special days the gramophone was ceremoniously uncovered, and, with the children gathered about her, Radha would sit on the floor, turn the handle till it was fully wound, then carefully lower the needle onto the record with the faithful dog that listened to his master's voice. A look of sweet contentment would light up her face as the reedy sound of Strauss's waltz reached out into the room.

It was here, in the wide space to the left of the staircase, that the children played their imaginative games during the monsoon rains. Roy was now a weekly boarder with the Brothers. In his absence Paula invented and performed stories to amuse her sisters. The actual performance was often in English, for, if Radha was attempting to improve her knowledge of the language through her sympathetic but ineffectual teacher, Paula was striding ahead full steam.

Preparations for the entertainment were almost as important as the performance itself.

'Right, we are about to begin, soon,' Paula warned. Clash of improvised cymbals to accompany the portentous announcement. 'And now,' another clash of cymbals, 'it's time for the audience to take their seats.'

This was a *façon de parler* as the audience of two would be sitting cross-legged on the wooden floor. However, it never failed to work Leela and Mena into a frenzy as they fought, undecided whether to sit to the right or left of each other. In the end Paula decided, as always.

'Now, absolute silence while the stage is prepared, and shut your eyes. No cheating or the performance will be cancelled.'

'Cancelled!' they cried in unison, clamping their hands over their eyes just in case, by mistake, they saw something they shouldn't.

There followed intriguing sounds that were wildly exciting; the sound of furniture scraping against floorboards, soft rustle of material, something falling to the ground. Would the Prince manage, yet again, after perilous adventures, to rescue the hapless but beautiful maiden from the jaws of death? In today's story would he have 'bold blue eyes' or would it be a 'fierce black gaze that confounded his enemies'? And would the 'hapless maiden' resemble Paula as she had in other adventures? At last a voice, very like Paula's, declaimed:

'The story is about to begin. You may open your eyes. *The Princess and the Nightingale!*' and a thrilling trill could be heard, clearly the song of the nightingale.

'What's nightingale?' Leela asked in a loud whisper.

'A bird ... or insect,' Mena replied.

They opened their eyes to see the wonders before them. Leaning on a stool which looked vaguely familiar, lay a Princess (easily discernible as such by the glittery scarf round her head and the velvet cloth with fringe draped over her body). In her right hand lay the nightingale.

'Paula lying down – she sick. Why table cloth round her?' the whisper was now louder.

'Shush, that not Paula; that Princess,' Mena explained equally loudly.

'Look same like Paula,' Leela insisted, no longer bothering to whisper, 'and that my tin whistle in hand – not nightingale. Why she –?'

Her question was drowned out from the stage by a loud groan,

'Woe! Oh, woe is me!'

'She sick,' Leela said triumphantly as one who'd been right all along, then, began wailing, imitating the princess, 'Woe, oh, woe.'

From the stage a still louder moan rang out.

'*When, oh when, will my handsome Prince hear the song of my nightingale and come to rescue me?*' And the trill of the nightingale could be heard even as the Princess covered her face with the glittery scarf and laid the 'nightingale' to her lips.

'Prince? That Roy. Roy not here; he in school,' Leela announced in a voice of authority to the stricken princess.

'One more interruption, and there'll be no story,' Paula shouted.

And that worked as always and the story was allowed to reach its happy ending.

If Roy was home, the performances were replaced with snakes and ladders or other such games. Ludo was their favourite. Leela, who had no notion of board games, traipsed around with her mother, complaining endlessly of Mena's treatment of her while Radha soothed her with promises that things would improve.

In one corner of the garden, the children were each given a tiny area to plant seeds. Only Mena tended her patch, watering the plot with devotion. At last something shot up and she ran to her mother with the exciting news. They watched the plant grow at an impressive rate. Finally, it put out a disproportionately small flower which Radha cut with great pomp and placed carefully in a vase though it threatened to topple over. They stood back and admired the monstrous weed. Radha declared with absolute truth she'd never managed to grow anything as fast as that. It proved, she claimed, Mena had green fingers.

A clump of sugar canes grown partly as a screen but also to please the children, shut off the view to this rear garden. There was always an air of festive ritual when the gardener cut the canes into segments and handed each child a length to suck the sweet juice.

Life round Radha was carefree for the younger children. School ended at one. This was followed by lunch and then a short siesta after which there was tea, their favourite meal. The tin of Huntley & Palmer biscuits was somehow always miraculously full and offered a delightful variety of choice. Then homework followed by playtime. Supper was on the dot of seven thirty, a short interval to digest, and finally bed. The routine had been established by the Doctor and Radha saw no reason to vary it.

It would ensure a smooth continuation when he returned.

Chapter 25

Radha now planned to take advantage of her husband's absence to instil some of her own culture in the two youngest children. When Agnes next arrived, she found her friend in a state of great excitement.

'What d'you think – Mena and Leela – I thought they could attend the local Tamil school, just the odd afternoon. They'd learn some literature and it would keep them busy. No reason why my husband should know about it; he'd probably not approve, at least, not straightaway.'

'Topping idea.' Agnes confirmed. 'Why to be worrying him with such drivel? I'm knowing headmaster of Tamil school; fellow looking same as butter can melt on him. School is stone's throw round the bend. Tamil literature class on Tuesday and Thursday afternoon. I'm knowing all this. You yourself can be going on two pins.'

Radha got the gist of her friend's advice but didn't want to risk her husband finding out; best if she wasn't seen outside the boundary of the house.

'Mena could surely get herself and Leela there, don't you think? Besides, the girl can accompany them.'

'Easy as pie because school is nearly bent. Self will instruct headmaster to be seeing you. Now, must be going. Tootle-oo and cheerio-bye.' So saying Agnes left, happy to be entrusted with this important assignment.

The headmaster duly came round the next morning when the children were at their English-speaking school.

'Leela may have learning difficulty,' Radha explained, 'but I'd like her to attend to see if she picks up something since it's in Tamil. Besides, I don't want her to feel left out.'

'I understand, Mrs; both girls are welcome in my school,' he mumbled, calculating how much he could ask for child-minding.

'Of course I'd pay the full fees for both.'

His calculations told him he was onto a good thing. Of course he knew whom he was dealing with. However charming he found Mrs Mentem, he had a deep-seated grudge against the Doctor though he'd never met him. Nothing like envy to kindle the flame of hatred.

' ... learns quickly but she'll be starting from scratch; I hope that won't be a problem?'

'Problem, Mrs? School is there for teaching children. Happy to have her, to have both, very happy.' God, how he resented the idea of these privileged brats appearing sporadically to interrupt his classes and for whom his school was not good enough except as an amusing little extra.

' ... particularly written Tamil and Indian myths.'

'My speciality. I'll be teaching her, that is, them, myself.' He didn't add there were no other teachers in the school, nor that it was killing him to keep up this ingratiating pose.

His life, he told himself, shouldn't be a round of polite, worthless chat such as she was putting him through. This very morning, for this interview, what with his bicycle having packed up last month, he'd had to run like mad to get here on time, then look as if he'd stepped out calmly from a trishaw, and any minute now, he'll be running all the way back to open his school on time. And by then, sweat will be pouring down his face and the length of his back, even before he administered the first caning to some culprit.

He knew all about the 'English' Doctor who was no more English than he himself but whose wealth and reputation placed him on another planet. Only the other day he'd caught a glimpse of the tall iron gates in Ampang Road where the Doctor's mansion was being erected. A sultan on either side for his neighbours. Not that these people had neighbours as such to nod a friendly greeting to. Wouldn't even recognize each other, screened forever behind the fortification of their walls and drivers. Though husband and wife were separated, he couldn't be certain of the outcome were he to show disrespect. He therefore bowed and smiled with every word, and all but pulled his forelock. God, what a performance!

'Send them along, Mrs, whenever you feel like it. I shall do my best to instruct them.'

As he set out on that sprint back, the wad of notes in his shirt pocket lent him wings to reach safety. They certainly had money to burn, paying like this, a full term of attendance for both children, though term was already half over! And, they'd only be there two afternoons a week! Too good to be true, he thought, through gritted teeth. Visions of a replacement bike acted as balm on his sore feet.

Knowing her husband would disapprove, Radha kept the transaction to herself. On the Tuesday afternoon, she led her two youngest children through the back gate and watched as they disappeared down the lane with the servant girl. There were curious glances from the few loafers who were hanging around. Yes, an unusual sight for the Mentem girls to be seen on foot. The stand at the end of the lane caught her eye – flattened tamarind. How curious not to have known that before! She'd tell the servant to pick some up next time.

When Leela and Mena arrived at the school, the very sight of them confirmed the teacher's worst forebodings. Each of their ridiculous dresses, Western-style of course, must have cost as much as he earned over several months, and there was the anticipated disruption as they joined the class.

'Settle down quietly,' he ordered, 'You, here, next to the aisle and as for you, over there by the wall.'

'Can't we sit together pl...' Mena began.

'Say 'Sir' when you speak' he barked. 'And the answer is 'No'.'

There were twenty-three pupils and that was in fact the entire school. Their ages ranged from six to twelve. The teacher picked up the book that was lying on his desk, opened it at the marker and started reading a story about a crow that was rather pleased with itself. Eventually its vanity brought about its downfall; it was out-smarted by a fox.

A well-trodden path but he'd chosen the fable feeling it was particularly relevant: the clever fox was obviously him, but the crow, well, it was anyone who puts on airs, and, without wanting to be too specific, there were a great many people who did that. He took immense pleasure in pointing the moral, not that the brats would make the connection. And now it was time for questions and answers.

'Who can give me an example of flattery?'

Many hands shot up, Mena's among them. Someone whispered loud enough to be heard, his hand waving wildly, 'It's what you put in a car to make it go.' Much to his frustration, the teacher ignored him.

'Let's see what our new pupil has to say, speak.'

'You're the strongest man in the world,' Mena said.

One or two hands remained up while the teacher threw her a hostile look.

'Silly girl, can't you remember to address me as Sir? Well, why would that be flattery?'

'Because you're not Tarzan, Sir.'

At this point a wild array of alternatives were offered which had nothing to do with flattery. This was turning into a fiasco. Never mind, he'd get his own back with a dictation. Ignoring Mena's pleas, he proceeded.

The sheets of paper with their names on top were gathered at the end and deposited on his desk. They'd be returned on Thursday at the next literature class.

Once they were home, the girls recounted their experiences amid peals of laughter.

'No Leela, me first, *Umma*, listen to this,' Mena stood very straight, her hand up, trying not to laugh, "Sir," that's his name and if you forget it, he jumps around as if bitten by a thousand ants shouting, "Start again, you silly girl and don't forget Sir."'

'Sir, Sir, please Sir,' Leela chanted, skipping around and Radha caught the infection and clapped delightedly.

But when Radha heard the theme of the story that had been read to them, she was indignant, saying it wasn't Indian. There were endless tales he could have picked out of the Ramayana which were equally instructive and amusing. She'd take him to task over this at the next opportunity.

Chapter 26

When it was time for the girls to set off for their Thursday class, Mena started dragging her feet. Finally, she was persuaded to continue with promises of tamarind and strips of salt/sweet cutlefish. But the lesson turned out to be an awful trial.

No sooner had the sisters settled at their separate desks than the teacher brought out the corrected dictation sheets. He started handing them out with elaborate gestures, praising some, encouraging others. Leela's sheet was returned to her without a comment; it was clear the hieroglyphics corresponded to no known script. Shortly before the end of the sheaf, Sanjy, who came top, received his accompanied by prolonged praise. Mena, who was still waiting, began to wonder if by some odd chance, she'd done brilliantly. Either that or her sheet had been mercifully lost.

The teacher now turned to her with the very last sheet. He sauntered down the aisle and returned to stand pointedly next to her. He held her dictation flat against his chest as he looked down at her. The class held its breath. It was obvious something of interest was about to happen. Would this new pupil be praised to the sky or ... finally, holding the paper above his head with both hands, and turning slowly to make sure the whole class got a good look, he spoke in a whisper so that the children had to crane forward to catch his words.

'And you, Mena, have earned yourself – an egg.' A pause, then, raising his voice, he added, 'Not an ordinary egg but an extra large duck egg.'

Mena was not sure what all this meant but as the class erupted into loud hilarity she supposed it referred to the zero that she too saw at the bottom of the page.

'Can't do dicta ... ,' she began.

'How many times do I have to remind you to call me Sir?' he cut in angrily. 'Can't you hold anything in that head of yours? There's nothing in there – it's as empty as this nought.' More laughter all round as he pointed to the unmistakable zero. It was quite enjoyable though he'd have preferred a few tears. This was the trouble with these people; they were brazen. Just because they had money, they thought they were superior. A child of seven, and he couldn't cut her down to size, not properly. But, though she looked at him unflinchingly she couldn't be enjoying it; that, at least, brought some satisfaction.

'You don't have to tell me you can't do dictation; I can see that for myself.' He looked round the class for support and got it.

'Sir, *Umma* sent me here – for you to teach me, Sir.'

He stared at her, somehow resisting the urge to throttle her. This was not their cue but by now the class was out of control and he had to shut them up with loud threats and the odd knock on the head.

When Mena told her mother about the uproar, Radha had difficulty understanding the antipathy of the man against her daughter who was so well turned out and had such quiet, nice manners. She hoped it wouldn't put her off attending.

Well, she needn't have worried. The classes didn't continue though it wasn't Mena or the Tamil teacher who ended them.

The next Tuesday, just as the two children were about to set off (and yes, there had been a certain amount of whinging from Mena who asked if she could have some Tamil lessons before going back to that school), the driver suddenly arrived with a note from the Doctor. It hardly needed Paula's translation from the English for Radha to know its contents:

It is extremely irresponsible of you to expose the children in this way. And for no better reason than to make them join the riffraff of Kuala Lumpur. Are you aware of the kidnappings that have become so prevalent? This must stop at once.

Radha couldn't know how well founded his fears were for she didn't keep abreast with the news. As the economy began to boom in post-war Malaya, the division between rich and poor became marked. Children of merchants who were unwise enough to exhibit their wealth with plush cars and servants in uniform were particularly vulnerable.

The Doctor kept a relatively low profile but news travelled fast in the capital and it was widely known that he ran two substantial households, of which one, albeit not yet completed, was in Ampang Road. Seven acres in the Mayfair of Kuala Lumpur couldn't be hidden under a bushel. And even if his car, an Ambassador, wasn't showy, he had a driver who would soon be lodged with his family in the separate cottage behind the grand house and there were any number of servants besides. Such details tend to leak out. The Doctor was right – he could have been a target for a kidnapping.

Radha dismissed the idea of a kidnapping, but she was deeply disturbed to think her husband seemed omnipotent: how on earth had he found out? And so soon.

As far as the two little girls were concerned, the driver's arrival and the subsequent veto were a merciful deliverance. The lesson on the Thursday had been an hour long torture, and they were happy there'd be no repetition of it.

When the two women met the following week, Radha told Agnes about the end of the Tamil classes. Agnes was shocked.

'Dear friend, when almighty men want to know, how to be stopping them? Your husband is all-knowing. Informants everywhere. Every man a snake in the grass that bite the hand that feeds. And that headmaster the biggest snake of all. May he be downtrodden by the spotless foot of the Virgin Mary and made mincemeat in the tongues of hell.'

'Maybe,' Radha said, feeling anything to do with the Virgin Mary must be all right. After a pause, she began tentatively, 'Agnes, I think you must have heard ... about the baby.' Agnes bowed her head to show she knew Radha was talking about Luk's pregnancy. Neither of them said anything further on the subject. At last, Radha got up, shaking herself free of that thought. As she did so, she noticed her friend's bare hand; she'd been wanting to ask for some time. 'Agnes,' she now said, 'no ring? Have you never thought of ...'

Agnes slipped into Tamil, feeling her past could only be related in that language.

'Five whole years I was engaged to him, wore his ring, never looked at another man. He travelled a lot and when I asked him what he did he said it was Government business; very hush-hush; I mustn't ask. All the women were after him, or so it seemed to me, but he told me he only had eyes for me. At last my mother, feeling the full responsibility of a widow, asked him to name the day. I was now twenty five. He named the day and we celebrated with wine which we never touched normally but that was, after all, a very special day. The first time I tasted alcohol. It was the last I saw of him. Can you believe it, never saw him again, ever.'

'Never saw him again!' Radha repeated in disbelief.

'Never saw him again. Of course we made enquiries but it wasn't easy. Even his name wasn't a certainty. Eventually there were stories of him having a wife in Mysore. At that point I removed my ring and gave up the hunt.'

'Poor Agnes, and you've been so kind listening to me.'

'Radha, my dear,' said Agnes, switching back to her English, 'I'm not knowing if it's you who should be listening to me or me to yourself. Both is what I'm thinking; birds of a feather are forever hatching together.'

Radha acquiesced with a nod although she felt certain Agnes and she were not in the same league.

'Problem comes,' Agnes said with a sigh, 'when women use foul play. Then they are certainly winning.'

'Foul play?' enquired Radha. 'What d'you mean?'

'Magic. How can your husband be thinking of you if Pigface is practising foul play with magic?– I'm thinking you are already knowing.'

'Dear Agnes, how am I to fight against that? No wonder my prayers haven't been answered. Foul play – a frightening thought!' After a moment she said, 'I sometimes wish I'd never left my mother in Pondicherry.'

'We're both blessed with a mother still, though mine is constantly growing old and health is no longer in the pink.'

'Yes, my mother too is no longer young, and in her last letter spoke of her diabetes which has got worse. Her eyesight ...' Radha shook her head and sighed, 'life is not easy.'

'Valley is flooded with tears,' Agnes echoed. 'But, bottoms up and chin-chin,' she added brightly.

When Radha was alone once more, she decided to replace the small statue of Our Lady of Lourdes with a larger one, install a veritable shrine to the Virgin in that room where her husband had surely sinned. That, she felt, was the first step towards protecting herself against the wiles of the Chinese woman.

Chapter 27

S he was flicking through the old photo albums that she'd dug out of the sandalwood chest to show Agnes, pictures of her mother and others, as promised. Ah, there was Ravi's wedding photo showing almost the whole family, and here, a lovely one of her godson, Julius, named after her first born. A photo of her with her husband at Port Dixon; what a mirage! How he'd teased her shyness as the wet sari clung to her body!

There were sounds at the gate and she heard the servant running to open it. When Agnes came in, Radha saw how flustered she was; all thought of photos was forgotten. Something was the matter. Her friend's opening words rang further alarm bells.

'Sometimes I feel God tries us too hard.' The fact that she dispensed with English altogether was the surest sign that whatever she had to say was so upsetting she wasn't her usual self. With fearful foreboding, Radha led her upstairs.

She sat her friend down and took the chair next to her. The servant came up with the fruit juice; when they were alone once more, she tried to say something to show she wholeheartedly agreed about God trying everyone too much, but her voice refused to make itself heard. She waited, gazing intently at Agnes.

'We've known for a long time the day would come and yet knowing it in advance doesn't help one bit. The child is born – a boy. They've called him ...'

'No!' Radha cried out, 'Not a boy! Why does God reward the wicked and punish the innocent so cruelly! Agnes, how can this be just?'

'This has nothing to do with justice. Here on earth, the devil looks after his own and we can safely count Pigface among them. Our task is to bear all patiently. Don't weep; God will reward you, if not here on earth, then surely in heaven.' So saying, Agnes tried to comfort her friend though she herself had difficulty holding back her tears.

Between sobs Radha learnt they'd named the boy George and that her rival had been pleased with the name, knowing that one day the child would be educated in England.

'All this information has got out because there was a problem,' Agnes said finally. 'If it's any consolation, there will be no more children – it was a difficult birth.'

'She can have as many as she wants,' Radha gazed without seeing. 'A dozen children, more – it's of no consequence to me. But *one* with my husband is one too many and I curse her and her child from the bottom of my heart. Nothing good will come to her from this child she's stolen from my womb.'

Agnes gave a shudder. A cold current seemed to blow through the sweltering heat and she hugged the sari round her. They sat in silence for a long while.

'Why did it have to be my husband, joined to me before God? That, Agnes, is why no good will come of it.' She gave a deep sigh, then spoke in a low voice more to herself than to to her friend, 'In the early days, life with him wasn't easy; everything so different; especially him. Bit by bit, he let me be myself, my hair, saris ...'

'Saris?'

'You see, at first, he wanted me to wear dresses, oh, yes, he really did! And to have short hair, to speak English, even drive a car! You can hardly believe it but that's how it was, at first. Then he began to talk with me, give me presents. These zircons – our second year, just after the miscarriage. He was so gentle, wiped my tears away saying, "One day, we'll have a son; but for now, you must be brave. I'll help you. Look Radha," he said, "isn't this a beautiful colour – turquoise zircons? I thought they'd look good on you."'

'They're beautiful,' Agnes murmured, wiping a tear furtively.

'The very next year, Julius was born. Summer breaks to the seaside, a pet dog for the baby, laughter and chatter the whole day long. More children. So many plans for our future. God help me I thought it would last forever. But the devil can't bear to see so much happiness. He came disguised as a Chinese nurse! I saw through her at once, but it didn't help. Agnes, what depth of wickedness to take a man who already had a wife and five children! Then the war, the devil's ally, sealed the shame.'

Agnes took her friend's hands in hers and held them.

When the children came home from school, Paula, seeing Agnes hovering in the background, guessed something had happened and that the bandyman had orders to return later with his rickshaw. Paula wondered what it was about, feeling, at the same time, a twinge of annoyance at her curiosity. It would all be revealed anyway the moment Agnes left and that was the rub – at thirteen she didn't want to be caught up in the gloom of this adult world, having to side with her mother and listen to the unending complaints about her father.

Not that she was complaisant about his living with that Chinese woman which necessarily meant that she, Paula, was deprived of his company. All the same, it chafed her to be drawn into criticising someone she loved so much.

Her mother and Agnes didn't join them for lunch which made it more unusual than ever. Radha said she had a headache and asked Paula to make sure her sisters behaved themselves and ate properly. From then on things proceeded exactly as Paula had foreseen.

The moment Agnes left, her mother called her into the prayer room, telling the two younger children to play quietly upstairs. Radha told her daughter the news, unable to stem the flow of tears.

'It changes everything,' Radha said, tears still misting her eyes. 'A separate family though an illegitimate one, makes his return less ... it complicates things. She turned him against me a long time ago. Now, with this child, I'm afraid for you children. How can he do such a thing if he really loves you?'

Paula tried to keep in check the anger she felt against Luk as well as against her mother who was, in some inexplicable way, responsible for things getting so out of hand. Even if she didn't want to join her mother in her grievance, for once, it looked as though they were in the same camp. She saw it was serious.

'He may not be free to do as he pleases,' she remarked, adopting as matter-of-fact tone as she could muster, 'If she's managed to turn him against you, why not against us?'

So, there it was again; confirmation from a new quarter, albeit a thirteen-year-old, that her rival was resorting to some other means, no doubt 'foul'. As Agnes had implied her husband was not 'free' to do as he pleased.

'You're right,' Radha readily agreed, 'She's done it with the help of magic.'

'Magic!' Paula let out with a derisive laugh, 'Is this the last chapter of the fairy tale with a new twist where the wicked witch gets the prince?'

'It's real, Paula!– how else could he have left us as he has?'

Well, that was an argument Paula couldn't deny though there was something self-fulfilling about it.

Radha sensed Paula had understood the implications of the birth of this child. It was a comfort having a daughter old enough for her to confide in. And she thanked Heaven she had Roy. There was her consolation. This George would never equal the beauty and excellence of her son. And the two youngest children – she must somehow shield them from the unhappiness that shrouded this family. But how was she to protect her children's birthright?

Despite the massive strain, she presented a calm exterior to the outside world. At Mass that Sunday, her face was so serene no one would have guessed the turmoil within.

Conversations with Paula became more urgent. Paula listened but she'd already learnt to switch off her emotional connection with her mother. Radha didn't know how to engage her feelings. Nor was she aware to what extent she was restricting Mena and Leela's development; her one priority was to keep them out of the ferocious reality of her world.

Chapter 28

R adha lay awake, staring at the top of the mosquito net.
For how long would she be able to protect her children
from this engulfing unhappiness round them? Paula at least
wasn't affected; it made her strong and angry. Strong enough
to be a consolation to her mother.

But for Paula herself, being thus promoted to
adulthood was particularly unwelcome mainly because her
sympathies did not lie with Radha. She knew what she
wanted in life, and it was definitely not to be stuck at home
with her mother. Days followed one another in a prolonged
waiting, peaked every now and then by some acute and
excruciating crisis that bounced from one parent to the other.
Paula was caught between a distraught and unhappy mother
and the father she loved. She ended up resenting Radha
whole-heartedly

She'd never forget that birthday, her fourteenth, when
the driver picked her up and drove her to the mansion which
was now ready. Saturday morning, her father standing,
waiting for her (normally he'd have left for the dispensary
by now), his eyes shining with delight.

He handed her a drink, pomegranate juice, she thought, and a piece of cake. A cracker, just like one of those Christmas crackers, lying on the low occasional table that was covered with a velvet cloth. He asked her to pull it with him. They crouched down, opposite each other, and pulled, her father down as low as she was. The only time she'd ever seen him crouch. Something tumbled out onto the cloth. A diamond bracelet. She stared, disbelieving, then, murmuring thank you, picked it up and stood gazing at it. He took it from her, undid the clasp, and spoke softly as he put it on her wrist.

'One day, Paula, would you like to leave these backward countries and go to Europe?' Paula held her breath as he went on, 'To England. There you'll be able to read Shakespeare and the Bible in English.'

'The Bible? I do already, a bit; the parables,' she said with a smile, but her heart was racing with excitement.

'The Authorized Version. I'm talking about literature, not the scriptures. From England you could step over the Channel to Europe and then on to Switzerland where they make cuckoo clocks and watches. Watches with precious jewels set in platinum, as exquisite as a diamond bracelet and more intricate. D'you think you'd like to go there, one day?

'I would,' she murmured.

'Good girl. The rest of that set will be ready before long. I'm also having a set made for Mena and Leela; a little less elaborate but it should keep them happy. Come, I must get to work now; the driver will drop me off first, then take you back to your house.'

On her return, Paula said nothing about the cuckoo clock or Shakespeare. Nor Europe. Women with bare legs, touching men to shake hands! Paula, taken from her mother's side. It would have unloosed an avalanche of grief. Instead, she held out her arm to show her mother the glittering jewel. When Radha saw it, she felt dismayed.

'Why has he done this?' she cried. 'Diamonds shouldn't be set in silver!'

'It's platinum,' Paula corrected.

'Makes no difference what you call it. It looks just like silver; or silver plate.

Radha was seeing in her mind's eye her daughter's wedding – gleaming, yellow gold to go with the gold sari would have looked right. Not this cheap looking stuff. She sighed – such mishaps were inevitable given the situation.

*

When the Doctor moved out of Jalan Inai, he rented a house nearby for Julius, Luk and himself while the mansion in Ampang Road was being completed. Julius was pleased to get away from the rest though he quite liked Roy. Roy wasn't a threat of any sort; a mere tuppeny-ha'penny minor, four whole years younger than him. His father was unlikely to take much interest in him, especially as he was his mother's pet.

Besides, being the eldest placed Julius at a distinct advantage – he knew that because his father had gone on about the British tradition of primogeniture. But his sisters were a different matter altogether; he had no time at all for them; especially Paula, who was clearly father's favourite and had already mastered a certain amount of English.

Soon after they'd arrived, he'd given a full scale performance on his banjo. It turned out to be his first and last. Hardly had he struck up the first few notes, when the two older ones stole out of the room, suddenly overcome with a fit of coughing. The other two stuck it out, but he noticed their stealthy nudges and brought the concert to an untimely end.

But, what a measly lot they were! First it actually was measles, then chicken pox, then mumps. He of course had already had everything. Why, he wondered, had they saved it up till they got to Kuala Lumpur?

Then there was real drama when Mena went down with whooping cough. That was rather more problematic. For a start, he hadn't had it. Nobody was allowed to go near her except his father, her mother and Ayu. She made an awful sound; more what he'd always imagined to be a death rattle. She was going to die for sure, and he tried not to breathe in too deeply when he was in the house. He practised breathing out the whole time and was relieved to find it worked – he didn't catch it.

But she didn't die, though she looked not far off it, and her mother had looked as though she'd been crying nonstop although that might have been for some other reason.

Anyway, now that he and Aunty and his father had move out, that was all over. He never went to see any of them, though the rented house was just down the road. His father had been back – Mena ill again. He did see Roy at school, but it was tricky being in enemy camps. Paula occasionally came over to the house, but otherwise, it was almost back to the good old days, though it was a bit annoying knowing they were occupying the big house and here he was cramped into this downmarket shack, even if it was temporary.

With the move to the rented house, life returned to normal for Julius and should have been more to his liking. But things started to go inexplicably wrong. For a start, Aunty changed overnight, and that made him jumpy.

His father, on returning from the dispensary, as always paced up and down the sitting room of the rented house, firing questions at him – dates, battles, kings and more dates. Or geography – lakes in far away countries that were of no interest to Julius so that his mind wandered.

By now his father had moved onto some other subject on the school curriculum that he wanted to forget even more than the geography. He kept quiet, knowing that the wrong answer, which it was bound to be if he had a wild guess, would only provoke a greater fury than his avowed ignorance.

School wasn't great either though it was less of a strain than home, mainly because Brother Leo, his uncle, made sure he was all right.

Much to the Doctor's annoyance, Brother Leo was fond of Radha and went to visit her from time to time. The two of them got on really well discussing Roy for the most part, but also (this was music to his biological mother's ears), Brother Leo did not approve of the Doctor's behaviour.

The Brothers, he learnt from a chance remark, had rumbled his father's irregular domestic set up. Disgraceful behaviour. Could Brother Leo have let the cat out of the bag?

Unlikely, family solidarity being what it was. The point was, they clearly couldn't punish the Doctor himself; would they then have recourse to the next best thing – his son and heir? Julius shuddered at the prospect.

No one had told him there was about to be an addition in the family; a half sibling sixteen years his junior. But there'd been enough talk and argument when he was supposed to be fast asleep in bed for him to know all about it. And it made him very uneasy.

This new addition-to-be was even more unsettling than the Indian connections who'd been sort of forgotten. Julius sensed the newcomer could turn out to be a cuckoo in his nest. No chance of ignoring him; rather, he, Julius, could be shoved out and forgotten for good, and there was nothing he could do about it.

At last they were installed in the grand house and he had to admit it had been worth the waiting.

Chapter 29

Julius had just got back from school one afternoon, when he saw Luk standing on the grand top step that led to the very grand front door of the new house. She looked enormously fat as he looked up at her. He tried to sidle past the bulge he was meant not to have noticed or to know anything about, but not a chance. She caught him by his wrist.

'Eat supper, then bed,' she snapped.

He could hardly believe his luck. This was the period he dreaded most, when his father came home, the gruelling question and answer drill. He was clearly to be spared that. It was important to take advantage of the opportunity before something happened to reverse it. So that he rushed off, gulped down his supper which Ayu had laid on the table, dashed to the bathroom to brush his teeth, changed into his pyjamas though it was ridiculously early and that made him laugh as he pulled them on, and dived into bed.

Soon after, he heard the car return bringing his father from his surgery. Footsteps, his father's, terrifyingly recognizable striding into the house. A moment of silence.

'Where's Julius?'

Gulp! Would he be hauled out of bed? Would his father believe him if he pointed a finger at Aunty? Would he dare point a finger at Aunty? Aunty was no longer 'Aunty' as he'd known her before. These days she was more likely to land him in the soup than attempt to bale him out. In any case, she'd only ever made a show of sticking up for him, he saw that now. It had all been a pretence.

He couldn't help feeling a thrill of excitement. This was better than the time he'd tried to run away from school and been caught even before he got to the bottom of the road. Luckily for him it was Brother Leo and he'd not had a caning or even been reported to his father. He had never dared to try it again.

'Bed.' That was Aunty's voice.

'Oh? Sick?'

'Not sick. We talk. Now.'

Oh,oh! Julius knew what this was about. The 'talks' had become more frequent of late, though generally they took place later in the evening. They were rather fierce, and it was odd hearing his father getting beaten up.

Julius dived under his pillow out of habit to block out whatever sound was coming, not that it ever blocked it out, not completely. The mansion was open-plan and that meant no secrets. Also, though he started out not wanting to hear, he nearly always ended up straining to catch every word, sometimes even creeping out of bed right out to the landing.

A deep sigh. Sounded bad, as though his fierce father was scared of Aunty.

'Luk, be reasonable, I've told you.'

'Nuttink! You tell me nuttink I want. I tell you, I kill myself. Now.'

A groan. Yes, that was definitely his father, and he sounded very bad. Julius slowly and softly removed the pillow from over his head to listen unimpeded.

'Don't say that. Look, I *will* send him away, but not yet. My money's tied up, and I'd lose heavily if ...'

Oh, no, his father wasn't handling this right. Aunty was screaming her head off now.

'Why you talk money? Tink me. Tink baby. You say no, I kill myself.'

He'd heard all that before, but it was the pitch that was different, more feverish. Julius carefully slipped one leg over the edge of the bed, then the other, and crept forward, the better to hear, keeping low the while.

'Try not to get agitated, it's not good for the baby. Hush now, you'll wake Julius. No, it's not just the money. Time of year isn't ideal. Winter, cold and wet. I read that last year it was so bad even those who'd lived there all their lives suffered badly. Arriving for the first time would be hard on him. You see that, don't you? We have to think of the boy.'

'You tink boy, tink money, tink you. You not tink me. Me and baby. I cry, then I kill both,' and with that Luk let out a louder scream than ever.

Julius dived back into bed, hoping the killing wouldn't include him. There was no saying what Aunty might get up to these days. Why hadn't the servants run in to see what was happening? Perhaps they'd got used to it. Or they had instructions not to disturb.

Then, all of a sudden, peace was restored. The battle had been fierce but brief. Sort of final climax to long drawn out introductory movements which had taken several weeks if not months of *crescendo* reaching this *fortissimo*, only to die away suddenly to a *suave e dolce*.

'I'll arrange it in the morning; put Sen onto it.' His father had found the formula. 'Cargo boats are frequent and cheap, should be able to get together enough for that. Ships no longer needed for troop displacement.' A pause while he worked out further manoeuvres. 'Only the other day, Suzenathan was talking about a school in Devon, famous old place, south of England, warm, that is, relatively.'

Julius was not just relieved, he was overjoyed. Back in bed, he stuffed the pillow into his mouth to smother the sounds of jubilation. There'd been hints during previous 'talks' but each time his father had put off his departure. Julius had always known he would one day be going to England; his father had spoken about it for as long as he could remember. It hadn't meant much to him although he realized from the beginning it was a privilege only allowed to a few.

With the return of the Indian contingent, followed by the move to the pokey, interim house, the atmosphere had changed; Aunty was decidedly unfriendly. He knew the house was a temporary stop but it was difficult to imagine her reverting to what she'd been before, teasing him and giving him treats. He was right. The 'new' Aunty held her ground right into the grand house. Everything, especially Aunty, had changed since the talk of the new baby.

Aunty, Julius decided, was like a chameleon. The smile was switched on when she was buttering up his father or fooling him, like when she met his mother; then, it suddenly turned into a fearsome scowl. These days, Julius tried not to catch her eye as she looked accusingly at him, as if he had no right to be there. Well, thank God he'd be off at last and not a moment too soon. He imagined himself wrapped cosily in that greatcoat his father had talked of, like the one the Emperor Napoleon had worn shortly before his dreams of conquering the world were finally dashed. Who knows what he himself might not achieve wrapped within the folds of such a coat?

It was thus the Doctor finally decided, or was persuaded, it was time to send his elder son to boarding school in England. Yes, he'd always intended to give his children the best education available. True, he would not have chosen this precise moment, mid-winter, to send Julius there, but in other ways, there could be no better time to start than now.

The Doctor knew something of psychology: Julius had come to see himself as an only child. Luk had spoilt the boy more than his own mother might have, making him feel he was the centre of her universe. He could have problems, the Doctor judged, adjusting to the new arrival.

All things considered, it would probably be for the best if he were settled elsewhere for now.

Chapter 30

It was August the thirteenth – the day for the treat; though how it could be called a treat when he dreaded it so, wasn't easy to see. Roy, who'd be thirteen before the month was out, wanted the coming year to whizz past. He was still superstitious about anything to do with 13 in spite of his mother telling him it was her lucky number. She didn't seem to him a lucky sort of person, and that didn't help at all.

The day was hot and sultry. The rains had been fitful, insufficient when they came. Too many trees being cut down, changing the climate, carrying monsoons elsewhere; or nowhere. At least, that was what his geography master went on about. And for once Roy saw what he meant – the heat was uncomfortable, making his clothes stick to him in a way he'd never noticed before. By eight the sun was already an angry spread across the sky.

The boy tried to amuse himself, doing tight turns on his bicycle – over to the right, then left, one hand only, steady, pretty good, now no hands. Hey, that was good. Suddenly he remembered the treat and lost balance. Picking himself up, he thought how unfair it was to have this thing looming over him just when it was the weekend. Boney, their puppy, was squirming and yelping with excitement but even that didn't help.

Ludo hadn't been fun either. As always he and Paula had cheated, pretending Mena hadn't won when she had ages before. In fact, a whole round before. Part of the fun of Ludo was cheating Mena. But he'd looked up at one point and seen the expression on his youngest sister's face – she knows, he thought. But then, why carry on playing till either he or Paula declared themselves the winner? Why should anyone, especially Mena, who everyone said was bright, allow herself *knowingly* to be beaten in the end? Girls were silly sometimes. Actually, most of the time, though he wouldn't tell Paula that; she would not be amused.

The memory of the imminent treat came back with a nasty ferocity. Ludo, puppy, bicycle, nothing worked today. Some sort of pattern had recently established itself and this treat now looked to be a monthly cert. Roy groaned; there must be something he could do to show himself unworthy of such a favour.

When his father had moved out to another house two and a bit years before, his life had suddenly become easy: school was fine; St John's where Julius had been in middle school, was not too bad. And when his brother had left to go to England something like a year or two ago, things had got even better. The Brothers were really nice to him, never told him off, not even when his homework was a bit rushed. Nothing untoward ever happened. Until now.

Last month, the first invitation to the cinema had come out of the blue. It had been all right that time; not just him on his own. It had been for Paula and him. Going together had been quite good fun because they'd been able to hold each other's hands, figuratively speaking. Paula, anyway, had loved it, saying their father could be counted on always for anything and everything. Hmm, he'd kept quiet, knowing they were never going to agree about that.

This time, the driver had handed him the note before dropping him home after school, just like the previous month. Only, when Roy handed Paula the envelope, she pointed out it was addressed to him only. They opened it:

Roy,
I have something in mind which will further your
education. The driver will pick you up, on your
own, tomorrow at 2.30. Be ready.
You should wear your new outfit.

'He doesn't say what film,' Paula remarked. 'And you've got to wear your new clothes. That plus the fact I've not been asked must mean you're going to meet someone; a private tutor, I bet.'

Groan. He'd have dearly liked to change places with Paula who was disappointed at being left out. She was right; it didn't make sense – she was just as good if not better than him at English. Oh, no! He'd have to speak in English to his father! Scary stuff! If only he could change places with Paula! But an invitation from their father wasn't something you bargained about. As for meeting a private tutor, it sounded even worse than having to go to a film. Or maybe this tutor-man was going to the film as well, which was why he had to wear his new clothes. An extra long gr-o-a-n.

Not even the certainty of the ice cream in the interval cheered him up. Nor the thought of being driven straight up to the entrance while everyone was milling about outside queuing for miles into the street. And most of the queue might not even get in, which was probably why they always stared at him; him, the son of someone important; not like one of them. His father of course had reservations upstairs in the air-conditioned area where Roy would have difficulty stopping his teeth chattering. It was horribly freezing. Probably catch a cold at the end of it all. What a treat!

As he tinkered aimlessly with the spokes of the wheel, he imagined the deep boom of his father's voice. If his father laughed it was like a sudden bark and there was a flash of large, ivory teeth. Then the dark lips would close over them again. But the bulging eyes would still glare at him. If only he could think of something bright to say, but his mind always went blank beneath that stare. He knew he was scared of his father, but so was everyone else except, perhaps, Paula. And there was Mena. But she was too young to know him properly and, anyway, after that game of Ludo that morning, he couldn't be certain her mind worked properly, if at all.

His father always stood out, not only because he was so tall, but his European-style white cotton suit made him look different. Roy once heard someone mutter that the Doctor may have a gift for diagnosis but it didn't mean he had a vocation, otherwise he'd be more caring with his patients. Roy felt a twinge of envy for his patients – they had the great advantage of either going away cured, or dying. His children, on the other hand ...

His mother now called him in for an early lunch. She was anxious he should be ready when the car arrived. She thought she could woo back 'her man' with exemplary obedience (that's what Paula said). His mother was convinced his father would return one day; leave that woman who had used magic to entice him away, then, they'd all live happily ever after.

Roy couldn't remember a single moment of peace when his father had been around. Nor could he imagine it. The lengths his mother went to preparing for the day his father would return were beyond his comprehension.

His mother kept saying the war hadn't helped but she was now certain it had been that woman's idea to have them all sent away to India so as to have him to herself and poison his mind against her, his lawful wife.

Weird, he thought, that she should hanker after the one person that anyone in their right mind would run a mile from.

It was two o'clock. The car would be there in half an hour. Boney had already been shut in the back so as to make sure he didn't make a nuisance of himself and the gate was left invitingly open. To Roy's surprise, his sisters too were told to put on their prettiest frocks and Radha had combed out the tangles which were forever forming in Leela's hair, and tied a satin bow in Mena's which looked silly in her short hair. Surely his mother couldn't be expecting him to come in!

Roy put on his white trousers and short-sleeved, white cotton shirt. All brand new, as were his shoes. He was following the instructions in the message but with each new item his nervousness increased. He emerged from his room, a little self-consciously, to the round-eyed wonder of Leela and Mena. Paula nodded her approval, his mother smiled at him with pride. He knew he looked good; if only he felt better.

So many presents were being showered on him; never had as many before in the whole of his life, not all in a heap like this. There were the new clothes he was wearing, a new wrist-watch (he'd been promised one by his mother for his birthday in two weeks' time; now she'd have to think of something else), new shoes and even a new pen, a real Parker. The watch and the pen were being engraved with his name in tiny, black lettering, but he knew they'd be ready soon – perhaps this afternoon. Still, he'd have happily foregone these presents if it meant slipping quietly back to not being noticed.

His mother had put on a pale yellow, silk sari (as though she wore silk for everyday round the house!). Even if he didn't come in, she no doubt thought her husband might catch a glimpse of her, just by chance, if he craned his neck through the car window.

But when the car arrived, it was parked a little past the gate, screened by the tall bamboo hedge and therefore not visible from any part of the house. That of course meant no one in the house would be visible from it. Roy had guessed right. The driver walked down the long curving path to the front door.

The boy went to join him with the excited cries of his two younger sisters shouting in Tamil, 'Have a nice time,' as each one tried to out-shout the other.

'Shush,' Radha said as though afraid their father might hear them across that distance. 'Roy, come here; the driver can wait. Remember to use your handkerchief,' she said tucking it into his pocket. 'And don't let the ice cream dribble onto these nice new clothes.' She almost missed his pocket altogether, her eyes were so busy searching the gateway. It remained a yawning space. The boy was as anxious to stay as his mother to hang onto him but the driver was standing there, hovering in the porch, and he made as if to pull away.

'You mustn't keep your father waiting,' she murmured, still holding onto him.

'I must go, *Umma*,' the child whispered, looking over his shoulder at the driver.

She smoothed his hair one last time. Finally, accepting there would be no sighting of her husband, she gently pushed him away.

'Yes, run along now,' she murmured, her eyes still searching the distance.

Chapter 31

When the driver returned two hours later, out of deference he left the car on the road. With a sinking feeling Radha wondered why he'd come back so soon, and alone. Had her husband decided to take Roy, as he had Julius? Surely not an accident? – the man looked too calm, though he wouldn't meet her eye. He was trying to hand her a note, his eyes cast down.

'Where's the young master?' her voice was already out of control.

'Madam, I know nothing; just told to deliver this note. No answer, Master said.' He was still holding out the envelope, staring at it rather than meet her gaze.

She was afraid to take it, but in the end, one hand covering her mouth in case it let out a cry, she reached out for it. She closed the metal shutters of the front door to barricade themselves in from outside forces though something told her she was too late. Clutching the letter to her heart, she made her way to the privacy of the upstairs room. The three girls were standing, waiting; no one said a word, not even Leela. Radha made out it was in English and she shook her head, her eyes wild with fright. No, she did not want to know. And yet ... she handed it to Paula to read it for her.

The message was short and straightforward, but no one seemed capable of grasping its meaning. Radha stood there before her daughters, her eyes dilated unnaturally, lips slightly apart, face frozen in its stillness as she listened to the brief message:

> *By the time you receive this, your son will be safely on the train to Singapore and from there he will take the boat to England. You can console yourself with the thought that, there, he will receive a good education, far better than anything available here.*

A cry of pain, like that of a wounded animal, escaped from Radha's throat.

'Translate it, Paula,' she whispered urgently, 'translate it into Tamil. Tell me word for word what he's written.'

Paula's voice was none too steady but she did as asked, groping for the simple words which had suddenly become alien. The message swam before her eyes. A weird, high-pitched sound came from her mother and faded into thin air; it didn't sound like a voice at all. Now she was pleading in a rasping whisper.

'Paula, read it again, yes, again. Perhaps you read the message wrong.'

But the message was short and its contents refused to change however many times they were read out. There was no room for misinterpretation.

'What can I do? Paula, quick, what can I do to get him back?' Turning aimlessly towards Leela, she begged, 'Someone, tell me what I must do! Why didn't he ask me? Why not tell me he was putting this plan into action, part of those plans he told me about all those years ago? Why steal my son from me in this inhuman way? Why?'

'He must have thought you wouldn't agree.' Paula, by now, was used to giving her opinion, but this time, she was sobbing helplessly.

'Is that a reason for what he's done?'

'Maybe he was afraid your refusal would put Roy off from wanting to go.'

'Wanting to go! D'you honestly think Roy would have wanted to go even if I'd been in agreement? Never! He was happy here in this family; this is his home. I didn't say goodbye to him, not properly. His birthday – soon. I must see him just one last time, just ...'

She was so undemonstrative by nature he wouldn't know how much she loved him. She hadn't kissed him good-bye knowing she wouldn't be seeing him for – O, God, when would she see him next? How many years from now? If only she knew that she thought she could bear the pain. Radha clung to the back of the carved chair and wondered how it was her heart didn't break. She pressed her hand hard against her mouth and screamed out her agony with her mouth shut tight.

Sounds of sorrow echoed round the house which suddenly seemed vast and hollow. The servants hid in their quarters not daring to come near for fear of catching this inhuman grief. Radha held her hands against her womb remembering the months she'd carried her son within her.

Another wave of torture tore through her body. Her daughters felt her anguish and wept.

At last there were no more tears to fall. Late into the night in that upstairs room with its carved furniture, they sat, no longer talking or making a sound, but they sat together. Finally the mother stirred and with tenderness prepared a small supper and put the two younger children to bed. The unwonted attention subdued them further. They quietly slipped off their fine dresses and crawled into bed to fall asleep at once from exhaustion.

But Radha would not know deep sleep that night nor for many days and nights to come. She stayed there with Paula till the pale light of dawn announced another day. At last, they each went to lie awake on a restless bed.

Radha lay with her eyes wide open and asked God how such cruelty could exist in man. Why, she asked Heaven, could her husband not have told her that, for his own good, Roy should go away? Why pluck her child in such a brutal way when a few chosen words would have helped her part with him willingly? He had dealt her a mortal blow. Did he know or care that the wound would never heal? And the child – had he thought about the child, what it would do to him to be wrenched away like this so cruelly?

These were questions Radha would ask herself to her last breath.

*

The moment Roy climbed into the car, he knew something was wrong. Why was his father sitting in the front next to the driver? This stranger in the back seat next to him didn't look like a tutor. Were they going to drop the man off somewhere? The car was speeding along. Roy suddenly sensed he was in danger.

His father turned round and handed him his new pen and watch, his face bland, what went for a smile on his lips.

'I'm glad to say they're ready, only just in time.'

'Time! Why time for?' Roy cried, his English worse than ever in his anxiety. Ignoring the mistake and the question, the Doctor went on lightly as though joking.

'At least they've spelt your name right.'

But Roy couldn't focus on either what his father was saying nor the presents. He didn't say thank you as he'd been taught to do, nor smile to show his pleasure. He felt none. Just terror that numbed him. The road – there was no mention of dropping the man off – this road did not lead to the cinema. Where were they going?

'This not right road to cinema. Where you taking me?'

'Don't worry,' his father explained in that voice he dreaded. 'Everything's ready, not just the pen and the watch. A trunk with all your clothes, new ones, warmer than what you're used to wearing, has already left for England by sea; there's a suitcase behind in the boot with more clothes – things you'll need on the crossing. Yes, you're going to a boarding school in England, to join your brother, Jul...'

'*No-o-o*! I not going. I hating you! Take me home.' And though his voice was shaking as he cried out, it sounded strange, no longer a child's.

But his father replied calmly and yet with that frightening anger somewhere deep inside.

'Quiet. Don't make a fool of yourself. Let me introduce you to Sen who'll be accompanying you to London. There, you'll be met by...'

'*No-o-o! I want home. Umma-a!*' The scream was deafening.

They'd arrived at the station. Roy had to be pulled out. His limbs of a thirteen-year-old were powerless against the joint effort of the man who'd just been introduced and the driver, who was as much of an unwilling aide as Sen. It was a miserably sad scene of farewell with his father's displeasure clearly visible as the boy continued to struggle against his kidnappers. He was bundled into the carriage, screaming and struggling to the last.

Chapter 32

The Doctor knew from the many prospectuses he'd studied as well as from Julius that if you send your son to a boarding school in England, he should start at the beginning of the academic year rather than landing in the middle of it. He regretted having had to dispatch his elder son to begin in the wrong term, and, coincidentally, in January. No imagination was needed to tell him it was the worst month weather-wise in the calendar. Unfortunate business. Irritating that the boy seemed incapable of getting over it, still writing in his ill-phrased letters about the cold, and that the greatcoat (as he insisted on calling his overcoat) was not, had never been, any good. That his hands and feet were covered in chilblains.

The image of his son sitting huddled over the coal fire, one side of him warm, while the other shivered uncontrollably, was vexing. And now, five terms later, surely it was time he got used to the weather and the food and the people? But no, he refused to adapt, and was incapable of paying attention to any advice he gave him.

In one letter he'd really piled on the agony saying sixteen layers, made up of blankets, useless greatcoat and other garments, plus towel (surely not towel?) hadn't been enough to stop him shivering; that he'd rolled a moth-eaten rug into a long sausage and stuffed it against the bottom of the door because there was a gale blowing through the crack at the bottom of the door. Really, what next! How could a gale blow through a crack! Something decidedly wrong with that boy.

The Doctor brooded, frustrated by his impotence. All the ingredients had been there for a successful outcome. He'd seen to everything himself a long time ago. But this next step had to be taken by Julius himself. That was the problem. There was nothing he could do now but sit and watch his plans flounder.

He must discover a way of minimising his disappointment; it was important not to allow this initial failure to sap his energy. A lot remained to be done demanding his concentration and foresight.

*

Sen took leave of Roy in London, happy to be relieved of his charge at last. In all his years of practice as a solicitor, he'd not felt as doubtful of the ethics of what he'd just accomplished. The crossing had proved to be extremely stressful. It hadn't occurred to him when accepting the undertaking that the boy may not want to go to England; indeed, that he'd have no inkling he was going there. Not that Sen had a choice in the matter.

Some eighteen months before, he'd accompanied the boy's elder brother on the first lap of his journey to England but that had been far less arduous. Julius had not only known where he was going, and indeed welcomed the notion, but knew Sen personally through his father. And though the boy had seemed to be in no fit state to start life in a foreign country on his own, at least Julius himself felt he was lucky to be given such a chance.

Now, sitting in the train on his way back to Dover, Sen recalled another day six years ago; a day that had shaped his life decisively: waiting in the Doctor's surgery as the minutes ticked by. One hour three minutes, and finally it was his turn. He knew the Doctor refused house-visits, even to a friend such as Sen considered himself to be, having first met the Doctor and his 'first' wife years ago through his partner, Pradeep.

But, friend or stranger, the Doctor made no exception; he simply did not do house visits. In spite of knowing that, here he was, about to beg him on bended knees, if necessary, to visit his dying son. Sen was trembling. It was not through fear. But the thought of that little body lying cold and feverish, so near death, brought on uncontrollable fits of shaking in him. Somehow he'd have to persuade his friend to come with him.

He stood before him now, words refusing to make themselves heard. Or even to take shape in his head. The Doctor's eyes seemed to glare at him. Time was ticking by. Precious minutes that Sen was wasting. Words. What words could he use to touch his heart?

'It's my son. He's - he's dying,' he blurted out, tears starting involuntarily.

A moment of stillness as the two men looked at each other; the Doctor sat as he always sat, without moving.

Sen was standing, the shaking had stopped. Not a muscle twitched on the Doctor's face, nor strangely, on Sen's. Sen wondered what the man was thinking behind that impassive mask. He had children. But he was different.

Suddenly the Doctor stood up, his chair scraping loudly on the tiled floor.

'Let's go,' he said.

Sen stumbled after him, out into the blinding sun, almost running behind the long strides, his breath coming in painful rasps, oblivious of the usual terror he felt walking out in the open street , knowing he might be detained for no reason.

And the Doctor, in his white shirt and trousers, was a living target. But he seemed unaware of it. Not so long ago, he'd saved the life of a top-nob – a Japanese – it was known the Doctor made no distinction which side his patient was on. There'd been others since. So that he was, as it were, protected. There was always the idiot sniper. But the man was striding on with the courage of a madman or a daredevil. Or a saint. Not a saint, at any rate, according to Pradeep who was forever bemoaning the fate of his cousin, Radha.

They arrived at the house where Sen lived at that time, a modest abode fit for a young man starting out in life. The Doctor stooped to pass through the low door while Sen hung back so as not to crowd the space. He could make out his wife in the darkened room, two eyes red with sleeplessness, through weeping too, though she took care not to let him see.

The Doctor bent down, pulled back the layers of covering, and taking the tiny wrist in his hand, stood still, his eyes boring into the sweat-streaked face on the pillow.

He pressed gently on the right side of the child's stomach, then noted how dry his tongue was.

'A towel and a basin of cold water. And a teaspoon,' he ordered.

Sen only just stopped himself saying he could heat the water. What was the Doctor going to do with cold water, he wondered. He was back in no time – a clean towel, cold water in a basin and a silver teaspoon – the only treasure in the house.

The doctor handed the towel to the mother, his eyes never leaving the child's face.

'Dip it in the water. Wring it out. Now, wipe the sweat off him. Yes, with that towel. All over his body, not just his face. Again.'

He opened his leather bag and took out a blue bottle which contained what looked like syrup. The Doctor handed it together with the teaspoon to the woman.

'Six drops now; that's right. Repeat the dose this evening at six. Plenty of boiled water, boiled properly, ten minutes once it comes to the boil. Sponge him down if necessary, but as soon as the fever has left, don't let him get cold. You can give him clear, chicken broth this time tomorrow. Here,' he handed Sen a prescription, 'Get this made up at the dispensary. It'll have instructions for application.' He snapped his bag shut and turned to leave.

Sen was waiting at the door, his savings ready. But the man barely looked at him as he said, 'You'll need that to buy the chicken.' And he was gone.

Sen, a man of thirty eight, who had seen much pain in these terrible years of the occupation, stood still, and stared, unseeing, into space. He couldn't remember when he'd last wept so freely; the atrocities at this inhuman time had systematically dried up all access to tears. But now his cheeks were wet and he didn't try to dry them. Looking down at the money in his hands, he smiled to see the tears splash onto it. Yes, he'd go out now to buy the medicine; then the chicken. And there'd be enough left for a lot more.

The child lived.

Remembering that moment, Sen now shook his head perplexed – how could he have thought he could pay for the life of his child?

A month after that visit, when his son was past all danger, he returned to see the Doctor.

'I want to thank you for saving my son's life. If there's ever anything I can do to help, anything at all, any time, please let me know.' Sen despaired, wondering how he was ever going to find a way of paying for that act of salvation.

Which is how he found himself, first, accompanying Julius on the boat trip from Port Swetenham up to Penang. From there Julius was to continue on his own on a cargo vessel on to Singapore, then Colombo, Aden, through the Suez Canal, past Malta, then Gibraltar, ending up in Liverpool. Something like that. Good God, the poor boy was barely fit to travel on his own to Singapore let alone all those stops to Liverpool! And then what? Some stranger, an Englishman, was to meet him, take him down to London, then over to the West Country where it's warm (relatively) even in the winter months. England, warm in January?

But Sen was not there to question the wisdom of the man who had saved his son's life, rather to do whatever he could to show his gratitude. He'd done his best, helped Julius to feel relaxed with the officers with whom he'd be eating throughout the six to eight week journey. Being a cargo boat, docking dates were fluid. As for helping Julius feel relaxed, that was a manner of speaking; the child seemed afraid of his own shadow, mumbling his words so horribly as to be unintelligible. There were moments he seemed to be talking to himself. The English food hadn't gone down well but Sen could hardly blame him for that; vile stuff, no taste whatsoever. He had as much difficulty swallowing it as did the boy.

At the end of that trip with Julius, the solicitor felt he'd been useful. Of course it was not on a par with the service the Doctor had rendered him, but there was nothing on earth that would equal that. He'd be ready to help out again whenever necessary.

So that, when the subject of Roy came up, he'd been eager to carry out the Doctor's wishes. A longer undertaking this time: Sen would be accompanying the Doctor's second son all the way to London, in a passenger boat, sticking to a schedule. His round trip would last two months. That was fine. Pradeep was now permanently in Madras, but business had grown and there were four of them now. Sen could absent himself and the practice would not collapse. Besides, the Doctor had always paid a fair sum for his time.

However, this venture had turned out to be a fearful strain.

Roy hadn't been prepared for it. He hadn't wanted to leave his home, his mother or country. He thought of his own son and Sen hated himself for what he was doing. He was the child's jailor.

The first three days had been frightening beyond belief. Roy refused to eat a single morsel. What was he going to tell the Doctor if his son fell seriously ill? Roy wept as Sen had never seen a child weep. But then, he'd never before been with a kidnapped child. He was inconsolable and between his sobs he vowed to kill his father one day for this outrage.

Good God, how was he going to report that? Sen had agreed to write down word for word every detail of the boy's reaction, as he had with Julius; to send regular dispatches to the Doctor. That had seemed quite normal; any father would want to know how his son was faring. But now, everything was topsy-turvy. Sen would keep his word, but for the first time he found himself in a situation where duty was wholly at odds with his conscience.

Chapter 33

Radha was gazing at the gate from the upstairs window; it had become a habit of hers during the days that followed the kidnapping, almost as though she hoped to see her son suddenly and miraculously step out of a car, returned at last from the trip to the cinema.

It was five days after Roy had been taken, and as she looked out, a car did pull up and when the girl opened the gate, the old Morris Minor the Doctor had given his brother Leo drove straight round to the front porch.

Brother Leo was the only one of her husband's siblings to have remained a loyal friend to Radha from the beginning. (Anna, who had befriended Radha in the early years, had sadly died young.) Brother Leo had not only been a mindful uncle and kind teacher to Roy, but stood in also as a father figure.

God, how like her husband he looked, Radha thought, they might have been twins though Brother Leo was slightly less muscular. He had the same hair, cut short, and his features were similar except there was nothing fierce in Brother Leo's gaze. For all that, an extraordinary power seemed to emanate from him that outstripped even the

Doctor's, or so Radha imagined knowing his moral values. Her husband would have kept the school in the dark about his latest development for Roy, in case Brother Leo leaked it out to her.

'Radha, my dear, I want to tell you how sorry I am at what's happened,' he began.

She was unable to stop her tears at these words. He took her hands as he came in and they sat under the revolving fan.

'My dear, I understand what you feel.' He wanted to comfort her but found he too was moved and broke off. After a while he resumed, 'I thought I knew my brother, but this ... I'm deeply shocked by what he's done. Roy is a sound boy; with God's grace, he'll be all right. Try not to worry about him. You have the girls to care for, and yourself.'

'Brother Leo, I've prayed so hard and for so long; does God really listen to our prayers? Tell me what I'm doing in my life here that's so wrong; what is it that needs to be punished like this?' There was a long pause before Brother Leo answered.

'Not a single word of a prayer is lost, I'm sure of that. But the gift of Free Will is double-edged. Everything we do is done through choice; there is no constraint from Heaven or Hell. We live as we choose to live. We've been given a Law that teaches us right from wrong. But, the problem is, we're selfish.' He thought for a moment before adding, 'I have a personal belief that runs parallel to the teaching – as long as we live our lives without hurting our neighbour, then we will find grace in God's eyes.'

'Brother Leo, are you saying the teaching of the Church is not the final Truth?'

'It is the final Truth, but there may be more ways than one that lead to that Truth.'

Radha bowed her head and gave a nod though she was not clear what he meant.

'Take heart, dear Radha,' he said finally. 'You are always in my prayers; may you find the courage and inner peace to overcome these fearful trials.'

She thanked him for his kind words and as she watch him leave, she felt comforted saying to herself the prayers of so good a man would surely reach Heaven.

However, by now she was convinced Luk used witchcraft; how else could she have robbed her of her husband and both sons? Her husband was thus exonerated of all responsibility.

It was even as she knelt in church, confiding her worst fears to St Anthony who was generally so good at finding lost objects, that the idea came to her: this was not the way to fight the evil that was being practised. She would have to use like weapons. There was no other way to get her husband back.

Since knowledge of this malignant force had come from her friend Agnes, she decided to confide in her and to seek her advice about putting her latest plan into action. Leela was home that Tuesday as she'd picked up a chill. That often happened during the monsoon season but Radha wasn't bothered that she would be present; whatever she and Agnes discussed would go over her child's head.

Much to Radha's surprise, Agnes was so perturbed to hear her latest project, she forgot her role as English teacher and resorted straight to Tamil.

'Radha, this is not wise. Just think for a moment how quick he was to discover your plans about the Tamil school. Nothing will have changed since then. In fact, if he had spies then, he'll have twice as many now that he's even richer and more famous.'

'But Agnes, there's no other way. I've tried praying; it's the first thing I did. Look where it's got me. I could never have imagined he was going to rob me of the only son I had left. D'you think he's punishing me for not agreeing to a divorce?'

'Maybe he is, but even if your husband is no longer practising, he knows the ruling of the church. There can be no divorce.'

'He doesn't care about the Church, otherwise he wouldn't be living with that woman. By taking Roy, he's gone beyond any measure I could have imagined. Even so I didn't go and make a scene at the dispensary. I said to myself, my patience will get through to him. Nothing of the sort. How can you feel pity when you have no heart? She's robbed him of even that – his honour, family, his heart, everything.'

'Chinese woman bad,' Leela put in, 'She take everything! *Umma*, where Huntley and Palmer biscuit tin?' Radha waved towards the stairs.

'Now I'm convinced there is a remedy.' Radha stopped to study her friend, but the look of alarm on Agnes's face was far from encouraging. Radha ploughed on, 'I thought you might know how I should go about it; it was you, my one true friend, who opened my eyes to what was going on. You said, "foul means"; it's all so obvious now.'

'Yes, I did tell you about it. And I still believe this is how she's managed to get your husband; I've heard rumours to that effect. But you're forgetting one major fact – she's Chinese. They're good at that sort of thing. You and I wouldn't know where to begin. I'm convinced you should have nothing to do with it.' Radha appeared to acquiesce.

They sat in silence for a while. Finally, Agnes began, clearly unsure of her territory.

'Dear Radha, you know how much I admire your constancy, but, isn't it time to close your heart to someone who's behaving so unkindly? What has he ever done to deserve such devotion from so pure a heart?'

Radha's eyes misted over suddenly; this was a question she'd asked herself countless times. Suddenly, she wondered if she could tell her friend something she hardly dared admit to herself.

'Agnes,' she began hesitantly, 'before I met him, I knew a sweet happiness. My cousin Pradeep and I imagined nothing could come between us! D'you know, he looks in on my mother as if he were her son! But our – union – was not to be. Then my husband came and with him love. He spoke of a future. We became one unit in that future which would hold our children. Once he was in my heart, the door shut behind him. I know no way to let him out.'

Agnes was moved and pity knit her closer than ever to Radha. But what could she say to cheer her friend? The past was no longer open to her; the present a dead-end. So, she took up one of their usual themes and asked after Radha's mother. Radha sighed; leaning over to re-fill her friend's glass, she was about to answer when she was struck by a new scent.

'Agnes, you've changed your perfume; I seem to know it, but can't quite place it.' This was so unexpected, Agnes jumped and stared for a moment in confusion. 'Don't be alarmed, it's quite nice; just that it's different.'

'Same old hair oil, I'm thinking,' Agnes answered finally, reverting to English.

'No, Aunty Agnes, new. What name perfume?' Leela enquired.

Agnes put her handkerchief to her nose to smell deeply the scent on it.

'Maybe the pear tart I'm gulping before coming. Yes, maybe; I'm also smelling it now – very strong.' Then, somewhat abruptly, she repeated, 'What news from ailing mother?'

'They don't know as much about medicine over there as my husband does. She'd do better to come over here. I've been trying to persuade her, though I can't be certain whether it's more for my benefit or hers.' She smiled suddenly and Agnes was struck by how young and beautiful she looked. 'Mind you,' Radha continued, 'even if she does come, it won't be easy to get her to see my husband; they never got on. And now with this terrible thing he's done to Roy...'

'Poor Roy' Leela confirmed, helping herself to another biscuit.

Radha's non sequitur had brought them back to their current favourite subject – the Doctor and Roy.

Chapter 34

Father,
    You see I am here. Teacher said I must write but I
have nothing to say.
    I saw Julius on my first day. He is in senior
dormitory.
        I am in junior.
        I am well.
          Roy.

The Doctor smiled. The boy was still angry, but he'd
get over it. Had Doctor Mentem seen Roy's first letter to his
mother – *Darling Umma, I am so sad here. I miss you all so
much* ... he would have been less sanguine, but being spared
such a painful comparison, he told himself this was what
he'd expected; Sen had kept him in the picture. He was
certain one day Roy would see it had been for his own good.
That day, far from wanting to kill him, he'd feel grateful to
his father for having gone to so much trouble.

The operation had gone off almost without a hitch; he
should have foreseen that bit of rejection at the beginning.
Had it been Paula, that would not have occurred. He'd had

no idea the boy was quite so attached to his home. But there had been no other treatment that might have worked better. Because of his mother, it had to be performed through subterfuge.

Various tussles with Luk had taught him women are not reasonable. They cling to a certain idea and are incapable of seeing the wider picture. That was certainly true of Radha.

That 'trial' period came to mind, when he'd tried to establish a peaceful settlement between the two women. Radha had shown herself totally incapable of accepting the arrangement he'd made. The wider picture had eluded her completely. It would have been the same here; she would have refused to let Roy go. Therefore, there had been no choice.

Although Roy's letter was so terse, it filled him with confidence. True, the English was halting, but already, though he was four years younger than Julius, the writing was well formed. Before long he would leave his elder brother standing. This might be just what Julius needed; it could bring out the competitive spirit in him, buck him up a bit so that he stopped going on about the cold and all the other things.

The Doctor reached for the thin airmail paper and began his first letter to Roy. It would be short so as not to overload the boy at this stage:

I'm glad to hear you arrived safely and have met up with Julius. It's as well you have a certain amount of independence from your elder brother so that you'll be able to form your own opinion about life in England.

I trust Gomez's efforts will not have been in vain and that before long you will take your place among the second violins in the school orchestra.

On the list of extras, I left out Carpentry as well as Mechanics (both skills that can be bought) and chose Speech and Drama instead as it will improve your diction in the immediate present and prepare you for the future.

Affectionately,

The doctor was right in foreseeing Roy would not present the same problems as Julius. In a remarkably short time he adjusted to life at Probus. Towards the end of the crossing, when the boy no longer showed the fierce animosity he had at the outset, Sen went through the school prospectus with him. It made much of its founder, Oliver Cromwell. It had been difficult for Roy to appreciate the importance of this detail which appeared to be the school's main claim to fame.

While flicking through the pages, Sen had muttered something about the aftermath of war, but Roy hadn't understood.

On arriving at his new school, after the relative opulence of St John's Institute, Probus looked incomprehensibly small and ill-assorted. There didn't even appear to be a proper uniform. Some of the boys wandered about in little better than rags, and all of them gulped down the slurpy gruels as though they'd known nothing better. Then, there were these much prized things called ration books – they were for sweets!

It was utterly baffling to think such a violent act had been committed simply to dump him in this place.

Sen had left him in London in the care of a representative from Philip Randall who kept rubbing his hands together in a pretend-jolly, pretend-friendly gesture, repeating over and over that he'd met his brother, Julius. This might have been because the poor man could think of nothing else to say, or, he might have been uncertain how much of what he said was understood. 'Yes, your brother, elder brother, I believe, Julius, mm.' Frequent nodding of the head. 'That was at Liverpool, that's right, Liverpool.'

Roy didn't bother to say he and his brother hardly knew each other; nor that what with the age-gap and all the other things, not only had they not had much to do with each other over there, at home, but probably wouldn't here either.

The moment the master took Roy to the seniors' lounge to meet Julius, Roy saw he was right – Julius and he wouldn't have much to do with each other. It was as if they didn't share the same parents, same family, same country, same anything.

Roy was an immediate 'success' (to use his father's vocabulary) at Probus; he had no difficulty fitting in with the system. Nor did the cold affect him unduly. As for the food, Julius had a point – it was inedible – but no use bashing your head against a brick wall. Therefore, Roy swallowed whatever was dished out and survived.

The Doctor was right on another point – Roy's murderous intent on him faded in a very short time, and as the years went by he grew into a witty, handsome young man. Hard–working too. And he took up the same profession as his father. He came to understand what a very generous man his father had been in monetary matters.

Roy became quite an eminent surgeon and his friends thought him amusing and suave. So that to all appearances there were no ill effects from that distant trauma he'd suffered. He didn't believe in God but that didn't single him out from many of his contemporaries. He rarely missed an opportunity to discomfit people, wittily, of course. He wasn't a great believer in human kindness because, as the boat pulled away from the harbour all those years ago, his heart strings, which were tied to those he loved, snapped. There were no visible marks on the outside but there where his heart had been, there was a void.

He trusted no one and nothing. But he understood the power of money. Therefore, in time, long after Radha's death, when his father died, Roy welcomed into that empty space where his heart had been, his father's rich widow, Luk, whose influence over the Doctor had caused so much unhappiness to his mother and to all of them when they were young.

In time, Roy's children learnt to call Luk "Granma".

Chapter 35

But, at the time of the kidnapping, Radha had no intimation of Roy's eventual development. Her main preoccupation was to get her husband back; everything else would fall into place once that happened. She therefore decided to see a sorceress on her own, albeit without Agnes's approval.

She turned to her trusted servant who'd been with her since her husband's departure. After making some enquiries, the servant told her it meant seeking help from the Chinese community. From what she'd found out no one else practised the art of magic.

Well, Chinese it would have to be and it was in a quarter unknown to Radha; but the girl gave clear instructions how to get there. Radha's command of Cantonese was now adequate, and if that failed, thanks to Agnes, she also had sufficient English if need be.

She took a rickshaw that made its way through the mud-caked path that led God only knew where. There'd been a huge downpour the previous afternoon as there would be again at the same hour that day. Season of rains; the ground was a quagmire. Pigs squealing in every direction, their stench so pervasive she could hardly breathe. As the man pulled her through the stinking filth, Radha was shocked to see a stall where some kind of fried food was being sold. Her husband would certainly not approve of this set up. Typical Chinese, she thought, forgetting the squalor and dirt on the side streets of Pondicherry.

As they jogged along, she used her sari to shield her from the polluted air. An overpowering nausea made her want to turn back. This was a mistake; she should never have come.

The bandyman stopped in front of a shack. She got out, instructing him to wait, and was immediately shown in by the sorceress herself. No doubt this efficiency and speed were to avoid too much unnecessary exposure that might embarrass clients.

The woman was dressed in black trousers and top in the usual style of Chinese servants except this material was shiny. The air was heavy with incense burning in various pots, but the perfume from them was thick and unfamiliar and Radha had a fit of coughing as she settled on the low stool. The sorceress began immediately in pidgin English.

'Husban' come back one day.'

Radha caught her breath. Just one look and the woman knew what she'd come about!

'Husban' good man. Yes, Madam vely light – he not going, only witchclaft make him go. Bad woman using stwong witchclaft. You ask how long – I tell you long time. Now not easy for husban' come home.'

'I know,' Radha agreed miserably, 'Eight years, long time. Five in war-time, and three years now.'

'That woman, she see me,' the woman continued smoothly, 'Yes, same time you say now – eight years back-time. She ask help her. I not help.'

Radha felt this was something more than coincidence that had brought her to the same woman as her rival.

'Only help people wanting what is light – like Madam. I not help other woman.'

At least, this is what Radha understood her to have said. So great was her need for help she didn't pause to question the woman's credentials.

At the end of the session she paid the hefty fee and took the powders she was given (though how on earth she was going to scatter it 'over her husband's head preferably, but if not, some other part,' she couldn't imagine.). She'd find a way. She was given further powders to be taken immediately. They would make her irresistible to her husband when they next met. Radha stumbled out promising to return for a second consultation.

Chapter 36

The car drew right up under the porch of no 10, Jalan Inai, and the driver turned off the engine. The three girls watched their father as he climbed out of the Ambassador. He said a few words to the driver who nodded, shut the passenger door without making a sound, then moved the car further up the drive.

Radha too watched: second visit in one month. The first visit had been a disaster. She had talked, shouted more than talked; first time ever with him. She didn't recognize herself though memory stirred, bringing into focus the girl she'd been before the burden of accepting without a murmur whatever life heaped on her head.

Since his last visit she'd taken the enhancing powders. This visit coming so soon after the other surely meant he'd cancel that disastrous decision he'd announced about Paula. Hope burgeoned anew.

The other visit three weeks earlier, the driver had arrived with a note to say her husband would be coming that afternoon. Radha's heart had quickened with apprehension. Since his departure from the family, he'd only been back twice; both times when Mena had been sick. That had been the year before Roy was taken from her.

So, three weeks ago: he'd come in, barely taking in the three girls who watched him in silence from a short distance. Then he'd shot a quick glance at Radha, but not enough to notice the pale pink of her sari or the gold chain round her neck.

'Would you like something to drink?' she asked in Tamil. Courtesy of two strangers. Illogically she wondered if he'd registered the girls' hair was now long.

From him, an indistinct noise that she interpreted as assent so that she sent the maid away for fresh orange juice. They sat down opposite each other, the low table between them, the girls not far behind her, by the opening to the dining room.

'I've come about Paula.' An awkward pause, then, 'It's time she went to England.'

'No!' She shot up from her seat, aghast, her voice so shrill she didn't recognize it.

'It's for her good.' There was that deadly, cold, inflexibility she knew of old.

'Her good?! Roy's letters ... I *know* what it's like over there: ice drops from a black sky, freezing night that eats into day, and the day short and so dark they use electric light to see at noon. Food you wouldn't give to a dog; the people cold like their climate. Sending a young girl, alone, to such a country, where all the customs are strange, where the sun never shines, the people so different, a different language, everything different and so far from her home and family! How can you say that's for her good?' She was crying by now.

'You don't know what you're talking about. Is it better to keep her here, by your side, to rot in outworn Indian ways? To marry her off to some fat Indian – is that it?'

'You weren't ... ,' she began, but he hadn't finished.

'Or is it so that you can send her on your little errands, to tell me where my duty lies?'

'That is not fair.'

'Do you deny it?'

Still shaking from her outburst, Radha slumped down in her chair, suddenly defeated.

'Just once.' She looked across at him, pleading, 'Don't do this to her, please don't. She's not yet fifteen. Her life is already reduced – no brothers, her father ... How will it be when there's no mother, no sisters; having to fend for herself on her own in a foreign land?'

'What, in your opinion, will it do to her?'

'Paula isn't easily affectionate. Out there, in an uncaring world, she'll become hard.' It was barely a whisper, even so, Paula was too near not to hear every word.

'So much the better if she learns to stand on her own two feet,' he countered with a harsh laugh. 'A woman should be independent today. My daughters shouldn't be at the mercy of their husbands, ever. The world is changing fast. The old order that shaped you, clinging to your family, your relatives, is no longer here. It's gone forever. Swept away by the cleansing flames of the war. Had you been here, you'd understand. '

'What? Are you suggesting I *willingly escaped* to the safety of Pondicherry?' She was outraged. 'Have you forgotten how hard I fought to stay? Don't you remember any of it? Is that how you manage to live with yourself?'

'I'm not here to discuss the past with you; merely to let you know my plans.'

He stood up abruptly. The meeting was at an end but Radha hadn't finished.

'As for my clinging to my family and my relatives, you should know better than anyone that is not true. Not once have I turned to them in all this time. You and our children are all the family and relatives I have since we took the sacred vow. That is the truth.'

'Don't hold me responsible for your limitations.'

'What limitations?'

'You've brought everything on your own head.' Doctor Mentem turned away from her and strode out of the house before any further discussion.

In the shocked silence that followed that first visit, Radha had turned to see Leela on the verge of tears as she herself was, Mena staring wide-eyed, and Paula tense and excited.

His words echoed round the walls of her mind: a woman should be independent; not be at the mercy of an unloving husband ... Oh, the irony of it! It just wasn't as simple as that. What about the heart? Did that not tie you as indissolubly to a man, to your children, your home?

Out there there would be no one to protect Paula from loose western ways. She could not allow her to walk down the primrose path without doing her utmost to guard her from such a ruinous course. Even if her husband didn't listen to her, her daughter might.

'Paula, don't go. England is far away, at the other end of the world. You've read Roy's letters, the food, you remember what he wrote, don't you?' No answer. 'A friend of Agnes's heard it was so cold, all the leaves fall to the frozen ground and the trees die, ice hanging from bare branches. Everything dead and frozen. Teeth drop out when you brush them. Instead of water, droplets of ice fall out of the tap! You mustn't go, Paula, say you won't.'

But it was soon clear she was wasting her breath. Of the two ideals, the Doctor's forward-looking, Radha's traditional, in the light of subsequent developments, it is not obvious which would have brought their children greater happiness and fulfilment. But on that day, Radha was on a losing wicket.

Even after the cruel theft of her son, it hadn't occurred to Radha her daughter might one day be taken from her. It was true she'd written to her mother asking her to come over and, almost as an afterthought, mentioned it would soon be time to consider a husband for Paula; but it didn't mean the marriage would take place straightaway. These things had to be arranged years in advance if you wanted a suitable partner for your daughter. How was she to proceed if Paula was in England?

This second visit: if he was back so soon, perhaps with a change of plans to say he'd re-considered and agreed Paula should remain at home, then, it was her assertive argument that would have brought about the conversion. That would be a pointer for future negotiations with her husband.

He came in, and, ignoring Radha completely, turned towards Paula.

'As a concession to your mother,' but he didn't look at his wife, 'I'm arranging for you to go to a convent school in the West of England.'

Radha was shocked by this abrupt opening. Nothing had changed. Her impassioned words had had no effect except it would be a Catholic school. Of course this was better than losing her child without any warning, and yes, it was better it should be a convent, but still ... no discussion, no recognition of what she might be feeling. Was there nothing she could do to make him change his decision? No, she had tried and failed.

She saw by the way he kept his gaze averted, he'd not come to bring her good news. She would not be allowed to hold on to her daughter. Forgetting, for a moment, the disastrous effect it would have on Paula, how about what it would do to her? With Paula gone, who could she turn to? Leela was not yet twelve and anyway she was afflicted with this strange mental disorder which made it difficult to gauge how much she was taking in. As for Mena, not even ten, what could she understand of her mother's problems?

The Doctor looked at Paula. She flashed back her most dazzling smile, dimple-cheeked and eyes sparkling with the knowledge she was his favourite. She had no doubt which of the two ideals suited her. In his halting Tamil which he chose to use so as to avoid any misunderstanding, he told her about passports, photos and thumb print, inoculations for smallpox, cholera and typhoid, her wardrobe – warm, woollen material would have to be sent for –, did she have a preference for a particular colour?

Her sisters listened awed and uncomprehending though the words were almost familiar. From next week Paula would be attending the English-speaking Convent School in KL to get a taste of things to come. England was different from Malaya – agricultural. Did Paula remember the two lambs they'd had at the bottom of the garden before she left for Pondicherry? In England she'd see whole flocks of them. He'd made plans for her future long ago, he said, smiling at her, sensing a depth of understanding that was beyond her years. Suddenly, he turned to Mena who was nine-and-a-half.

'And you, don't you want to go with your sister?'

Her father was smiling at her – Mena. This was new and exciting. Panic. What should she do? Since that occasion with the injection and the ice cream, she couldn't remember his ever addressing her directly, and now here he was, asking her to decide if she wanted to go to England. At least, it sounded as if that was what he was saying. Talking to her and smiling at her as though she were grown-up. Taking a step away from Leela, Mena looked straight into her father's eyes, and said, 'Yes,' in English.

His guffaw of approval almost drowned Radha's stifled sob as she sprang forward as if to shield Mena. Then she drew back, digging her nails into the palms of her hands till the pain shut out all else. This was an end.

'There now, you have a companion on your adventure,' he said to Paula who looked thoroughly put out.

Radha did not remonstrate even though her life's force was being ebbed. She remained silent knowing her youngest was being stolen from her. How could she pit her strength against his? His retaliation would be violent, without warning. Roy was a precedent.

Or was it a culture where disaster struck and you prayed God for strength to bear the unbearable?

Radha stood alone, watching her children gazing at their father's smiling face. In the deepest recesses of her heart, she thought God in His mercy, had given her Leela, whose affliction meant she would not be taken from her, and she thanked Him with all her heart.

That night as she lay in bed exhausted with weeping, she remembered the powders she should have scattered on her husband. They lay at the back of the drawer in the wardrobe which she kept locked. She hardly reacted except to reflect she'd not get such another chance for a long while. If ever.

Little Mena, her baby, her Minupa, gone. Gone before she'd had a chance to teach her the important things in life. There'd be Paula to look after her, but Paula had never had time for her. Minupa in a cold land where the sun wouldn't shine on the gold of her skin. Her poor little darling. Her baby – gone. Roy – gone. Julius – gone. Paula – gone.

All her children, except Leela in whom he had no interest, they would all be gone. Lost in a strange distant land without a parent to hear their heartbeat. He had them all. There was nothing left at home to bring him back. Then she smiled sadly in the dark of the night thinking that even if she'd remembered the powders that lay in that drawer, at no point was she close enough to have scattered anything on any part of him. And as for those enhancing powders she'd taken – they'd had no effect. How could they when he hadn't glanced at her once?

Something stirred within her. She opened her eyes wide and stared into the dark netting above. This man, her husband, why was she still true to his memory? Everything he'd done over the last three years showed a total disregard for her. If she hadn't known about his dreams from the beginning for their children, she'd have said his one aim in life was to thwart her, to destroy her.

Radha felt bewildered – was there *any* good in him? Even his love for the children was so distorted. He'd done so little to see them since his departure. Always the grand gesture. The diamond bracelet, engraved watches and fountain pens, but not once that silent moment together, his arm round the child's shoulder.

And now, to snatch a child who was not yet ten! To say it was for her good to be sent away from her home and her mother! The man was unnatural.

His next step, once they were all gone to that faraway place, would be, no doubt, to say she was free to visit them, knowing she could not leave Leela behind. Knowing too she would not vacate this house. In her absence, he would move her and Leela to something more modest, she was sure of that. And when the day came for the children to come home from England, they would have to stay at the grand house with him and that woman because there would be no room for them where she was.

It had taken her long, but that night, in her misery, it seemed to Radha she was seeing the man for the first time, and she wondered how she'd ever loved him as she had.

She closed her eyes tight, wishing the tears away. Then, slipping the rosary over her fingers, she prayed to the Virgin Mary to bring her comfort and strength not to lose hope.

Chapter 37

Preparations went ahead at full tilt. Mena was transferred from Bukit Bintang where she'd been doing well, to join Paula at the English-speaking Convent. If the lessons were a struggle for Paula at the new school, they were utter gibberish to Mena. The teachers tried to be fair and include them but on hearing their stay would not outlast the term, they kindly left Mena in peace. At the same time, much to everyone's relief, Leela's schooling came to an end.

Adrenalin pulsed through the Doctor's veins. His dreams were coming to fruition sooner than he'd hoped. Paula – yes, he'd expected nothing less – an intelligent child, mercifully untainted by her mother. But Mena – why, that had been an unlooked for victory in the war he was waging against ignorance and wilful backwardness. The suggestion had not been entirely unpremeditated, but if the child had shown any reluctance, it might have been difficult.

The girls now attended ballet classes on Saturday mornings with a Miss Naomi, a retired English dance teacher, who had been persuaded to tie the ribbon of her *pointes* one last time. Through her the Doctor learnt of the private viewing of *Red Shoes* which had recently been released. What timing! – to kill two birds with one stone – excellent practice for their English and an inspiration in their ballet.

For the two sisters, the film outing which was in the evening was an unsettling foretaste of things to come. They could make very little of the film itself, but because there were no other non-English present, nor indeed any other children, they came under close scrutiny. Miss Naomi presented them to her friends as she might two rare though curious birds. Mena reached for her sister's hand, but had to be content with the wooden arm of the chair instead.

Their first ballet lesson. Both girls stared in embarrassed astonishment as the scrawny Miss Naomi who looked ancient beyond belief as she leapt around, almost naked, kicking her legs in all directions. They stole surreptitious glances of her in the huge mirror that covered one whole wall rather than look directly at the papery white of the naked strips of flesh.

They'd been told to come in leotards. A modified costume with a short pleated skirt was found at Whiteaways and now they stood, self-consciously listening to these strange orders, '*Pliés, pas-de-deux, arabesque, demi-pliés*' and all the while to the accompaniment of an old crackly gramophone and the no less crackly humming from Miss Naomi. The gramophone was the only familiar item in an otherwise alien score.

'Gels, gels!' A clap of the hands, not an applause, but rather, to stop them midstream. 'Higher, much higher, and now down, right down, turn, round and round – Oh, it doesn't matter, just watch me.' And Miss Naomi gazed at herself in the mirror that covered the entire wall and smiled at her image as she bent and swooped and leapt.

The girls looked at this same reflection and wondered that Miss Naomi should look so pleased at such a sight.

Now it was the girls' turn to try once more: however graceful the movement of their arms, their legs refused to reach the desired angles of abandonment, and Miss Naomi looked closely at their limbs as though trying to decide whether they really were the same as hers.

On returning home Mena tried to reproduce for her mother the high kicks; Radha found this a good opportunity to remind them of the contest between Shiva and Parvati which naturally ended with the god winning precisely because of these immodest excesses. Women were never meant to excel at such wanton gestures. Radha's fears for her daughters' morals deepened.

The days leading up to their departure were filled with feverish activities: fittings, jabs, packing. Mena's feet had difficulty with the heavy leather lace-ups, but Paula reminded her the choice had been hers to go to England. That shut her up. But Radha looked at the shoes that seemed to her more fitting for a boy than a little girl, and her heart ached for her child.

The two large trunks, one for each girl, bearing their initials in bold Roman characters on the lid, had already been sent off separately by sea.

On the appointed day, the car arrived to take them to the station. The Doctor would be waiting for them there. The driver, with the help of the gardener, arranged the luggage on the roof rack and the smaller bags went into the boot. Mena hugged Boney and told him he would have to learn to bark in English while the dog yelped with excitement. The child suddenly wanted to take Boney with her and Radha realized with anguish how little Mena understood what she was embarking on. Unable to take any more, Radha had the dog shut in the back of the house and they all piled into the car and set off.

The magnificent domes of the railway station came into view. The car stopped and porters rushed forward to take the two expandable 'Revelation' suitcases and the two smaller bags that carried Paula and Mena's clothing as well as various other bits and pieces on their long sea voyage. A great deal of shouting as the men staggered off to the first class sleeping carriage to stow the bags on the rack above and the suitcases under the seats.

Dr Mentem stood slightly apart, an angry scowl masking his awkwardness at finding himself in a public place with his wife. Leela hovered, her handkerchief ready, should her tears catch the contagion from her mother. But Radha smiled though her heart was breaking; she didn't shed a single tear till the train disappeared from view and she could no longer see the girls' hands waving out of the window.

That week, Radha did not see her friend, Agnes. She phoned to say she wasn't up to it.

Chapter 38

Paula and Mena were the only children on board during the long four week voyage. The second day was marked by a small act of rebellion when Paula persuaded Mena to cut her hair short with the aid of nail scissors. The result, to everyone's surprise, projected Paula into Europe with her new fashionable bob.

At Marseilles they were met by the faithful Sen who accompanied them to London and there, put them on the train to Cornwall. He sighed with relief to think his services had at last come to an end; George, he felt certain, would be accompanied by his mother when it was his turn.

Soon after their arrival at the convent, the two girls were given a sheet of paper and told to write home. A tall order, given it had to be in English as Tamil was forbidden whether spoken or written. Mena was studying her finished version with a certain amount of pride when the nun in charge took it and after studying it, placed a clean sheet before her.

'Now Mena, write a nice letter to your mummy.'

'*Umma* letter finish,' came the reply.

'The word is Mummy not *Umma* and what you've written is not a letter; it doesn't tell your Mummy how you are. No good just writing *mising you* from start to finish (and, by the way, missing has two *ss*). That's like writing 'lines' a hundred times when you've been a naughty girl. And what are these funny squiggles? They look like a spider crawling around.'

'Tamil. *Umma – um-* mummum teach me Tamil.'

'Goodness me, Tamil! You must write in a proper language that everyone can understand. We'll just tear this up, shall we? There, gone. Lucky we did it in rough first, wasn't it? And now you can write a nice letter. Tell her you like it here. That'll make her happy, see?'

So, Mena re-wrote her letter to make her Mummy happy and Radha never learnt how much she was missed.

Despite the odd disruption, the two Mentem girls settled down quickly to their new way of life. And yet, what a dramatic change there was!– no more showers whenever they felt like it, or daily change of clothes knowing the servant would wash, iron and leave the garment in their room that same day. Instead, bath – once a week; change of underwear – once a week; hair washing – every other week; change of blouse – every other week; tunic – once a term.

At first, they thought they'd misunderstood. Then, when realization dawned, Paula asked for a more frequent laundry service, but it was not granted.

That first term, to everyone's amazement, ten pounds of powdered egg sealed in an airtight tin arrived by sea mail. The nuns received it with jubilation. There was a treat of scrambled eggs for the boarders accompanied by a small ceremony as each girl in turn thanked Paula and Mena for their father's generosity. There was no further sign of it until, towards the end of the supply, Paula and Mena were singled out for another tasting.

Further food parcels arrived in the form of tinned meat and fruit which were proudly exhibited to the boarders though it was difficult to deduce which dish, if any, they later enhanced.

*

Letters to and from England were Radha's life-line. Her friend Agnes came without fail every Tuesday soon after nine. The two women would chat about the latest fashion in saris or what the government was up to – Radha still listened to the radio every morning but the exchanges with her friend brought everything to life. The days when there was a letter to be answered, usually from the two girls, sometimes from Roy, were always a high point and Radha could scarcely wait for the sound of the rickshaw outside the gate. Then, Leela too would catch the excitement from her mother.

'Letters coming morning-time Paula, also Madras uncle Pradeep – who uncle Pradeep, *Umma*? Roy, no letter this month? And Julius not write – why? He forget us, *Umma*?'

It was true there was not a single letter from Julius in the sandalwood chest.

'It's that Chinese woman,' was the usual answer. 'Uncle Pradeep never forgets to write; and Paula and Mena are good girls. Nothing from Roy this month,' Radha would say with a sigh.

Agnes had heard it all before, but it never failed to wring her heart and provoke a few words of encouragement; then she'd assure her friend she prayed for her more fervently than ever; God would surely take pity on her steadfastness before long.

That morning a letter had arrived from Penzance and Radha now waited impatiently to discuss it with Agnes. Of course she'd read it already and as always Leela and she had talked of little else all day. Also, as always, there were passages that needed clarification and Agnes was invaluable for these, but the arrival of a letter was in itself an event for all three of them.

When Agnes finally arrived, they sat in the friendly seclusion of the upstairs room with their glasses already filled with fresh lime juice, and Agnes began to read:

Dear mother,

Thank you for your letter. Next week Mena and I are going to The Isle of Wight to a sister-convent for our summer holiday. We'll be going by train to Portsmouth and there we'll take the ferry, which will be fun. I'm looking forward to it – no more grinding-organ-playing!

Apparently the island is full of different coloured sands and Mena plans to sift graded colours into a glass tube for Leela. I've warned her she might sink the ferry if she collects too much but she won't listen.

Affectionately,

Paula.

'I wrote to Paula all about my mother's sickness but she doesn't refer to it; d'you think she got my letter?' Radha asked. 'And why are they changing to a different convent? Is it because Paula doesn't like grinding the organ?'

'Here she is writing 'thank you for letter' therefore, letter arrived,' Agnes pointed out. 'Distance makes the heart grow fonder or forget; here, she is forgetting her grandmother. Simple answer, next question, yes please. Not changing convent; this time changing places for holidays. Organ not creating rumpus, no thank you.'

'Mena putting sand in glass,' Leela objected. 'I not want drink sand.'

'It's not like Mena to refuse to listen to her elder sister,' Radha reflected.

'Sisters always will be fighting. Mena and Paula same every sister. Paula giving her advice, Mena not listening. Result – ferry will sink.'

'Isn't that worrying? What exactly is 'ferry', Agnes?'

'Ferry is familiar word for toy made with fur; Paula thinking toy will be fun; but filled with sand, ferry-toy will sink.'

With the letter thus nicely translated and understood, everyone settled down to discussing the usual topics – the monsoon which was late coming, the Doctor whose line of patients was longer than ever, and the grandmother's health which continued to give much cause for concern.

*

Mena realized with a sense of panic even simple phrases in Tamil now eluded her; however was she going to communicate with her sister Leela who couldn't speak English? What was the Tamil for homesickness? Did such a thing exist? She tried repeating short sentences to herself as she wandered about the convent grounds but the sounds were no longer familiar. Her accent didn't sound right even to her own ears as her tongue twisted clumsily round the words that had become foreign to her.

Since that early unsuccessful attempt to communicate in earnest with her mother, she had learnt to write anodyne letters that would not distress her.

> *Darling Mummy,*
> > *How are you? I am well.*
> > *Last Sunday after church we went for a walk by the sea. It was cold and wet because it was raining. It is still raining. And my shoes hurt my feet. But not much.*
> > *With lots of love,*
>
> > *Mena.*

Radha held the letter to her heart. The old familiar phrases stabbed her each time she read them. She closed her eyes and saw her child standing alone in a cold country, with the rain pouring down. Alas, Paula had never taken to her sisters; Mena was too young to have left her home. Radha wept silently for her lost child as she carefully folded her letter along the lines that were there, and stored it away among her treasures in the sandalwood chest.

Chapter 39

Then came the afternoon when Agnes arrived a little later than expected and as she stepped inside, a hiccup escaped noisily.

'Sorry Radha dear, please be forgiving me. Here I am arriving late, but saying to myself – better late than never getting here.' And although she made a valiant effort to hold her breath, another hiccup exploded into the quiet decorum of that house.

'Agnes, are you all right? Are you not well?' Radha asked, solicitous, going towards her. That strange scent on her friend's breath reached her – pears – Agnes had said. But suddenly Radha saw, so clearly, he might have been standing in front of her – her father-in-law entering their house in Pondicherry that day her in-laws had come to visit her – drunk! And she knew, beyond any doubt, this was alcohol. The smile on her lips froze.

'Problem here, Radha dear, we're not accustomed to having one for the road. But, on no balance would I be staying away when you are here waiting on me.'

Radha remained silent. Her eyes filled with regret and the letter in her hand fluttered as she held it against her heart. Radha found she could not ask her friend to come in or offer her the cool drink the servant had already taken upstairs and placed on the table.

With embarrassment and confusion, Agnes too remained rooted to the spot as another unfortunate hiccup blasted into the silence, and her face crumpled into an apology. Some desire to distance herself from her present state made Agnes carry on in English.

'My godchild was inviting me for her pre-engagement celebrations; all the glasses looking the same, or nearly the same – orange juice – just one sip; tasting nice. Like orange juice, but better. One sip, maybe two. Knowing your objections to all strong beverages, I was limiting myself. And I myself am wanting to throw up drunken women. Bad company. Then someone telling me good luck one for the road. I should say no, but how to be letting people bumping down?' Here she made a gesture of hopelessness of one who'd tried to please too many people as another hiccup surfaced to destroy her composure. 'More than anything, I'm not wanting to bump you down by not turning in at all. I am here giving you my honourable word, it will be happening again on no balance.'

Nor did it happen ever again because she was never again invited. It was clear to Radha this was not a flash in the pan. Agnes had taken to drink.

The Doctor's first commandment had always been 'no alcohol'. With an alcoholic for a father, the son had learnt a few hard truths. Those rumours about the family that had so worried his mother-in-law were well founded. He put most of his father's excesses down to the evils of alcohol. His strictures applied to men. It wouldn't have occurred to him to include women for, at that time, Indian women rarely touched alcohol. So that the age-old tradition together with her husband's objection left Radha no choice. She did not watch her erstwhile friend stumble along the drive.

Would the trishaw be there, Agnes wondered, her heart thumping miserably against her ribs. What should she do if the man had left, hoping to catch a quick fare and be back in time to pick her up as usual? He did that sometimes and she'd never complained.

At the gate, she looked round the bamboo hedge and was so relieved to see him and his trishaw, a whimper escaped. Closing the gate carefully behind her, she took one last look at the silent house where she'd known hours of friendship. Too late she understood the evils of alcohol. And yet, she'd been warned; had known from the beginning there would be no second chance. She had become a teetotaller, refused to allow a single drop to pass her lips.

Then, little by little, she began, once more, to have just a sip or two. Nothing more, to start with. Now, she needed a little something when she got up. There would be no more visits to Jalan Inai.

Without a word, Agnes got in the trishaw and the man set off for her house where her ailing mother would be waiting for her.

Radha walked slowly up the broad, wooden staircase, feeling with each step the weight of her loss. There will never be another Agnes to brighten her days; she knew that with absolute certainty. But she also understood her husband's aversion to alcohol. If only she'd had a choice! If only.

Leela was standing at the top of the stairs, agitation making every part of her tremble piteously. Her hands were clasped in front of her and Radha could see they were shaking. Her voice too was unsteady and there were tears in her eyes.

'Aunty Agnes? Gone! I see out window. Trishaw gone. *Umma*, why?'

'Yes,' Radha let out, trying to hide her emotion, 'Agnes has gone. It's better this way.' She took Leela's hands in hers to still them. Poor Leela, to increase her misery like this! She poured the lemon drink into two of the glasses and putting Leela's hands round one, she explained, 'Agnes has taken to drink. Just think what your father would say if he knew we were friendly with an alcoholic!'

'Oh, alcohol no good. Aunty Agnes coming back, we give lemon drink.'

'The problem isn't what she has when she's here. You didn't see the state she arrived in. But I should've known before. The pear tart. Not used to the smell which is why I missed it. It's become a habit with her.'

'Pear tart, no good. Bad habit!'

'Yes, well, drink is a very bad habit. Heavens, if your father got to hear of it!'

'Oh, the Doctor! No, no alcohol!'

'That's right – what would he think if he found us entertaining someone (and a woman at that! Though clearly I wouldn't be entertaining a man!) – someone who drinks! No, an impossible situation. I had no choice.'

They sat without touching their lemon and biscuits. Eventually, feeling that Leela was calmer, Radha unfolded

Mena's letter, there was another from Paula that had arrived the day before – no Agnes to savour these letters with her, she thought miserably. She deciphered Mena's childish writing and holding it down with her left hand, she began to write her answer in her beautiful script:

Dear daughters, Paula and Mena,

 Thanking you for yours. Happy so to be hearing both is well. Same here. We are, and Leela also, in the pink of health.

 By all means please be keeping well. I am here, praying and missing you. Up–to–date be writing please.

 Your loving mother.

 Ps, news of Ummachi – Granny – still no good. Sick diabetes. I pray she come here.

She folded the letter and slipped it into the envelope, then she smiled at Leela.

'The servant will post it tomorrow as usual.'

'Tomorrow usual,' Leela nodded and smiled back at her mother, pleased that in spite of the unforeseen catastrophe, some things would continue as before.

Chapter 40

The following Tuesday, the absence of so good a friend was hard to endure. Radha decided they needed to get out, do something different. Anything, rather than sitting, waiting for the moment when Agnes would have arrived. She therefore told Leela to put on her pale blue dress with the violets along the hem.

'We going out, *Umma*? You wearing pretty sari; I put on violets dress?'

'Shopping – buy you something new, shall we? I'll ring for the car as soon as you're ready.'

Radha was about to get her necklace out of the armoire when there was a small disturbance at the gate. Looking down from the upstairs window, she saw a man talking to the servant who'd run up from the back. From Radha's viewpoint, she could see little more than a mass of black hair which glinted grey in the bright sunlight; the man was clearly quite tall, and young if his bearing and build were anything to go by. Surely her single state was known to everyone; no man would dare present himself at her house!

Whatever he said to the girl must have convinced her she could let him in. The light-coloured Austin was now making its way towards the porch but Radha was none the wiser. Whispering in case her voice carried through the open window, she told Leela to change into her dress, and then made her way down quickly.

Her visitor was standing at the front door, smiling. Recognition was immediate; Radha ran towards him, her eyes shining with joy.

'Pradeep! After all these years! Come in. What are you doing here?'

'A long time, Radha! My letters were so inadequate. I wanted to see you, but what with, er, the problems at work' He'd prepared the excuse well beforehand but it refused to come out smoothly. 'Anyway, here I am. I can't believe it, you're more beautiful than ever!'

'Oh, Pradeep! Tell me, how is *Ummuma*? I'm so worried about her. And Pondicherry – is it the same as ever? Heavens, that word – such memories! You'll have a cold drink, won't you? Oh, of course, coffee! It's so nice to see you.'

The excitement of the meeting made Radha look so young and lovely, her cousin was genuinely taken aback. Or it might have been a trick of the light, coming in from the bright sun outside into this cool area of white and blue. Whatever it was, Pradeep stared at her, unable to believe the Doctor could have left such a woman.

While the servant ran off to make the coffee, they settled themselves opposite each other. Pradeep looked taller than Radha remembered, handsome with thick wavy hair, grey at the temples and a wonderfully spontaneous smile. His colouring was roughly the same as her husband's, but she thought he might have been an inch shorter. He was wearing long white trousers and short-sleeved shirt with what looked like tennis shoes and white socks. Very relaxed; very different from her husband.

'Vida ...' she began, then stopped. How silly to re-open the old wound!

Pradeep nodded and murmured something, but Leela arrived at that moment. She'd changed into her dress and Radha smiled to herself on seeing traces of face powder on her cheeks. Pradeep stood up with outstretched arms.

'This must be Leela. Last time I saw you, you were almost four, just imagine that!'

'Four!' Leela echoed, for whom numbers had little meaning.

'That was just before we left for Pondicherry,' Radha said excitedly, then suddenly fell silent, remembering too much.

Mention of Pondicherry was enough to trigger off Leela's current concern.

'*Ummuma* sick!' she cried.

'Yes, I know,' Pradeep said, 'I saw your mother last month; she may have written? Anyway, she never complains but she's a lot frailer than six years ago. The main problem is her eyesight, though she also has considerable difficulty moving about.'

'Poor dear *Umma*, she should be here,' Radha said sadly before coming out with a *non sequitur*, 'I should never have left him here on his own.'

'You mean you should have stayed here in KL during the war? No, it was a good thing you weren't here. Perhaps all wars are terrible, but that one ...' Pradeep shuddered at the memory and fell silent. In spite of the years of separation, there was nothing awkward in this sudden silence. He looked across at her with concern and sympathy, 'Of course I understand what you're saying; such a deep sorrow for you to bear.' He paused before saying, 'Just after the end of the war, I was sent out to open a branch in Madras.'

'I remember. My husband wrote telling me you might be in touch.'

'It's thriving now which is why I'm back here at long last. I had every intention of coming to see you then, but by the time I got round to it, you'd left.'

Pradeep knew his lie wouldn't be detected. How could he have told her the truth?– that he'd arrived in Madras, longing to see her, but guessed she was in the dark about her husband's life-style. What was he to do? If he told her, he would merely heap confusion and pain on his cousin Radha whom he had never stopped loving. So, he'd stayed away.

'Pradeep, *Ummuma* talks of you in almost every letter though, surprisingly, she didn't mention you'd be coming over.' Then, struck by a new thought, she cried, 'You must re-marry, it's what Vida would have wanted, a nice young wife. I'd arrange it for you except that here, coming back at the end of the war, I lost touch with everyone. No, I never really knew anyone. That's how my life here has always been except for dear Vida and you. And there was my friend Agnes ...' she said wistfully.

'A young wife! D'you want me to make a fool of myself?'

'I'm serious. You're only forty-five; a lot of young women would be –'

'Radha, if I marry again, it wouldn't be to some flighty young thing – worse than a millstone round my neck. But the idea of someone, say, roughly your age ...'

'Oh, you mean a widow – but you'll have her children round your neck – now, if that isn't a millstone for a young man, I don't know what is!'

'The thought of a string of children doesn't put me off. They grow up sooner or later and leave the nest. But, it wouldn't be a widow.'

'Why ever not, if the thought of her children doesn't frighten you? Anyway, I can't see what alternative there is.'

'No, not a widow; she'd have sanctified the memory of her late husband and there'd be no way of getting through to her.'

'You are hard to please, no wonder you haven't re-married.'

'But if I were to find the right woman, she'd have the choice of living in Madras or KL.'

'What a wonderful opportunity! D'you really mean you'd let her choose?'

'I most certainly do. I'm as useful in KL as in Madras; in fact, although I haven't been to see you till now (and the reason for that is somewhat complicated), I've been flitting to and fro between our two establishments. That's why, whether it's here or there, you – I mean my wife would be able to bring along her children, mother or any other appendage.'

'Oh, talking about that, I'm trying to persuade my mother to come here. I'm sure it could be done even though she's in a poor state. We could arrange it to coincide with someone who's coming over to keep an eye on her during the journey. What d'you think?'

'Why don't you and Leela go over there instead? I'd be able to arrange –'

'Me, over there! Oh, no, Pradeep, I've got to stay here because – because – this is where I belong.'

'Yes, stay here,' Leela put in, 'Jalan Inai, Imbi Road; nice big house, good for family.'

Pradeep bowed his head and remained thoughtful for what seemed a very long time.

'I'll see what I can do to bring your mother over,' he said at last.

When he'd left, Radha told Leela how her cousin and she used to play together when they were small.

'He was really kind; he should get married again. It's what Vida would have wanted.'

'Who Vida, *Umma*?'

'Vida was Pradeep's wife – we were good friends,' she started making her way up to the bedroom, Leela following close behind, 'We used to talk for hours on end, though never about – Oh, they were good times. Then the war came ... yes, I'm sure he's right, a terrible war in more ways than one.' Her tone became lighter as she held the hand mirror to check her hair at the back.

'Leela – the grey – is it very visible?'

'What, *Umma*?'

'No, never mind,' she said, getting up and taking off

her fine sari. 'We never got to the shops,' she said with a laugh. 'What a surprise seeing uncle Pradeep! So nice to think he's here now. Leela, we must get your hair cut, make you pretty. Prettier than you already are, buy you that new dress we were talking about.'

*

As the weeks went by Radha began to rely on Pradeep for news of the outside world. This was something new for until then, although she still listened to BBC World Service, her sphere of interest was strictly limited to the narrow tunnel of her life.

The change showed. Not only was her step lighter, but she laughed more readily. She pointed out the three children to her cousin from photos hanging on the half-landing; old snapshots of Roy taken by the Doctor in that brief period when they'd all lived in this house; more recent pictures of the two girls sent to her from Penzance.

'Look, Pradeep, Paula and Mena in this strange outfit. What's a reel?'

Pradeep explained that people in Scotland danced a reel wearing kilts with matching berets and sashes like those in the photo. He showed her in the atlas where Scotland was in relation to England. Radha listened, absorbed.

The transformation in her was visible. Pradeep found the change exhilarating and had to restrain himself from rushing too fast.

When he mentioned the seasons in England – certain trees, fully grown, that lose their leaves in winter, then sprout again the next spring – memory stirred. Radha felt a sudden and painful longing. But the moment passed.

'Radha, listen to this,' he continued, 'there are animals who sleep through the winter months so that if you come upon them in the middle of their hibernation, you'd think they were dead; in reality, they'd be in a deep sleep.'

'When I first learnt Paula was to go to England, I warned her water fell from the tap in droplets of ice. I believed it!' She laughed and Pradeep joined her, his heart full to bursting to hear her laugh. She continued, 'Someone told me that. I was hoping it would put her off. From what you say, it wasn't far from the truth. My poor children, what a life!'

Pradeep reached out towards her but checked his movement in time, smoothing his hair instead in a familiar gesture. Being there with her, he couldn't help thinking how different his life might have been but for superstition and star-gazing.

When her family had returned from Saigon, he and Radha had seen each other for five wonderfully happy months. Their cousinship had allowed the intimacy. Finally he told his mother he wished to marry her. That was when the stars came in to dash his hopes!

He had left immediately for Malaya to work in a law firm, and was thus spared the sight of Radha becoming someone else's bride. In Malaya, within a very short time, he lost his belief in astrologers and the like, but returned to Pondicherry at the end of three years to marry the young woman his mother had chosen for him. It made her happy, and it was of little concern to him whom he married. When his wife, Vida, met Radha and the two women became good friends, Pradeep lived in constant fear his true feelings might be detected. Somehow, they weren't.

'Your children,' he told Radha, returning to the present, 'won't have suffered too many hardships; the country is crippled after a grim war, but it's picking up. I'm told life in England isn't too bad though it's certainly more comfortable to clean one's teeth in tepid water. But imagine, Radha, in the summer months, you can, if you feel like it, sleep under the stars and not be bitten to death. And the sun does shine during those months, till ten at night.'

'Ten at night!' Radha murmured in wonder.

'Then rises again soon after four. So you see, there are compensations.'

In this way Radha learnt about the country where her children were living before they came home that summer.

Chapter 41

The Homecoming

From the moment Radha learnt her three children would be home in August, she thought of little else. She must plan ahead; make sure their stay was happy. That was vital. Roy would have his seventeenth birthday while he was home. Seventeen. Not quite a young man but no longer a boy. Old enough, at last, to understand.

Paula was already eighteen. The age she'd been when she got married. *Ummachi* had been right – eighteen *is* a good age to take on the responsibilities of life. Paula, of course, had always been headstrong; but the three years in the convent will have had a softening effect, made her ready to listen to others.

And Mena – Radha stopped short. She realised with a pang she didn't know Mena. She'd held her and loved her the first eighteen months of her life, a gurgling bundle of joy. Then everything had gone wrong. Those years in India, no thought for anyone but *him*. Migraine, tears. So many tears there should have been none left to spill. She did weep less these days though that might or might not be a good sign.

Mena had been there the whole time during all those years – Pondicherry, birth of the illegitimate child, the terrible kidnapping of Roy. Mena had been there but it was as though she herself had been absent, half-crazed in her grief.

It was time to make up for past neglect. They would be her priority. She would show them how much they meant to her, that being here was a genuine alternative way of living.

She must get the silver out from its hiding place under the stairs; get the girl to clean it; perhaps let Leela practise using the clumsy spoon and sharp-pronged fork. What an idea to resort to these tools when God had given us perfectly suited hands to do the job! But of course, Pradeep wasn't telling the whole truth – fingers were probably so stiff in those countries, they had no other way of getting food into their mouths.

Also, she must stop running round the house dressed in just the under skirt and blouse; not even in the heat of the afternoon. They mustn't get the impression she was letting her standards drop. She'd always stripped down during the day for as long as she could remember, but it made no difference. After these years in England, things will have changed – they might even have started walking round the house wearing outdoor shoes.

Radha stopped short, suddenly deflated. How on earth was she going to do it? To make their stay happy and carefree? It wasn't going to work.

There was *Ummachi* installed in the downstairs room. She'd arrived at last; brought over by Pradeep. A near miracle, that crossing, in her condition. It couldn't have happened without him. He'd been like a son to her.

Ummachi, a shadow of the grandmother who'd run the house in Pondicherry. Moving unseeingly in the semi-darkness of her room, the shutters permanently half-closed to let in the air but not the light. No need for light, the diabetes had wasted those dear eyes. Radha was filled with pity – all that vitality reduced to this skeletal form, groping her way in darkness.

She'd enfolded *Ummachi* in her arms and led her to the room she'd prepared. The altar had been moved into a corner to make room for the bed. The place had served long enough as a prayer room for earlier memories of the Doctor's *ménage à trois* to have been exorcised.

Pradeep had tried to warn her but Radha hadn't listened; she'd imagined her mother at least able to walk from one room to another on the flat level of the groundfloor, or sitting in the airy room downstairs, the two of them chatting together for hours, as they had in Pondicherry six years before. But the old lady was well past that.

Radha had known her mother wouldn't want to consult the Doctor. She hadn't made that fearful journey with thought of a cure, but to end her days near her beloved Radha. Radha wept silently, touched by such depth of love. Her mother was dying. It didn't need the diagnosis of the brilliant Doctor to know that.

It was going to be difficult to rejoice at the children's return within the space of this house. Dear God, she thought, can nothing in life ever be simple and joyful, not even for a brief forty days? She'd have to impose near silence because of the poor sick lady.

Three long years since Radha's daughters had been taken from her; Roy the year before that. How many days did that make? Four years in all. Almost one thousand, five hundred days. One thousand five hundred days of longing and now they were to return. Forty days at home. The question was – when exactly would *he* come during these forty days?

She forced her thoughts back to Paula. Perhaps the years of absence will have made her more understanding and sympathetic. Would Radha be able to talk about a suitor for her? With Paula's credentials: educated in England, School Certificate taken (had she passed? but that was of little importance), exceptionally gifted in needlework, cookery and music, why, she'd be able to find someone at the top of the list. Hopefully the convent education as well as the passage of time will have smoothed those scratchy feathers or, if not, pray God she'll have learnt to keep them well hidden. At least till after the wedding ceremony.

Good heavens! Radha had done nothing about consulting the charts to choose a favourable partner for her daughter! It was high time she got on with it.

The marriage would be sumptuous: she'd take Paula to 'Devendra's Finest Silks' to buy her wedding sari. It would be gold on gold as she'd always dreamt, and Paula's diamonds in their gold setting would look magnificent. She herself would wear her Benares sari of red silk with heavy gold thread; handed down to her by her mother; it was fit for a maharaja's wedding. They would have to hire the Anandha Reception Halls well in advance.

Here she floundered. Where was she going to find the hundreds who would normally be lucky enough to be invited to her eldest daughter's marriage? Radha had become a recluse. She knew no one. There'd been Agnes, her one true friend, but even she was lost.

Radha did not allow herself to be confounded by these considerations. There was a lot to do and not much time in which to do it.

The children were coming back; they would all, or almost all, be together again. So much cause for rejoicing! Radha said as much to the sleeping form of her mother.

Then her children arrived and everything was so different from what she'd imagined, she wondered how she could ever have thought it would be otherwise.

Chapter 42

When the three children heard from their father they'd be returning home for the summer holidays, all three were elated though each for a different reason. Paula at last saw her chance to escape from the detested convent. Mena couldn't wait to take up the thread where she'd left off three years before. And Roy needed a break before starting at a new school (wherever that was). After a valiant struggle over the centuries, Probus was finally to be laid to rest by Lord Attlee's astringent laws on death duties.

The flight back, with many stops *en route* to fix the radiator or propeller adjustment or some other repair, took twenty–seven hours. Kuala Lumpur at last.

What stifling heat! The air thick and humid with unremembered scents and smells! So, this is what *the tropics* means! So different! Tired and strangely lost in their own country, the first person who came into view at the airport was Luk.

Paula stood still for a second and stared at her – dumpy and graceless, an ingratiating smile masking venom – had she been a common servant sent to fetch them rather than her father's chosen partner, the sight would have been less distasteful. Suddenly all that had been wrong about this place assailed her. Her anxiety to leave the convent had blinded her to the reality at this end; now, with the realization, she felt an aversion she could barely conceal.

She should have guessed it would be Luk and not her father who'd be waiting to greet them. Officials would have to be bribed, the path prepared for the three of them to have an easier passage than the hoi polloi. The Doctor wouldn't have stooped to carry out such menial tasks.

Or, perhaps it wasn't that at all. Perhaps – no, it couldn't be! Was it possible her father was forcing them to accept this woman? Paula felt an anger that threatened to engulf her.

The children were dazed as they swept past the queue to the head of passport control; customs officials waved them on with an oily smile. An awkward greeting with their father, then they climbed into the back of the car while he sat next to the driver. Luk squeezed herself next to Roy who sidled away towards Mena. Long drive past quaint-looking *campongs*, the smell of *durian* through the open window, stirring memories of guzzling and nausea. Finally the car stopped outside their father's mansion. Now what?

The Doctor and Luk got out; the three children remained seated.

'Come in, come in,' came from their father, sounding too jolly in the heat and unfamiliarity of the surroundings.

They climbed out, reluctantly. So, this was the mansion. Paula of course had seen it before – the birthday present she'd never forget – but she'd forgotten how luxurious the place was. Either that or the interim years in the convent had given her a new perspective. They'd heard a great deal about it while it was being built, when he was still in that mean, rented house not far from them. Then more rumours after it was built. Air-conditioning. Wrought iron. Marble floors. Acres of land.

Yes, it looked grand. For a start, from the road to the porch was so long they'd forgotten before the end it was a private drive leading to the house. Then the house, that rounded bit on the first floor, green, curving all the way round – glass? – almost certainly the air-conditioned room everyone had talked about. Downstairs, wide open space, but no nicer than their home they'd be going to in a minute.

And these flowers – orchids – should have been a single plant, given pride of place on an occasional table, or in a greenhouse. Not this long hedge growing out of the ground. Only, this whole country felt like a greenhouse. Hot, humid, oppressive.

The trees on the other side of this screen were enormous and lush, conscious of their stature with space round them, lending a park-like feel to the place. A private park – that's what it was – not open to the public. Nobody allowed in through those tall iron gates, except them. And they longed to be elsewhere!

Their father's voice broke in on their uneasy thoughts as he turned to follow Luk into the house.

'I'm sure you could do with a cool drink after that long journey. Come in, come in.'

"Be careful what you drink in that house!" reverberated in Paula's head.

'No thank you. I'd like to go home,' she said, her voice taut but perfectly clear.

'What? No drink? Home! You'd like to go *home*!' His voice incredulous. Turning to Roy, his anger more audible with every word, 'And what about you?'

'Not thirsty, thank you.' Roy replied.

Looking at Mena who had stopped on the first step, his voice now a roar.

'And you're not thirsty either, I suppose.' Mena stood, uncertain, looking towards her sister. 'Right. No one wants a drink in my house.'

Mena still hesitated but he bundled her towards the car with the others.

So, here they were, he thought ruefully, back exactly where they'd been before their departure. All the old antipathy and anger still there. Nothing had changed. Yes, something had changed, but it was for the worse. Paula would not have behaved like that before.

Paula looked across at her brother and saw they thought as one. Thank heaven there was Europe! That is, if he was still willing to pay for them to return there.

The Doctor gave the order for the driver to drop them off at their mother's house.

*

Hearing sounds of their arrival, Radha hurried towards her children, half laughing but with her finger to her lips; even at such a joyful moment, she had to warn them *Ummachi* was in the next room. Roy had already stepped into the house. Roy, her marvellous boy, so handsome! Her son who had been snatched from her that terrible afternoon. She almost had him in her arms when she saw his hand and stopped – what was the matter with his hand? Why was he holding it out? His voice was deep like his father's. Unintelligible words. Of course – English. She'd let it slip in the last year, but given time, she'd ... ah, Paula, standing just behind Roy, her hand too, outstretched.

Radha took her son's hand in her own trying to shake away the tears – not of joy, but of defeat and shock. Then, she shook Paula's hand. Had Paula always been so much taller than her?

And here was Minupa, moving forward, standing right in front of her, waiting for something. Except that Mena stood six inches taller than her little girl who'd gone away. She was so much thinner, no Tamil, and she'd forgotten to put out her hand to be shaken. How was Radha to greet her European child if she couldn't shake her hand? She wouldn't risk hugging her – Roy had flinched in anticipation, ever so slightly, but ... Radha's palms come together in a formal Indian greeting. Strangers meeting for the first time.

Mena stands still, confused, lost in this alien culture. Where was *Umma* who had been in her heart these three lonely years? *Umma*, who would have held her so tight, she would have laughed aloud for air. Tears prick her eyes as she crouches down to stroke the dog who is barking excitedly. Could this be Boney, looking different? Does his bark mean he still remembers her after so long an absence?

The two older children shuffled their feet, feeling dejected. It wasn't just that there was something primitive about the place, but everything was hushed as if they were in mourning. They'd forgotten how mangy the dog was and as for their sister, Leela, she clearly couldn't understand English which was why she was standing there grinning at them, darting quick glances at her mother.

This sepulchral hush, there *had* been a letter from their mother several months earlier, before they knew they'd be coming home, saying something about their grandmother coming from Pondicherry. But in the excitement of later developments, this detail had slipped their minds. Now they learnt the old lady was not only somewhere inside, but that they had to be quiet because she was very sick. Dying.

'Sounds jolly,' Roy muttered to Paula under his breath.

On hearing they'd declined to stop at the mansion, Radha's spirits rose. This was surely a good start; God only knew what lethal concoction that woman might have slipped into their drink. That refusal gave her hope; they were good children; they understood the situation.

Chapter 43

A few days later, seeing Paula on her own, Radha embarked on the subject that had been at the forefront of her thoughts ever since she learnt they were coming home. Paula's Tamil, thank heaven, was just about good enough to have a serious conversation.

'Paula, I don't know what your father has in mind, but eighteen is a good age to ...'

'Forget it,' Paula cut in quickly in English.

'Forget it?' Radha wondered if she'd misunderstood.

'I have no intention of getting married yet. And when I do, it will not be here, nor will it be to an Indian. You will not be involved in any way. What surprises me is that you can recommend eighteen as a 'good age' to marry after your experience.'

Radha's hand flew to her heart. Had Paula always been as cutting as this?

'My marriage hasn't been a happy one, but there were unusual circumstances – a separation of five years is too long; wars knit together those who go through it side by side.

Also, she used magic. Under normal conditions, Indians make good husbands.'

'Then, perhaps you should consider getting yourself a new one; but don't bother on my behalf.'

Radha looked at her eldest daughter and realized with shock she'd never seen her in a sari. Now she never would. The earlier ill-founded optimism was replaced by bewilderment; how could she ever have thought it was going to work? The gulf that now separated her children from her was far greater than the thousands of miles that had stretched between them during the one thousand, five hundred days since first Roy, later, the girls, had been taken from her. Her heart beat dully within its cage as she registered all that she'd lost in that time.

Roy, she saw, had no time for anyone but himself. He would never fight someone else's battle. Seventeen but still like a little boy chasing after butterflies and sticking the poor things with a pin into a box. As for Paula, if her feathers had been scratchy before, they were positively poison-tipped now. No, there would be no wedding, no celebration of any sort. And Mena – lost forever. Only Indian in name and colour though even that had somehow faded in the cold, north light. How could she devote more time to her youngest child when there was no way of getting through to her? Her mother-tongue – lost. And with it, her Indianness – gone. Everything lost. Gone beyond repair. A hopeless case.

Radha turned away, closing her eyes from so much heartache. She prayed to the Virgin Mary to succour her flagging spirit as she silently repeated the sorrowful mysteries of the rosary that had been blessed at Lourdes. A gift from dear Brother Leo, her husband's youngest brother. It soothed her, and that, she knew, was a miracle.

*

Their first Sunday together, Radha got up early, apprehensive; it was clear by now there was an unbridgeable gulf between her and her English children. But it was Sunday, and they would all be together in her usual pew, and people round them would be staring at them, filled with curiosity and – how could they help it – envy. Small consolation. Never mind, it was something, and a drowning man must cling to his last straw, thought Radha, suddenly remembering one of Agnes's favourite English sayings.

The door of her bedroom was ajar as always, and while doing up her sari blouse (she would wear the rich green silk today since it was such a special day), she called to Paula.

'I took your gold set out of the bank; it's here in my armoire. It'll go with any outfit.'

'Why would I want it?' Paula sounded irritated.

'The diamonds are safer left in the bank; also, they're less suitable for church.'

'Church! What are we going there for?'

Radha stopped short; the pleats of the sari cascaded out of her hand; she must have heard wrong. No one who had spent three-and-a-half years in a convent could question Mass on Sunday. Perhaps Paula hadn't realized it was Sunday? After such a long journey, she could be muddled about the days. There was also the problem of language; Paula's Tamil wasn't bad, but it wasn't perfect either. So Radha resorted to her English.

'It Sunday. See here, gold chain, earrings, bracelet.'

'Very nice; I'll not be needing them. You wear them.'

'Thank you. Thank you, Paula. But, not needing. Mummy wearing garnets with green sari. Remember garnets set, yes?'

Oh,no, thought Paula, here we go – the story of that historic journey that father made when Julius was no more than two, and none of the rest of us had yet been born. A whole month on the boat to England to have a goitre operation, two weeks to recover, two weeks to sightsee, to have firsthand knowledge of London where, one day, he'd be sending his children.

'... all people looking Doctor Mentem children.'

Ah, well, at least she'd been spared the story of the garnets. Yes, she'd tag along, not in order to fly the flag for the family, but the alternative, that is, staying at home with the Ghost of Pondicherry, did not appeal.

'I'll be ready in five minutes,' Paula said, 'but I don't need any jewellery.'

They'd piled into the car when it came, Roy sitting in front next to the driver as was befitting a young man, and although Radha had that uncomfortable feeling her eldest daughter would have opted out if she'd had a choice, she did feel proud to have all of them with her; that is, all except Julius. Where was he at this moment, she wondered. At least Mena had looked suitably excited, and Roy, well, it hadn't been clear what he thought about church. Later, at communion, it had become clear.

The two older children had been inattentive throughout but Radha said nothing. She was about to go up to the altar for communion when she heard Paula whisper to her brother, "You going?" A slight shrug of the shoulder and Roy whispered back, '"All mumbo-jumbo anyway. In for a penny, in for a pound. Coming?"

And they'd all gone up to take communion though Radha almost choked with grief when the moment came to swallow the sacred host. She'd not understood Roy's words but the tone had been plain.

At the end of Mass, as they filed out of the side door, Radha wondered for a second if Agnes would be there, standing to one side with her quiet smile.

'Why, hello! The whole family, or almost.' It was her cousin. Dear Pradeep, she thought, feeling calmer of a sudden.

He smiled at Radha's English children. They were certainly eye-catching! Paula – unusually tall, confident and good looking in a European way with short hair and western dress. A beauty, with large soft brown eyes and flawless skin; pity she looked so haughty. Next to her, Radha's beloved Roy – slim, with exquisitely fine bone structure such as occasionally seen in southern India; less self-assured, hermetically sealed from the world. Over on this side, standing close to Leela – 'little' Mena who was almost as tall as Paula. Pradeep stared at her – the resemblance was uncanny – she was the living image of Radha as a child!

'Pradeep! I was looking for you,' Radha said in Tamil. 'Children, this is your uncle Pradeep; he speaks English perfectly.'

'A rather distant uncle, but I used to know you all quite well when you were tiny, before you left KL.' Seeing Paula's puzzled look, he said, 'Ah, I should have said left

KL the first time – when you went to India. I'd understand if you don't remember me; you were very small, probably no more than five or six.'

'Why don't you come back home, Pradeep? It would be nice if you got to know the children once more,' Radha suggested. 'You can follow us in your own car. We should be going back now so that the driver can return.'

Chapter 44

Once they were home, Radha looked in on her mother, then went to the kitchen to make sure everything was in order. The servant brought a jug of fresh lime with syrup and cubes of ice tinkling against the side and left it on the table near Paula.

'The sermon went on a bit, but Mass at least will have felt familiar,' Pradeep began.

'Totally barbaric!' Paula let out, forgetting her usual gentility in her pent up frustration.

'Really? The ritual of Mass is always the same, wherever you are. Why did it seem barbaric to you?'

'It's always barbaric, only, here, it was worse. A huge church, crammed full of people, for the most part illiterate, the priest with his back to everyone, muttering away in a language that's been dead for centuries, most of the congregation unable to understand a word of it let alone a whole phrase. Pure mumbo-jumbo; no other word for it.'

'But the people,' Pradeep replied mildly, 'will have received grace, inner strength, through the prayers they themselves will have offered up, as much as through the intercession of the priest. They were there out of their love for God.'

Roy, who was flattered Paula had adopted his phrase so quickly, now joined in.

'Doubtful; not sure about their love for God. Non-attendance means Hell-fire. I'd say it was either the Rule of Terror, or to do with vanity. If God is everywhere, why bother to go to church? Seems obvious it's to show themselves off. A social occasion.'

'That,' Pradeep said, 'sounds more like the Church of England than the Catholic Church.' He saw Radha come in and stood up, ready to leave.

'Pradeep, you will stay, won't you? Lamb biriani, I made it especially for the children. You'll see it's good.'

'I'm sure it is, but ...' Suddenly, sensing Radha wanted him to stay, he said, 'Can't resist. Thank you; happens to be my favourite dish.'

After the merest hesitation, Pradeep took the seat Radha indicated at the head of the table. Roy presided at the other end.

Sitting on Pradeep's right, Paula was able to study him at leisure: good looking, she mused, tall dark and handsome as the saying goes; his build was probably what's called athletic. Unruly hair, but it suited him. When had he entered this household, she wondered, there'd been no mention of a Pradeep in any of her mother's letters, or had there? Unexpectedly *chic* considering he was Indian. Fortunately they'd got off the thorny subject of religion. He was doing justice to the biriani, and now Mena joined forces with him.

'Super food,' she chirped in, 'Hey, Paula, better than Sister Raphael's rice, isn't it?'

'Tell us more; what's this story about Sister Raphael and her rice?' Roy asked.

'The food at the convent,' Paula began, 'was quite inedible. Whatever you have to say about the horrors of the dining hall at Probus, I assure you ours was a thousand times worse; honestly don't think words exist to describe the slurp that was dished out to us. Then one day, at long last, we were promised a rice dish. We couldn't immediately understand what Sister Dimsim was going on about –'

'Oh, Paula, did you really call her Sister Dimsim?' Mena asked excitedly, and Paula acquiesced with a smile.

'Getting nowhere with the word 'rice',' Paula went on, 'Dimsim eventually called it *curry*. This was early on, our English was, let's say, limited. By the time the rice *pudding* arrived (that, uncle Pradeep, in case you don't know, is a sort of gluey mess of rice, milk and sugar – totally unpalatable to the uninitiated), Mena's disappointment was such, at this point, she took her revenge by sicking it up all over the poor nun.'

'No, Paula, I didn't do it on purpose; it just came out, you know that.'

'I'm sure you didn't mean it,' Pradeep said soothingly, 'but it really must have been difficult going from your mother's cooking to that.'

Praise for Radha's cuisine was interrupted by the servant who came out with the grandmother's tray and was waiting for further instructions. On noticing the food had hardly been touched, Radha was about to coax the old lady, then decided to tempt her with the dessert – crème caramel.

'Is that a suitable dessert for a diabetic?' Roy asked, perhaps prescient of his father's chosen vocation for him.

'Poor *Ummuma*, bad diabetes. *Ummuma* not see,' Leela put in. Before Radha could say anything, Pradeep explained.

'Good point, Roy. You should make a good doctor one day. However, I think in this case, there's probably no harm. Your grandmother is too far gone for such precautions to be of any value. Anything you can get her to eat will be a bonus.'

And so the meal came to an end and Pradeep left soon after while Radha went to see if she could persuade her mother to eat a little something. The old lady looked so near her end, Radha felt a moment of panic in case she died while the English children were still at home. She could see it was difficult for them having to keep quiet, walking round on tiptoes, so much of her attention given to her dying mother rather than to them. And now, it would be the last straw if *Ummuma* died and they had to attend a funeral! What a home-coming!

Soon after, as if reading her daughter's thoughts, the old lady perked up visibly and when Radha went in to see her one morning, she found her sitting at her dressing table, more or less dressed, peering unseeingly into the mirror, combing her thin grey hair that fell in straggly long strands.

'What's this, *Umma*, you're feeling better then?' Radha asked in amazement.

'You remember that sari from Bina Bazaar? What a day that was! D'you remember, Radha? That's the one you must wear.'

'The turquoise silk? Of course I'll wear it, if you want me to. But, are you really getting up, *Umma*?' Radha asked, alarmed at the idea.

'There must be something suitable among the things I brought over. You'll find me something, won't you? All of us together in the photograph.'

'Photograph?' Radha asked, fearing her mother's mind was beginning to wander.

'One last photograph; what d'you say? Of you, me, and the children, all together.'

Radha said nothing, feeling the tears choking her again just as they'd done at communion, except there was something of joy mingled with the pain this time.

'I wanted you to have every happiness, Radha, but it hasn't worked out that way. I chose the wrong man.'

'Oh, no, *Umma*! Don't say such a thing. It's not you who chose wrongly, but in life, sometimes, we're tried to the utmost.' Radha's voice trailed off into the silence in the room.

A single tear ran down the old woman's cheek and landed on her hand. She neither felt it nor could she see it. Her voice was shaking badly when she spoke.

'You should tell the children to get ready; perhaps Paula will phone for the car to come in an hour's time. And Radha, the photograph – a good traditional arrangement.'

They took that group photo her mother wanted. An ordeal from start to finish: preparing the old lady, the walk from her room to the car, getting her in the front seat, out to the shop, sitting for the photo. And afterwards the whole journey in reverse.

One last shot of the three generations all together with the mother and grandmother seated in front and the four children behind. All exactly as the old lady had wanted.

Leela, standing just behind her mother, had learnt not to grin. She'd learnt through her mother's experiences that life was not a laughing matter. But Paula's and Mena's gaze held hope and expectation – there was a resemblance between them in that smile. And Roy, what exactly was that expression on his face? Could he be said to have no feeling if he looked so guilty at feeling nothing? On the old lady's face courage shone out most. And there, central to her family, Radha, a smile to fight through another day.

Chapter 45

That summer when the three children came home, after the car carrying them to their mother had pulled out of sight, the Doctor went in and sat down heavily at his desk, burying his head in his hands. The hours passed but he remained there, alone, fighting his anger. What a rejection! All those years away from the bigoted influence of their mother and they'd learnt nothing. It was as if they hadn't been away at all. Worse, their action had not been prompted by her.

During the intervening years since he'd left Radha, the Doctor's life had moved on. Had he wanted, he and Luk could have rubbed shoulders with the select of Kuala Lumpur. Radha had ceased to exist in his life. Payments were made automatically into her bank account, and that was that. He supposed he had that depressing fatalistic creed of hers to thank for not having been pestered over the years. He really was well and truly rid of her.

Yet the truth was, not a day passed without her image rising in the forefront of his mind to rob him of his inner peace. Over the years, he had come to loathe her for this invasion.

Now as he sat fighting his anger and frustration, he wondered how it was *she* managed to command such loyalty from the children. Letters, doubtless in pidgin English, that somehow won their hearts more than all the time and dollars he'd heaped on them. He wasn't asking much, not love or devotion such as she obviously got. All he wanted was their respect; their acceptance of his freedom to choose; their recognition of Luk. Instead they'd turned away, tantamount to slapping him in the face with their polite phrasing in English – the language they owed to him.

His children (not Leela of course), had become an essential part of his life. If he'd arranged for them to come home, it was because he wanted to see the change in them after living in a civilized country. To make sure there was no trace of their early upbringing. The new perspective should allow them to see he'd had a point in leaving their mother.

'New perspective? Hell!' he muttered aloud. Nothing had changed, though it was true they hadn't yet set eyes on her. The deuce! That proved more than anything how deeply her influence penetrated their psyche.

They'd not even seen her, but they rejected him out of whatever it was they felt for her. Each of their fares had cost as much as a year's school fees. No, it wasn't the money; he'd spent it willingly. It had been his choice and they owed him nothing for it. Even so, this was a humiliating blow. He'd not expected them to be still fighting a battle that had been won and lost a long time ago. But who had won, and who had lost? Nothing was clear now.

At almost seven-thirty that evening, Ayu, the servant, was ready to announce '*sec fana*' but she stood just outside the kitchen not daring to come further in. Earlier, she'd brought the tea tray but had removed it when Luk told her it would not be needed. Now she was wondering if supper too would go the same way.

Luk now stepped into the study and said, 'Must eat.'

He got up without looking at her and sat down at the dining table. Ayu served him the usual white fish of one sort or other, cooked to his specifications – steamed without salt. Luk served the vegetables after she'd helped herself to the lobster.

'Better forget now. Ungrateful children. Eat and forget.' Luk ventured, none too confidently.

'I will not forget them,' he roared. 'They are my children. It is to help them develop an independent mind I have spent so much time and money on them. I will not give up.'

'That is good. You misunderstanding me. Eat now,' she said, more conciliatory.

The rest of the meal passed in silence.

Two days later, he sent a message via the driver addressed to the three children:

I trust you are rested.

I suggest we meet this afternoon before I reopen the dispensary so as to discuss past progress and plans for your future.

The driver will come at two-thirty to pick you up.

Thus they met at the Doctor's house after a nervous lunch. No allusion was made to the previous visit. That episode might never have taken place except there was no offer of coffee or any other refreshment. The Doctor turned to Roy and began with a hint of jocularity.

'So, how's the future surgeon shaping up? Your report relating to Biology and General Science are luke warm. Not your favourite subjects?'

Roy tried not to gulp but failed. Surgeon! So, that's what he was going to be one day. Following in the old man's footsteps before the war had altered his course. Well, if his father said so, no doubt that's what he would be, even though science was definitely in the category of the mumbo jumbo. He cleared his throat before tackling the old man.

'It's OK; I'd say I was slightly above average.' He coughed, embarrassed by the lie which seemed to him so glaring. He changed the subject adroitly, 'I'd like to make a butterfly collection while I'm here; science master thought it a good idea. Hope you agree.'

'You haven't said much about your work but I suppose that means there are no outstanding problems. Butterfly collection, hmm, zoology is a recognized branch of biology and therefore not totally irrelevant to your eventual needs. At least it means you'll be spending your time profitably during these holidays. I hadn't foreseen Probus closing down; result of crippling taxation. Socialism! – fortunately, the timing could be worse as far as your schooling is concerned. I've managed to get you into Bishop's Stortford.' He paused an instant in order to work out the logistics.

Roy let out a silent sigh of relief: at least they were off the sticky subject of his report and, still more important, his return to UK was assured. Phew! Surgeon – that meant he'd be chopping up live bodies; which part, he wondered. His preference would be probably for the liver, because it reacted interestingly to alcohol. He had no time at all for the heart: it was unreliable, given to changing; stopping and starting. But the liver – he'd be able to find out exactly what happened when he sloshed all that wine into it. He had a vague recollection of his granddad whose body had been put on exhibit on a wooden bed in Pondicherry; cold mortality stretched out for the scrutiny of young and old. Pondicherry – place to be avoided – full of disease and death. His father's voice cut through his lurid images.

'... stout shoes. The ground will be swampy with leaches but the driver will have a supply of salt. The hot end of an extinguished match is equally effective as is a lighted cigarette.' Roy had difficulty taking it all in; his father was now saying '... jar of powdered chloroform. Take it with you so that you can drop them in on location. That way, you're assured of undamaged specimens. Driver will also show you where to get a suitable net and display cases.' The Doctor turned his attention to the girls.

Roy was thankful his turn was over. He had survived!

'I'm pleased to hear all three of you have a good grasp of English and speak it with the proper accent. Nothing more comic than a foreigner speaking a language with a regional peculiarity.' He let out a short laugh and the three children joined in, relieved to have passed that test satisfactorily.

'And now, tell me about St Gertrude's,' the Doctor said to Paula.

'Afraid you may be disappointed – if the standard was any lower, it would lie somewhere at the bottom of the Atlantic.'

The Doctor laughed at her turn of phrase and hid his disappointment.

'I had no idea! Bottom of the Atlantic, ha! The end of term reports were always most encouraging. Why didn't you let me know?'

'How could I? Our letters were always vetted.' Paula thanked her lucky stars she'd been prepared for that one.

'There are always ways ... but, let that be; no good crying over spilt milk. In any case, it's time you moved to somewhere more central if you're to make your career in an international organization. I've arranged for you to attend a finishing school next year near Oxford; after that, you'll be joining your brother Julius, at Trinity College Dublin.'

He became lost in thought. Paula felt like dancing with glee on hearing St Gertrude's was over. It had been on the cards mainly because of her age, but it was nice to have confirmation. That bit about 'international organization' was sweet music to her ears.

On the other hand, the idea of going to Ireland one day (a country that had never struck her as *chic*) and, to cap it, with Julius, was less cheery. Her last view of Julius, precisely three years before, a trip organized by the nuns (but no doubt masterminded by their father), had taken her and Mena from Penzance by coach to their brothers' school. Julius was definitely not, and never would be *chic*.

However, for the time being, there was plenty of cause for jubilation: she'd be free of her mother, and the Convent and, at last, Mena. Dublin was a long way ahead; with a bit of luck Julius would be somewhere else by then, or better still, she'd be sent to the Continent; perhaps to Switzerland where they made watches as exquisite as diamond bracelets.

'In all seriousness – how well taught is Science?' her father asked. 'I need to know if Mena is to continue there.'

'Science?' Paula laughed, 'There's no such subject as "Science". Anyone showing too keen an interest in that area, is likely to end up in Coventry.'

'Sounds drastic,' he remarked.

'It was – solitary confinement on bread and water.' she was delighted to expose one of the less well-publicized practices of the nuns.

'But this is positively Dickensian! From what I can make out, you've been confined to three years at Dotheboys Hall.' He laughed to cover up his annoyance. After a moment he asked, 'So, what were the 'Sciences' mentioned in the school report?'

'The nuns were not short on imagination,' Paula said, with glee. She'd waited a long time to get her own back on those nuns. The Doctor laughed again and turned his gaze to his youngest daughter.

'Well, no chance of your making it as General Practitioner if we leave you there, hm?'

General Practitioner? What on earth was that, Mena wondered. And now he was talking about his dispensary. Oh, no, surely not! He couldn't mean he wanted her to be a *doctor* like him. All those sick people waiting to be cured. No, that was not at all what she wanted to do. What she liked was poetry, and verse and acting and things like that. She bit her lip – should she, *could* she tell him? Was now the right moment?

But he'd already turned back to Paula.

'I shall write immediately to Mother Superior to thank her for raising the level of your knowledge to such a high point that you need no further education. Then I'll explain I acted too hastily in sending Mena away at such a tender age. I shall ask her to send both your belongings to Gabbitas & Thring.' He now addressed Mena once more, 'By the way, what was the mention of the drama prize in your report?'

'Oh, that was very exciting. That's what, that's what I really like – acting – it was the Cranborne festival of Drama and Poetry and I was the only candidate from the convent. A prefect had to go with me all the way there and back, by coach.' She stole a glance at Paula – was she talking too much? Paula was looking bored. She must get to the point. 'I recited a passage from 'A Midsummer Night's Dream' – it was Puck. Then a poem by Blake about a piper. I won first prize. That's what I like – poetry, and ...'

'Bravo! So, something good came out of that place after all. But after such a fiasco, academically speaking, I shall not relegate you to another convent simply so as to pander to your mother's conscience. Three precious years when we should have been laying foundations for your scientific career, lost through ignorance and superstition! It's important to learn from our mistakes and not repeat them.' He nodded gravely. 'Hmm, musn't keep my patients waiting. I'll certainly have plenty to occupy me during these 'holidays'.'

From the look on his face, it was clear he was not complaining. Paula, however, wondered how he managed to overcome the disappointment he must be feeling after planning everything so meticulously only to land them in such a dump as that convent. And for three whole years!

Chapter 46

Once they were back home, Roy heaved a sigh of relief, 'Phew, survived that skirmish,'

'What d'you mean?' Paula asked, knowing what he meant.

'A bit like a military campaign, wasn't it? I mean, a five year plan with pins marking the strategic positions on the board. Guess he's trying to equal, if not beat, Gandhi and Nehru. We, under his generalship, are no doubt destined to become world leaders.' Seeing Paula was not entering into the spirit of his banter, he quickly added, 'Not that I'm complaining – a surgeon commands a lot of respect. Looks as though Mena is to take over his practice; she didn't look thrilled about it.'

'Actually, he didn't have much choice – I started out too late – in any case, he's chosen the right career for me.'

'What exactly is it? Thought it sounded a bit vague, "international organization".'

'Not absolutely sure, but he'll know what he's talking about. Can't wait to return to civilization. Got a bit of a shock seeing Luk at the airport. Can't imagine how father actually *chose* her! As for her English, mother's pidgin effort used to infuriate him; why replace her with someone even less gifted in languages?'

'The surprising thing is *he* sounds as though he was born and bred in the Palace of Westminster.'

'Hey, you're right, but don't you agree about Luk?'

'*She* probably chose *him*. Besides, we don't know what his criteria are in choosing a – er, companion. But I shan't lose sleep over it – he's got the sheckles; he can do as he pleases. As long as he keeps paying the bills, can't say I'm bothered who he chooses to spend his time with.'

Paula was momentarily struck into silence. She hadn't been aware of this gap in their separate attitudes to their father. No, it was more fundamental than that – it was, rather, to life in general. However, no point in dwelling on their differences while stuck out here.

'At least he cares about us,' she concluded. 'He realized something had to be done and is getting on with it. My knight in shining armour, come to rescue me from a fate worse than death, which, I can promise you, is what that convent was and life with mother would be.'

Leela who had been hanging around, hoping to be included in their conversation, recognized these words from the days when Paula used to entertain her and Mena on wet afternoons with her theatrical improvisations. Thinking there was a chance for more of the same, she now urged Paula enthusiastically.

'Fate worse than death – play, Paula, play. Princess Paula and fate worse than death. Prince in shining armour. Roy, here. Play, come.'

'What are you jabbering about?' Paula asked.

'Think she wants you to play the piano,' Roy translated with a wry smile.

'Piano! Not likely – bet it hasn't been tuned since I was last here.'

'No can do. Piano cracked,' Roy told Leela with an apologetic gesture of his hand.

'That's not the only thing round here that's cracked,' was Paula's opinion.

Leela in the meantime wondered what the piano had to do with it but she moved away, sensing she was not wanted. The problem was, she didn't want to join Mena who had returned, somehow taller than her and a different colour. She didn't like it. The sooner her younger sister went back on that terrifying thing they called a plane the better, she decided.

Paula continued in a conspiratorial tone.

'Mother hasn't budged an inch since we were last here; actually tried to arrange a marriage for me! I told her what I thought of that. And this house, have you noticed – not a thing changed in all this time: same two portraits on the wall with the two of them glaring at each other, same 'precious' vases, trophies of an earlier period, same curtains, same dog, same servants! All older and more dilapidated, needless to say. Has anything happened during these three years other than the old girl coming here to die?'

'There's a definite hidden advantage in the G of P being here –'

'G of P?'

'Ghost of Pondy. Her being here means the 'prayer room' where some sort of minor ritual goes on in front of the idol, is out of bounds. We've been saved all sorts of mysteries.'

'True; I suppose we have to be thankful for small mercies. Hey, did you notice the way Leela was holding her spoon? There's been a definite regression in that area; it was upside down! As for the fork, she was eyeing it as though it might have been an instrument of torture. I suspect cutlery hasn't been in daily use. Either that or she's not all there, and that is more than a distinct possibility. Hearing the two of them gabbling away in Tamil, which now sounds thoroughly vulgar to me, makes this place more of a hell-hole than ever.'

'Mmm, that old friend of mother's, Agnes? I think she's the scribe behind the quaint letters we get; she hasn't cropped up in any of the conversations. A bit odd; they were such close chums. Not that there's been much conversation as such; my Tamil's pretty shaky. A shade better than Mena's, however, which is non-existent.'

'Oh, don't you know, the Actress has other things on her mind!' Paula said, rounding her vowels in mock grandiloquence.

'Not sure she'll be allowed to pursue that career though Father did seem pleased about her prize.'

'Yes, Father was generally helpful; he saw straightaway what you were talking about re the butterflies.' She paused, then said excitedly, 'Hey, what about Valentino? I imagine he accepted mother's invitation to lunch because he was intrigued by us.'

'Wrong track. Seems quite obvious to me what he's up to.'

'Really? What?'

'Totally smitten. Pradeep only has one interest and that is mother.'

'What? You've got to be joking!'

'He's sweet on her, no doubt about it. Gazes at her with those doggy eyes; he'd do anything for her. Did you see how he leapt to her rescue? – the crème caramel – he virtually jumped down my throat. As for lunch, she only had to ask and he says – couldn't resist!'

'But she's so ancient! And primitive. D'you think it's reciprocated? Hey, what'll happen to us?'

'What d'you mean?'

'Hold on, this is a disastrous scenario – both parents hitched up with new partners! Nothing good ever comes to the first batch. And what about Leela?'

'Nothing will happen to us. Not exactly under mother's wing, are we? It's father's dosh that counts and, hopefully, since there's enough to go round, he won't do anything unfriendly. As for Leela, that's not negotiable. But Pradeep would accept anything as long as he gets his beloved.'

'I hadn't foreseen anything like this,' Paula said, feeling inexplicably put out.

'Mind you, all that is purely hypothetical. The fact is,' Roy added with a snigger, 'nothing will happen. Having said that, I can't be one hundred percent certain, if you see what I mean. She does look rejuvenated when this Pradeep character is around, and there's no denying it, it'd be a smart move on her part.'

In this way, although remaining on parallel lines, brother and sister managed to while away the tedious hours that stretched before them till their return to England.

Mena was not invited to join their discussions, nor would she have understood what they were talking about. The eagerly anticipated reunion with her mother had turned out to be non-existent. Her inability to formulate even simple sentences in Tamil was frustrating for her and distressing to her mother. She longed to reach Radha but the outward, physical changes that had taken place while she'd been away, made her a stranger to her own mother. She felt rejected, and so did Radha. And where Leela was concerned, Leela, her childhood playmate, the sister who in her heart had seemed to care about her during those lonely years of separation, now, Leela too was out of reach. Perhaps she always had been. The distance was so great she would not have known where to begin.

There was no one at home with whom she could communicate. The very house was no longer familiar: the shutter in the upstairs room resisted as much as ever, making her smile whenever she used it, but the air within the house smelt different – a joss-stick now burned each morning before the statue of the Virgin and, though the gardenia still graced the vase, its scent was overpowered by the smell of incense.

*

The six-week-holiday was over. The time had come for her three children to fly away to England. The three Revelation suitcases stood open on the upstairs landing, waiting for last minute additions. Radha walked past them, trying not to look, trying to stop the terrible pain in her heart. Just three boxes, that's all they were, made of card and covered with canvas, containing clothes and bits and pieces people collect and discard as they go along. And yet they seemed to her as whole as three lives. Three children she'd brought into this world and who were now leaving for ever. She sensed she'd never see them again.

Trying to keep her voice even, she handed each of them an envelope.

'Inside is a photograph of all of us together – a family. It will help you to remember.'

And now it was time to put on her red sari: red the symbol of joy. All the joy she wished them in their young lives. May they have happiness in everything they touched. A mother's blessing on their head. She'd hardly thought of her husband that morning, but now as she pinned the slim gold brooch across her shoulder, she remembered he'd given it to her for her birthday, just days after she'd given birth to Roy. It had felt like a present for bringing Roy into the world.

Leela was already dressed, waiting nervously near the suitcases, refusing to look at them directly. It was a confusing moment for her: she was pleased not to be going off in a plane herself, and she wanted all three of them gone. All the same, these minutes of waiting made her feel muddled.

Mena was subdued; she'd hardly uttered a word all morning, but she too was ready and now shut her case with a finality that made it hard for her to breathe. Paula asked Roy to hold the lid down while she shut hers. Roy checked his, one last time, before shutting it and putting all three in a row for the gardener to take down.

Radha put on her favourite record to fill in the silence that had crept in between them. A Strausss waltz played in the background, the tone cracked with age. Before long Roy and Paula, she knew, would stop writing. Mena, she supposed, would persist, but though the messages would come regularly, they'd be meaningless – what would either of them ever have to say to each other? They had so little in common; no language between them, no common culture. But the letters would begin with 'Darling Mummy' and end 'With lots of love' just as they always had, and she was moved.

The children were scattered into the wind to be buffeted over the corners of the earth. That is how it was, and she had to accept it.

So that when the three of them returned to far away England, Radha only spent one night crying the hours away because she couldn't help it. Leela soothed her, telling her they were better off on their own. And, sadly, that was true.

Chapter 47

The old lady never left her room these days. The bathroom was at the far end to the left; a shallow step down, though even that had to be carefully negotiated. She'd adapted to the modern convenience without a word; nothing Roman about it. Printed on the white china, Radha had read out to her, *Thomas Crapper*, the name of the man who'd designed it. Anyway, no one but she used it and that was fine. These new contraptions had their good points as long as hygiene was strictly observed. As for her room, although it was comfortable, she was ready to die.

She should have come a lot earlier but how was she to know? Not that she'd have been any use. But she could have given Radha support, helped her to feel less alone, been there to listen to her. There was Leela. Leela would still be here when she herself was gone. Leela – a mixed blessing.

A few days after the English children had left, when Radha looked in on her mother one evening, she found her sitting on the edge of her bed, a sari wound loosely round her, her hands lying in her lap, clasped as if in prayer.

Several strands of hair had escaped the bun at the nape of her neck. Her feet were bare. No sandals in sight; perhaps she'd thrown them away, feeling she had no further use for them. Even so, the old lady had gone to some trouble to prepare herself; it was clear to Radha she was waiting for her. Going over to the bed, she sat down next to her.

'The children,' the old lady began, 'they were all here; all except Julius.'

'Yes *Umma,* not easy for you with all the bustle over the last six weeks. But it's quieter now. Back to normal.'

'That's not what I meant; not what I was thinking.' Several moments slipped by as she tried to gather her thoughts once more. 'What was I going to say?' Another long pause.

'What's bothering you, tell me. You know we have no secrets between us.'

'Should have come years ago,' a deep sigh, 'Not like this, just at the end.'

'Oh, I'd have liked that! – to have had you here. When I came to you with the children, when he sent me to India, I remember thinking – but for the war, a war that was wrenching me from him, I wouldn't have been coming to you.' Taking her mother's hand in hers, she said, 'Not so different now – if he'd been here, it would have been difficult for you to come.'

'Difficult?' the old lady shook her head slowly, 'Impossible.'

'You see what I'm saying, don't you, *Umma*? Out of the saddest things in life, we sometimes get our dearest wishes. I'm so glad you're here. To think I might never have seen you again! I'm really happy you came, happy you gave me this chance to do something – so little – but still something in return for everything you've given me.'

'You, Radha – my dearest – I had to come.' The two women sat in silence for a while.

'How the children have changed!' Radha said, trying to keep the pain out of her voice. 'If I'd tried to tell you in a letter, I wouldn't have known where to begin.'

'The children – that's what I wanted to tell you – they were all here.'

'Yes, *Umma*, you said that; all except Julius. And now, I'm afraid you may never ... that is, I don't know when Julius will be over next.' If ever, she thought.

'But *he* never came!'

'Who never came?' Radha asked, knowing exactly who, but unsure if she was ready to discuss it. Besides, her mother was so frail, to be reminded of that distant past now.

'Their father. He never came to the house while they were here.'

Radha had lain awake, wondering if he'd put in an appearance. The last time he'd come, it had been to take Paula and Mena from her. She shuddered at the memory.

Three years had passed since then, and in that time, all thought of a united family had slipped away. It had been an impossible dream. She wondered if she'd known all along it was nothing but a dream, but had clung to it, just to keep going. Now that the illusion was gone, what was there left?

She sat next to her mother and said nothing, because there was nothing to say.

'Radha, my dear child, it's time you stopped waiting for him.'

'Stop waiting?'

'Listen, Radha,' she let out a deep sigh, 'at your age, I too was alone; had been for a while. But I got on with life. There's no need to bury yourself like this, waiting endlessly.'

'If I was waiting, it was because I wanted the children to have what you and *Uppa* gave me – a loving family.' (God, how she'd longed for that!) 'But, in his absence, my every thought became concentrated on that void. I ceased to be. My children – orphans; no father, no mother. I should have stood in for him; been a father *and* a mother to them as you were to me when *Uppa* died. I failed most completely there where I wanted most to succeed.'

'No shame in failing. In life, things happen and we do what we can. We may not always take the wisest course.' Her voice trailed off and Radha, remembering the marriage arrangements made all those years ago, squeezed her mother's hand gently. The old lady murmured softly, 'We're weighed down with our hopes, our expectations, our experiences; but we do our best.' A nod, then, turning to Radha with renewed vigour, she continued, 'if, later, time grants us a clearer vision over our past, and we see where we went wrong, it does no good to brood over our mistakes. Nor to carry on as though we hadn't seen.'

'What you're saying is so different from what I've always thought you wanted of me,' Radha murmured, scarcely daring to follow her mother's thoughts.

'When I say it's time you stopped waiting for him, I don't mean you should end your marriage though God knows you've done more than your fair share to keep it going. But you could live your life, knowing it's whole without him.'

When Radha began to explain, her voice seemed to come from a long way off, a wave surging from the depth of the ocean to break in a whisper into the silence of that room.

'This waiting, if that really is what I've been doing, is part of me. It is what I am; what I've always been. It's a way of living; there are so many ways of living, this is mine. Think of it as no more than that. My task and my trial. My vocation, you could say.'

'It doesn't have to be. No one is worth such a sacrifice.'

'But the sacred vows, I thought you ... how am I to know this isn't part of His design?'

'To live again doesn't mean you have to go against His laws. You will not be breaking your marriage vows simply by leaving this place. You could go to your brother Ravi.'

'But you can see why I can't go to Ravi. *You* could have gone to him; moved two streets down from your house, remained in the White Quarter of Pondy. It would have been so easy, so convenient. Instead you're here. What a journey for someone in your state, sick and almost blind! Ravi's loss is my gain. No, I am where I should be. This is my home.'

Both women had grown used to silence; much of their life had been made up of it, and now, they sat without saying anything for a long time. Finally, the old lady smiled to herself and nodded.

'Radha, you're your mother's daughter – stubborn as a mule! – but for all that, I love and admire you.' She sighed softly, then murmured, 'I feel tired; think I'll sleep now.'

Radha arranged the sari round her shoulders and helped her lie down, pulling the sheet up as the old lady felt cold. She sat on the edge of the bed, her mother's words whirling round her head.

Until now she'd never doubted for a moment the virtue of her conduct. The certainties she'd lived with, the clear-cut line that had dictated her way of life, it was all wiped out in an instant. The towering edifice had come crumbling down. No banner, no garland to honour its passage. Simply a void. Far from clothing her in a virtuous garment, this waiting suddenly exposed her with its hollowness. She'd buried her life within a living dream; where would she find the courage to stand once more in the glare of the real world?

Stirring herself at last, she was about to steal out of the room when she became aware of a stillness too profound for sleep. Radha caught her breath: surely death cannot come as peacefully as this?

But the old lady had unburdened her heart and shared her last life force with the child she loved.

Radha had known from the moment her mother had come she would die soon. That, after all, was the reason why she'd come – to die near the one person who meant so much to her. And yet, when it happened, that moment when Radha, sitting on the edge of the old lady's bed, suddenly wondered at how very still she seemed, she felt an anguish she could never have imagined. And Leela, coming in and seeing her mother, knew immediately what had happened and the two of them held each other and wept.

Chapter 48

Pradeep arranged everything: the requiem mass, the burial in the Catholic cemetery. Brother Leo was there. Agnes had never met *Ummuma*, but she heard of her death in the announcements in church. She therefore sent her friend a kind letter of condolence. Radha was so moved, her tears made it almost impossible for her to read the words:

> *My dear friend, you cannot imagine how sadly I miss you, and how much I regret my weakness.*
> *But I remember the times we had together, and know that they were among the happiest moments of my life. I will always remember you and Leela with true affection.*
> *Accept my deepest sympathy at this moment of your great loss.*

After the funeral, Pradeep would have stayed to help in whatever way he could but Radha felt she needed to be alone.

That morning, standing in the cemetery, watching her mother's coffin being lowered into the ground, she felt her world slipping out of control. She tried to pray but her mother's voice was quietly insistent, *You don't have to. No one is worth such a sacrifice. Live a whole life.* What was a whole life?

Radha's hand flew to her mouth, good God! What was that thing about talents her husband used to go on about? Had she, like the foolish servant, buried God's gift of a life, to whimper year after year without making the least effort to live?

She felt she might pass out. Slipping Leela's hand through her arm, Radha pulled herself together with difficulty. But the disturbing thought refused to lie low.

Her cousin's voice now pierced through the haze.

'Will you be all right? When can I come and see you?'

'I don't know. I need time to think. Pradeep, I 'm sorry.

'If you need anything, any time, any time at all ...' For a moment, he sat still, looking down at his hands, fingers interlaced, lying open in his lap; a begging bowl waiting for alms. Capable hands, gentle and strong. And yet, at this moment, how useless they were, powerless to soothe away the pain from the woman he loved. Why couldn't he act decisively? Was he not known and valued precisely for that quality? What was the use of his reputation if here, when he needed to take over, he was paralysed into inaction! He took a deep breath and stood up. 'Radha, I'm here if you need me. Don't forget, will you?' With that he left.

A war was raging within Radha which she alone could resolve. She looked in on *Ummuma*'s room which the servants had cleaned and returned once more to a prayer room. Leela, who'd been following her around, pointed out the vase was empty – no gardenia. It made Radha smile; yes, it would be as easy as that to pick up the thread where they'd left off. Another year, and yet another, of waiting for– what?

Ummuma had been here such a short time, yet nothing would be as it had been before.

Radha was crushed by a sense of failure. So many years which of a sudden had no meaning. *No shame in failure.* Hadn't Brother Leo once said there were more ways than one to the truth? Radha's head ached. Endless questions without answers turned round and round.

She went upstairs with Leela to the sitting area. A letter from Mena had arrived that morning; it lay unopened on the table. Radha picked it up absently and held it a long time, looking at Leela the while. What if ... she stopped short. Could she really change the course of a lifetime? Had she played the forlorn, abandoned wife, and all the while been waiting, not for that lost love sanctified by marriage, but to be free of him?

The thought took her breath away. To have lived all her life, certain of controlling the vagaries of her heart; certain no one but Manicasami could enter there, and now, of a sudden, free fall! Oh, God, thought Radha, *Ummuma*'s words had never meant this! She felt dizzy as the question formed itself again – what if ...?

'Leela, what if ...' she gripped the chair and began again, 'What if we go away from ...'

'Not go. This, good family house. Not want aeroplane. Stay here.'

'No, I promise no aeroplane. But this house – no one will come now. We've had all the family that's ever likely to be here. They've gone to live their lives somewhere else. Whole lives that will bring them happiness. We too will have to learn to live.'

'What, *Umma*?'

'What indeed! I'm talking in riddles. The truth is, I myself don't understand or know what to think. But whatever happens, we, Leela, you and I, will always be together.'

*

Several days went by. Then, one morning, Radha sat down at the table upstairs to write a letter. How should she address him? Husband – he no longer was. Doctor – sounded foolish. It would have to be the old name she'd once loved, though never used. And it would have to be in Tamil. Would he need a translator by now? Hopefully, the man will do an adequate job:

Dear Manicasami,

My mother's death has left a void in my life here in Kuala Lumpur, which is hard to bear. I have therefore decided to return to Pondicherry with Leela. You no doubt know my mother left me our old family house.

My decision to leave has nothing to do with what you might or might not want; it merely happens to coincide with what you have been wanting for a long time.

You have always made all the moves in our

*life together and apart. Even now I am unsure how
to proceed. Perhaps you will instruct me in your
reply.*

Radha.

She read the letter again and knew she was going about
it the wrong way. She needed advice and Pradeep was the
right person to give it. But he was also the last person she
wished to involve in this matter. He could interpret it the
wrong way.

And so she sent it off, feeling, with a twinge of bitterness,
it would be welcome at the other end.

*

A whole week had passed and there was still no reply.
Each day felt like a month. Heavens! – did it mean he wanted
to keep in touch? Of course it didn't! Radha scolded herself
for allowing the thought to form.

Such silence all round! Not just from him. She was
sitting at her dressing table, fixing the gardenia she'd started
wearing once more in her hair. Why had *no one* been in
touch? Had she, of a sudden, become a pariah, she
wondered, more to herself than out loud, but Leela heard
and now added her own thought.

'Yes, *Umma*, why no one coming? No Uncle Pradeep,
no Aunty Agnes, Doctor not coming.'

Radha looked at Leela in the mirror, and took in the
full import of her words.

'What you've just said is so true! But it needn't be like
this, at least, not quite; Agnes ...'

'Yes, *Umma* – you saying Aunty Agnes? Not wanting alcohol?'

'Agnes – we can help; she only has fruit juice when she comes here.'

'Doctor say no alcohol.'

'That is the Doctor's strictest rule; he never touches alcohol. We all have rules. Leela, don't you think ours could be to be a true friend to our friends?'

'Aunty Agnes – friend. When Agnes coming, *Umma*?'

'Next Sunday, after Mass. We'll look for her then, that's what we'll do.' And Radha smiled with anticipation.

Chapter 49

S udden sounds outside made Leela run across to look out of the window. She cried excitedly it was Brother Leo's car. Brother Leo here today, thought Radha, so soon after seeing them at *Ummachi*'s funeral! He did come quite regularly, even so, not quite as often as this. Radha put on her sari with speed, and made her way down, followed by Leela.

Although Brother Leo did not know the full story, he understood how devastating *Ummachi*'s death must be for Radha. He listened attentively while she unburdened herself, then went on to take him into her confidence, that is, up to a point.

'I wrote to – Manicasami – yes, you're no doubt surprised to hear me call him by his name, but at last, I feel he is no longer my husband.'

'Radha, I know you've written, and I want to tell you straightaway how entirely I agree with you – my brother hasn't been a husband to you since the early years of your marriage. He isn't worthy of the title of husband.'

Brother Leo and Radha had always been as brother and sister, even so, the frankness of his words astonished her. She was also amazed to hear he knew about her letter but she remained silent, waiting to hear what he had to say.

'I'm here partly because of your letter; he hasn't replied because he wants to know if you'll give him a divorce.'

It was true. She had studiously avoided all mention of divorce in her letter.

'You know the ruling of the Church better than I,' she replied, 'When he first asked me, I told him I didn't have the right to do that. Was I wrong? Brother Leo, I'd – I'd like to give him a divorce, but I don't know if ...' She broke off suddenly. The moment she said it she knew it was true. That is what she wanted – a divorce!

Brother Leo looked at her searchingly and she looked back without flinching. He nodded; she thought it meant approval, but of what? Smiling gently, he began.

'I want to speak to you as a friend; to give you my personal opinion. The Church doesn't have much leeway on issues of this nature. She's unable to look at each separate case and give a ruling that fits that particular one. It happens occasionally when the Holy Father himself is asked to intervene.

'I know my brother's nature; he has gone too far down the wrong road to turn back now. He won't do it. You've been a model of patience and faithfulness; I'd understand if you felt enough is enough. It isn't right to waste your life waiting for him. He won't come.'

'More or less *Ummachi*'s words,' Radha said, softly. 'Brother Leo, can you tell me – if I grant him – this divorce, will my life – what I mean is, I don't think the Church will let me share a life with someone else. Is that true?'

'Which is why I told you I was speaking as a friend.' There was a pause while he put his thoughts in order. 'I'm helped in what I'm about to say by the knowledge your decision would never lead you to act selfishly, or in a way that's harmful to another.' Another pause. Finally, looking straight at her, he said, 'Whatever the Church's ruling, whatever course you decide on, you will always be very dear to me. Radha, if I, an ordinary man, can tell you that, is it likely that God in His mercy, who loves us beyond all measure, would be harder on you in His judgement? I really think you will not cease to be one of His children simply because, after so many years of trial, you choose to live.'

There were tears in Radha's eyes. She supposed they were of relief, perhaps gratitude too that Brother Leo, whose opinion she valued so greatly, had dared to step outside his discipline to encourage and support her just when she needed it so badly. Radha took his hands in hers and held them as she whispered, 'A true friend.'

*

Up till now, Radha's life had been complete in one sense, filled with the certainty she was doing the right thing. Waking up from an illusion could have left her bewildered. Instead there was a dizzying sense of freedom.

She'd sent off a second letter to the Doctor to say he could have his divorce. His reply was prompt and the settlement seemed clear and fair. She felt an unexpected pain; it felt like a final dismissal. So many years of yearning for him. No, she had not yearned for him! She'd needed his love. It had been no more than that. The truth was, whatever he'd been a long time ago, he had become the one person who was totally incapable of giving her the love she was looking for. She knew that now.

Although there'd been little discussion, Leela seemed to know what was going on better than Radha herself. After her initial reluctance, she'd welcomed her mother's plans, whatever they might be. And Radha had reassured her that a move would not entail a flight in an aeroplane which had seemed to be Leela's main worry.

It was only after she'd given instructions to the agent in charge of her house in Pondicherry that Radha decided at last to contact her cousin Pradeep to help with the legal and financial details.

Chapter 50

He came over at once. That was so like him; but now that he was here, he didn't know what to say. The coffee arrived as usual. Desperate to hide his nervousness, he drained it at once which only made him feel more jittery than ever. His new lace-ups pinched his toes and the tie round his neck was strangling him. Why on earth had he got himself up like this?

There was nothing he could do about the shoes but he could at least loosen the tie. His hand was halfway there when he realised that would only draw attention to his ridiculous get-up; instead, he grabbed the second cup of coffee which had arrived. She, as always, was looking so cool he longed to embrace her. The very thought made him hotter and more bothered than ever. But that brief glimpse showed him something was different about her. What was it? Sort of independent and quietly radiant. Or was he imagining it because he hadn't seen her for one whole interminably long week?

Radha wanted to thank him but her thoughts also were in disarray. The list of things she could thank him for was endless but that wasn't at all what was foremost in her mind. It was he himself, the man he was, that touched her so deeply. Could she thank him for that?

A lock of hair had come loose somewhere along the back of her neck; she could feel it, but didn't risk tucking it into the bun in case the whole lot came tumbling down. She'd been all fingers and thumbs doing it in the first place; that little gardenia Leela had plucked hadn't been easy to fix.

Looking across at him, she wished she'd put on the blue sari which was more dressy. He looked amazing – like a film star, she thought – shiny shoes, even a tie that suited him so well she couldn't help staring at it. First time she'd seen him so dressed up; on his way, no doubt, to see an important client.

Suddenly, they both began at once.

'I –'

'You first,' he said, feeling unaccountably relieved at not having to go first.

'No, really, you,' she said, trying to remember the order in which she was going to thank him.

'Yes, of course; me first. Um, Leela, could you ask the girl for a glass of water?'

'Water, Uncle Pradeep? Not want cold coffee?'

'Ah! Yes, a glass of water, please Leela, to go with the cold coffee.'

Leela ran off to supervise in the kitchen.

Pradeep felt he'd handled that rather well but now that he was alone with Radha, it wasn't any easier. Perhaps he should start by telling her how well he was doing at work? It would reassure her if they, that is, if she agreed to ...

'I feel it's time for Leela and me to think of Pondicherry,' she said, knowing he'd approve since the idea had come from him.

'Yes, I'm glad you mentioned Pondicherry,' he said with an emphatic nod. 'We're doing very well over there. One of our bright spots, you might say. As a matter of fact, we might even open a branch in Pondy itself.' He came to a sudden halt. What was that she'd said? Surely not that she might ... He looked at her and the smidgen of thought he'd retrieved went out of the window – her sari a shade of pink, so pale there should have been another word for it. Perhaps there was another word for it; he'd have to look it up. Not that pink was the only colour that looked good on her; any shade of any colour ...

Radha was puzzled. Surely Pradeep should have said something about her going to Pondy; his idea, after all. Once she was over there, she'd be able to find him a good wife. She knew what sort of person would suit him – not a widow, not too young either, horde of children in tow not a problem. Odd, that! Ravi could point her in the right direction.

Now Pradeep was looking hard at her in silence. Perhaps he didn't trust her to make the right choice? He regretted ever having suggested she should go to Pondy to look on his behalf! Not that he'd said that in as many words, but he'd have known she would once she was over there. Pradeep had changed his mind knowing she'd been out of it too long. That was it!

She turned away to hide her confusion. The tiny white gardenia in her hair shone bright against the glossy black where there were one or two highlights of grey.

'I love you, Radha!' Pradeep suddenly cried. What inspired him to come out with it at long last? Was it the gardenia? A feeling time was passing?

'Pradeep, I'll find someone perfect!' She stopped short and stared at him.

Having spoken his love, Pradeep now couldn't stop.

'I've always loved you, always,' he declared, rising impetuously and drawing her to him, shoes and tie forgotten in the frenzy of the moment. 'Everything about you, not just your beauty, a wonderful, special beauty, but everything else about you too. Apart from now, the happiest time of my life was when you came back from Saigon. Remember those months?'

'I remember. We used to walk along the sea front. Remember that time when ...?'

'So many shared dreams! And one day ...'

'In the Botanic Gardens, Pradeep, d'you remember sitting in the miniature railway? We talked of going to Kodaikanal one day.'

'O, Radha, you really do remember! Can you believe me, I have never stopped loving you. Now I'm asking you what I should have asked all those years ago, marry me, my dearest love, and we'll join together indissolubly that time and this.'

'Pradeep, such a wonderfully kind man!' She stopped, then murmured so softly she might have been in a confessional, 'my first love! But, I'm no longer young.'

'Radha, for me you're eternally yourself! Age could never make any inroads there.'

'I'm not a widow, and, the children! Pradeep, that day, when we were talking about a wife for you ...'

'My dearest Radha!' With that he took her in his arms and laid his lips to hers.

The tinkle of glass made Radha look round.

'Hot coffee, Uncle Pradeep, very hot. No cold water, I forget,' Leela said, as the servant put the tray down.

'Leela, my Leela,' Radha murmured, taking her daughter's hand and Pradeep's in her own. As she did so, she felt a joy that was too deep for words.

*

The chest with Radha's treasures now also contained the three precious vases carefully wrapped in sheets, then wedged into cardboard boxes. Souvenirs of happy times long ago. There were heavy silk saris below them and cotton ones on top to give further protection. She took down the photos of her children from the landing and removed them from their frames. Holding the few prints in her hand she stood for a moment feeling lost – they were so heart-rendingly insubstantial. Then she put them in an envelope which she slipped down against the side of the chest.

Two large new suitcases held the rest of all Radha's and Leela's belongings.

She left the two oval portraits on the wall downstairs.

With Pradeep's help, Radha wrote to her children:

What I have to say will come as a shock but I hope you will understand – your father and I will be getting divorced.

I have decided to go back to Pondicherry with Leela, to the house we lived in with Ummachi when

*we all went over there, that is, all except Julius. I
shall keep the upstairs floor permanently ready for
any of you in the hope you will come to see us.
India is a little bit closer to England than Malaya.
If everything goes according to plan, we should be
there before the end of the year. Leela remembers
the house well and is looking forward to the move.*

*This is a very big change for me and I owe it
to Pradeep that I can take it on without too much
difficulty. He has been wonderfully kind; I think my
future will be shared with him.*

*You, my children, are always in my thoughts;
I pray God He will look after you and keep you far
from harm at all times. Your letters are my dearest
possessions.*

Your loving mother,

Radha

Postscript

No one would deny Radha had earned the years of joy and love that awaited her in her life with her cousin Pradeep. And happily, fiction is here to give us just such fulfilment. However unjust we know life to be, we eagerly accept, or even expect, our heroes and heroines to receive their well-deserved reward in the end. From our earliest childhood, we know what the ending should be – "And they lived happily ever after."

But the real world doesn't give a fig for our just deserts. In the real world we are often tried beyond endurance, then tossed onto the rubbish heap, while villains thrive, going from strength to strength.

For those who want something more than the easy comfort of Radha's fictional ending, I have set down, in the following pages, what actually happened after the death of Ummuma.

Chapter 51

What really happened

After the funeral, Radha and Leela returned home, and Pradeep went with them. He knew the time had come to talk to his cousin, both, for his sake and hers. He'd rehearsed the scene a thousand times; it still didn't feel quite right but he knew it never would. They sat in the space downstairs, saying little, each one preoccupied with thoughts for the future. Not for the first time Pradeep let his gaze wander from Radha to Leela and back again.

'I'm thinking of returning to Madras,' he said at last. 'We're expanding the office there. I was wondering, that is,' he paused, searching for the words that might reach across the gulf that separates one heart from another, but they refused to come. All that rehearsing, as he'd known, had been a waste of time. He tried again, 'You know it would do you both good to go away from here. Just for a while, you understand. You should have a break; forget, if you can, what you've been through.' Her continued silence prompted him to say, 'There's your brother ...'

'So kind, Pradeep,' she replied softly. 'So very kind. Thank you, but we'll be all right here.'

'It need only be for a short ... well, as short or as long as you wish it to be. I'd accompany you, so that you'd have nothing to worry about, you know. I could arrange everything – tickets, passports, anything you say. Anything at all. I'd be happy to.'

She smiled sweetly and shook her head. He looked helplessly at Leela, but she too shook her head.

'All right here, thank you, Uncle Pradeep. Write, please,' Leela urged. '*Umma* like letters, huh, *Umma*? Letters from England, Madras, Kuala Lumpur – You come back, come Jalan Inai.'

Pradeep sat without moving. He was so close to Radha he could have touched her. He longed to take her in his arms, hold her face, to touch her lips with his.

'Leela,' he said, 'could you ask the girl for a glass of water?'

'Water, Uncle Pradeep? I go now.'

When he spoke, his voice was so low only the silence in the room carried it across.

''I love you, Radha!'

'I know, Pradeep, fond heart.' Her voice was as soft as his.

'I've always loved you. The happiest time of my life was when you came back from Saigon. Remember those months? The more I saw of you, shared your thoughts, the more I wanted to keep you by my side. Then, all my hopes were dashed! I cursed my stars and fled, but it changed nothing. Just imagine Radha, nothing changed – I still loved you as much as ever! Radha, I respect your lonely vigil; admire your courage, your tenacity. No wife could have shown greater loyalty to her husband. Now I'm asking you what I should have asked all those years ago – marry me and we'll share our dreams together.'

'Pradeep, a long time ago, and yet not as long as the time you speak of when you and I wandered in the gardens of Pondicherry, our hearts entwined with hope. Even so, it was long enough ago that I married Manicasami Nanamentem. A marriage is forever. I am still married to him, always shall be, to the end.'

When Leela returned the silence was not even broken by the sound of the lizard.

'Here's water, Uncle Pradeep,' she said, handing it to him.

He took the glass and put it on the table. Pradeep looked down at his hands, fingers interlaced, lying open in his lap; a begging bowl waiting for alms. Capable hands, gentle and strong. But as they lay there, he thought they looked useless, powerless to soothe away the pain from the woman he loved. He took a deep breath and got up, saying, 'I'll be leaving for Madras soon; can't say how long I'll be needed over there ... and, yes, I'll write; you'll write back, won't you, Radha, my dearest cousin?'

'Yes, Pradeep, I'll write. You've been much more than a cousin to me. My life would have been,' she shook her head, trying to find the right words, 'no, that's not it.' After a long pause she said, 'I owe you so much, dear Pradeep.'

Pradeep left the house. A gentle smile played on his lips; a strange peace, almost happiness, in his heart. At last he'd spoken his love. She knew.

'*Umma,* Uncle Pradeep forget to drink.'

'He had a lot on his mind.' A mere whisper for Leela to guess at their meaning. She resumed with a gentle smile, 'He was remembering the past, a very distant past.'

'Your eyes, wet, *Umma* ! You crying?'

'No Leela, just remembering. Like Uncle Pradeep, remembering a time, long ago, before our mistakes; happy now with our memories, our lasting friendship.'

Epilogue

Some twenty-five years after Radha's death, Mena, the youngest of the Mentem girls, tracked down her sister, Leela, in a Home run by nuns near Pondicherry. Recognition was slow in coming – Leela remembered the names of her sister, Paula, her brother, Roy, even her elder brother, Julius, whom she'd hardly known. But Mena meant nothing to her until the third visit.

Mena's efforts to talk about Radha were met with stony silence. At first, though she found it hard to believe, the repeated failure to excite some sort of response, made her wonder if Leela had actually forgotten Radha over the passage of time. Leela, she could see, was a survivor. Otherwise the transition from that large, comfortable house with an adoring mother by her side to this shabby institution for old women, unloved, unwanted by anyone, would surely have killed her. Forgetting Radha would be one way of not being hounded by a terrible sense of loss day after day.

Mena persevered. Year after year she travelled to India to see Leela. And she always asked the same questions; sitting in Leela's spartan room, walking along the seafront in Pondicherry laughing into the wind to bring the sound of happiness to her sister, resting in the hotel after lunch, 'Leela, remember *Umma?*' Not a single crack showed in the wall of silence so that she finally gave up. Her Tamil was pathetically inadequate. And it was all so long ago.

Then, one day, after eleven years of visiting her sister in January or February before the temperatures rose too high, she at last found herself back in Pondicherry, unusually, towards the end of March when the heat was oppressive. They were to have lunch at the Rendezvous roof-top restaurant.

As they made their way up and up, Leela became increasingly nervous. At the second flight where the steps are uneven and steep, she balks. She's overweight and her legs have always been unsteady. Leela wants to turn back without attempting the final hurdle but Mena is right behind her and gives a gentle prod; there's no option but to go on up. On reaching the flat haven above, she slouches down onto the wicker chair, refusing to smile even when the waiter presses the button on the camera that Mena has handed him to record the event. One of the many photos that will find their way back to Leela with the monthly letters.

They are alone in the vast dining hall. The waiter tells them it will be full that evening as it's Saturday. Leela remains morose, dreading the return journey down the perilous flights of stairs. She can think of nothing else. Mena assures her she will go in front, hold her hand and there's the metal rail on the right. Reassured a little, Leela nods and smiles.

The smell of the spices reaches them and teases their appetite: there's ginger with garlic and chilli. Leela does not want chilli or onion, 'Weakness,' she murmurs, touching her stomach.

'Like father,' Mena concurs softly.

The huge expanse of the thatched roof above them is held by massive bamboo rafters that span over fifteen metres across the width from one side to the other. The light is diffused through the hundred potted plants that stand on the parapet, the pots cemented down.

'Look Leela' Mena remarks, 'Just like at home; like the potted plants in our porch that mother used to tend. Remember the plumbago and the gardenias?'

As always, Leela nods distractedly without looking at the plants or at her. Does she hear her? Or see the plants or the thatching that reminds Mena of Malaysia and their childhood? Does she notice the wicker chairs so like the ones they used to sit in when they were children? And now, there's the smell of the fish that the waiter is placing before them. Ginger and garlic that Radha loved in her food. Doesn't any of it trigger off a distant memory? Doesn't she feel the cloying humidity in the air? Mena's hands are sticky and warm and the air she breathes is so familiar she is suffocating with the memory.

'Jalan Inai.'

Mena holds her breath with disbelief.

'Yes, 10, Jalan Inai,' she finally says, cautiously, 'Our home, Leela.'

'Huh, 10, Jalan Inai. Imbi Road. Kuala Lumpur. She lock me in.' Leela's whisper strains to breaking point.

'Who Leela? Who locked you in?'

'Chinese lock me in, in room. Alone in room.'

'You mean Luk?'

'Huh, Luk. Father – Chinese woman.'

'I remember. Do you remember what we used to call her?'

'Pig Face.'

And they both laugh. Mena wonders at how innocuous and childish the term sounds for one who brought so much pain into their lives.

'Yes, Pig Face. Where did she lock you in?'

'Big room. Upstairs room with box. Mother's box.'

Mena remembers it all: the large room on the left as you go up the steps, just on the other side of Radha's music machine. And the sandalwood chest which was carved all over and which, whenever their mother opened it, filled the room with its scent. The chest with its treasures – not her jewels which were in the bank, but other mementoes gathered here and there, souvenirs of a life. She sees the peacock feathers shimmering in the light from the window with the stiff shutters.

She sees it all – Radha admiring the feathers, each time she sees them, holding them up, murmuring, 'Beautiful', but not daring to have them out for fear they'd bring her bad luck. It was here she kept their letters, tied neatly with lengths of ribbon; and her old albums of photos that Luk will burn after her death, as well as the mysterious letter in the Doctor's writing to his favourite brother, with the earliest, perhaps the only mention of Luk. When Paula once asked her mother after she'd deciphered it for her, how she'd come by this letter, Radha explained it had lain in the inside pocket of her husband's jacket for so many days that at last she'd removed it and there had never been any mention of it. He would have known she wouldn't have been able to read English in those days even if she found it.

Leela touches her sister's hand and whispers although they are alone.

'Mother in hospital. High up room in Kuala Lumpur Hospital. So sick. So sick. Putting this on face,' and Leela covers her nose and mouth with her cupped hand.

'An oxygen mask? Did she have oxygen, Leela?'

'Huh, oxygen. Cannot breathe. So sick. Alone.'

'In hospital, alone; dying of cancer,' Mena says, her voice, too, barely audible. 'Twenty years of waiting – is that how long? Twenty years, and father never came back.'

'Father come back.'

Mena's eyes are round with amazement, 'Father came back? Back to the house? Are you saying he came back to the house, Leela? Was it to nurse *Umma*? Was it?' Her voice is too taut. Surely Leela will hear and take fright, her thoughts lost for ever.

But Leela only hears the voice of her memories, '*Umma* not want nurse; only want father. Father come back, one week, three, two. *Umma* say all family come back now.'

'God, how I wanted to! And so nearly made it. So nearly! But that's another story ...' Mena shuts her eyes, remembering that year, so long ago. Her eyes are still clouded with the memory of that past when she murmurs, 'But he never really came back, not in the way she wanted. Her last letter to me – I now understand. Such an awakening! In the end she knew.'

'*Umma* more sick. Morphine. Go to Kuala Lumpur Hospital in ambulance. Chinese ,she lock me in room.

Cannot go see mother. So sick. Alone. Lock all day, alone in room, all day. Crying; crying.'

How can Mena bear to sit there in that pleasant space listening to these words that tear her heart to pieces? She imagines the ear–splitting screams from that room on the left of the landing as Leela pounds the locked doors with her helpless fists. Poor, sad Leela, longing to be with her dying mother. And Radha dying alone, the truth at last sealing her dreams in a shroud.

Mena's eyes are dry as she gazes up to the tall rafters and asks herself how any God could have witnessed such desperation and not hurled down his thunderbolt to smash to smithereens that door and its keeper. Words suddenly echo in her mind: '*My ways are not your ways.*' And she is curiously quieted, and comforted by this thought.

When the coffee arrived, Leela asked with the casual ease of two sisters discussing absent siblings, 'Julius – you see him?'

'Yes, I see him from time to time. He lives in England. It's quite far from our house in France. But I phone him sometimes.'

'And Roy? Roy never writes.'

Mena had long ago given up trying to get Roy to send Leela a word, so that she said nothing. How could she explain to her sister Roy refused to get involved in case it cost him money, that money for which he'd paid so dearly.

'And Paula not write. Woe, woe is me,' Leela said laughing, briefly transported to a happier time long ago. She continued, 'Poor princess waiting to be rescued,' another small laugh followed by a questioning gesture of her up-turned hand that reminded Mena of their mother, 'Why nobody write? Only Mena write.'

Again Mena nodded without saying anything; there was nothing left to say.

As they got up to negotiate the staircase once more, Leela's thoughts were still far away and she murmured, 'Jalan Inai. Nice house. Big trees, coconuts, rumbutan. Nice fruit.'

Mena did not tell her their palm trees were no longer there, nor the gardenias, nor the clump of sugar cane that had brought them so much pleasure, nor the rumbutan that their mother had loved, nor even their home where Leela had brought Radha some comfort in her sad, lonely life. Everything gone, house and trees and garden, all razed to the ground with a bulldozer long ago to make way for the 'luxury homes' that now stand on that land.